Literature of the Supernatural

Editorial Direction   Joy Littell

Design   William Seabright

Literature of the Supernatural

Robert E. Beck   Editor

McDougal, Littell & Company   Evanston, Illinois

To E. B. G.

Acknowledgments: See page 190

Copyright © 1974 by McDougal, Littell & Company
Box 1667   Evanston, Illinois   60204
All rights reserved   Printed in the United States of America

Contents

The Undead

The Man Upstairs   Ray Bradbury   9
The Real Dracula   J. Donohue   21
Dead Men Working in
    the Cane Fields   William Seabrook   25
In the Vault   H. P. Lovecraft   35

Spirits Abroad

The Considerate Hosts   Thorp McCluskey   44
The Haunted and
    the Haunters   Edward Bulwer-Lytton   55
Sweet William's Ghost   Anonymous   78
Footsteps Invisible   Robert Arthur   81
The Black Cat   Edgar Allan Poe   95

Beyond Eyes and Ears

Readings, Forecasts,
    Personal Guidance   Kenneth Fearing   104
The Furnished Room   O. Henry   108
The Tradition   Algernon Blackwood   115
The Demon Lover   Elizabeth Bowen   120

In Ghostly Japan　　Lafcadio Hearn　　126
The Other World from *The Book of*
　the Dead　　Translated by Robert Hillyer　　129
Charts from *The Divine Comedy*　　Dante Alighieri
　The Universe　　131
　Purgatory　　132
　Hell　　133

Witchcraft and Black Magic

The Witch Mania　　Charles McKay　　135
Witches' Spell
　from *Macbeth*　　William Shakespeare　　145
Pollock and the Porroh Man　　H. G. Wells　　147
A Way of Thinking　　Theodore Sturgeon　　163

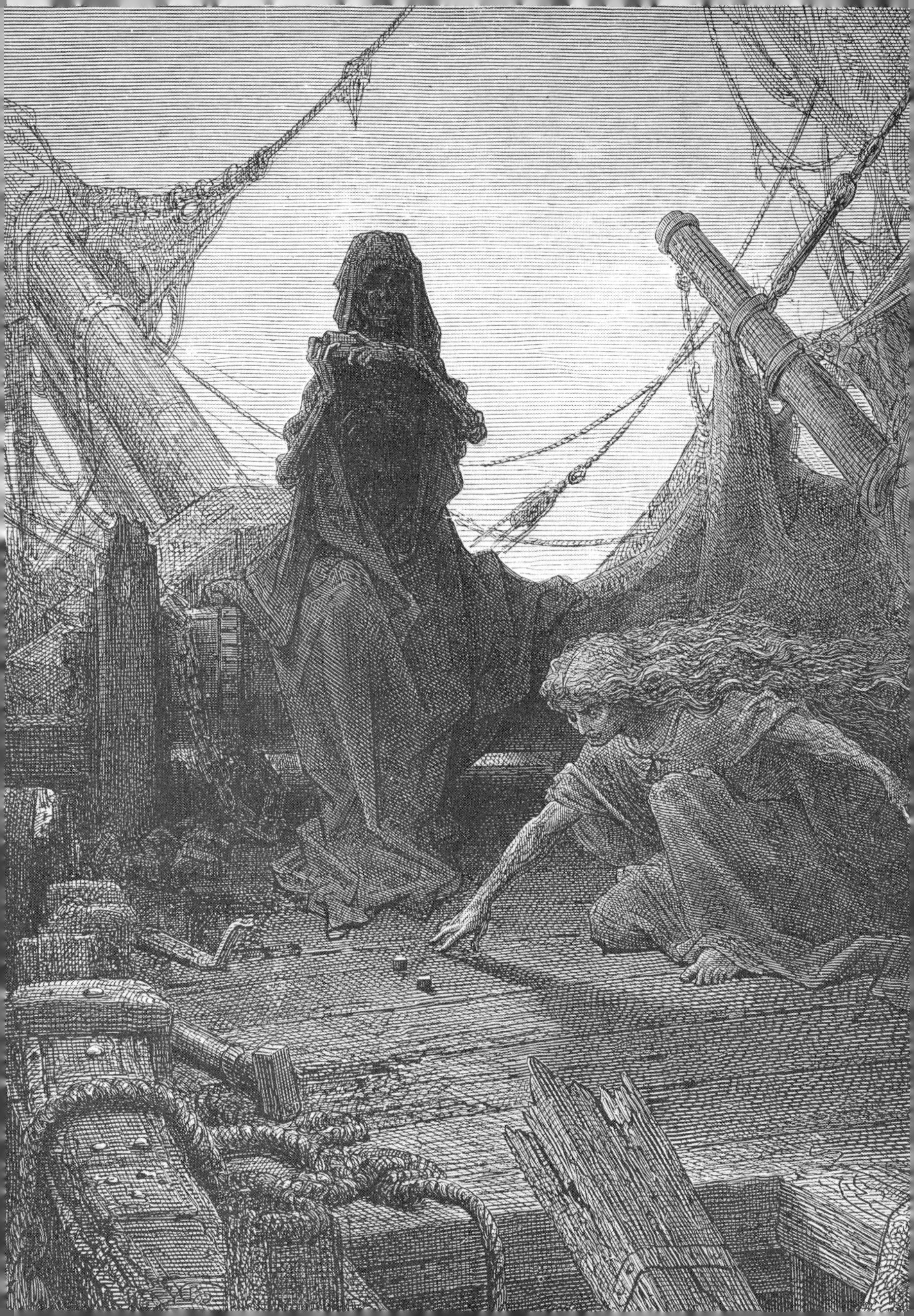

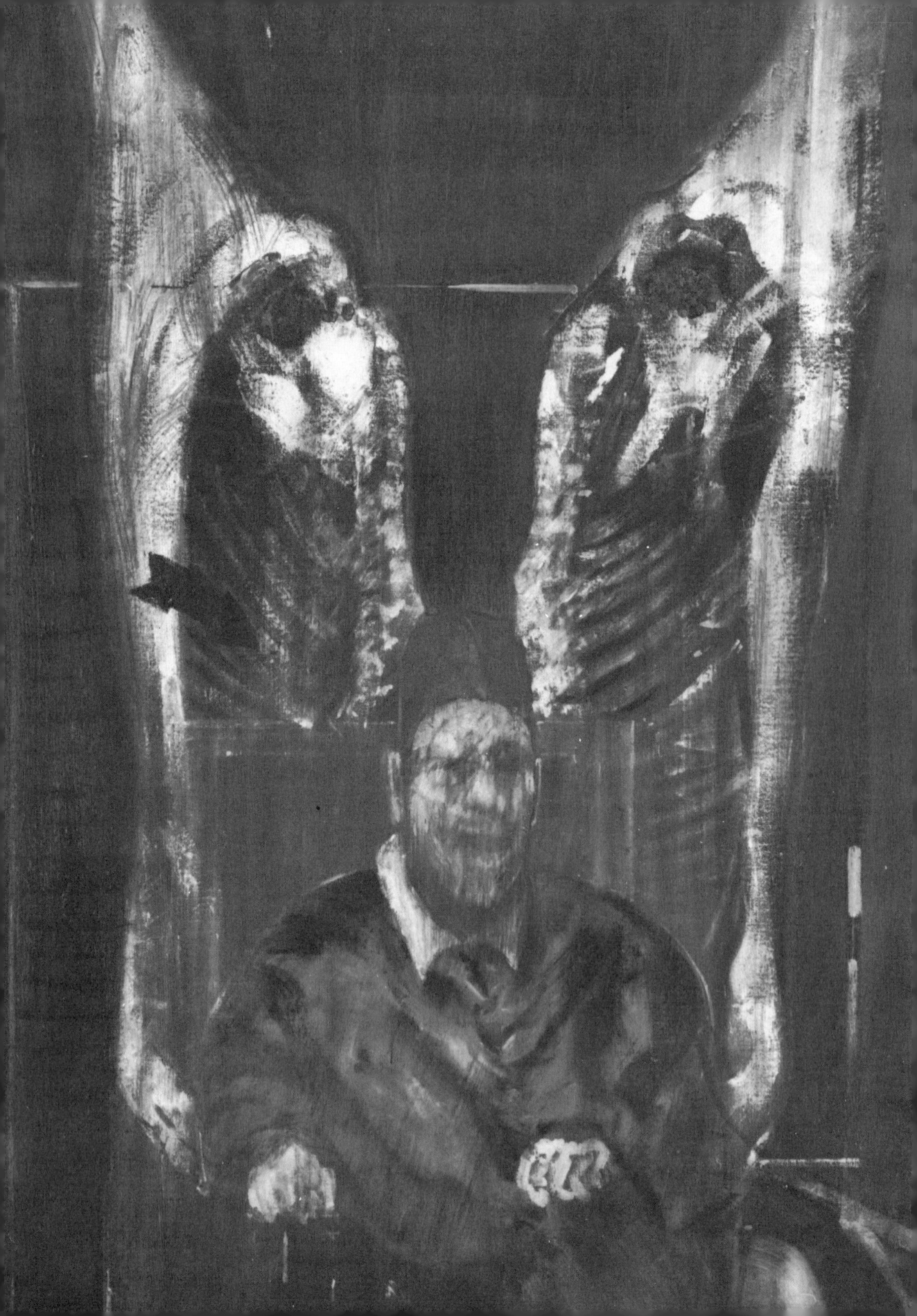

The Man Upstairs

Ray Bradbury

He remembered how carefully and expertly Grandmother would fondle the cold cut guts of the chicken and withdraw the marvels therein; the wet shining loops of meat-smelling intestine, the muscle lump of heart, the gizzard with the collection of seeds in it. How neatly and nicely Grandma would slit the chicken and put her fat little hand in to deprive it of its medals. These would be segregated, some in pans of water, others in paper to be thrown to the dog later, perhaps. And then the ritual of taxidermy, stuffing the bird with watered, seasoned bread, and performing surgery with a swift, bright needle, stitch after pulled-tight stitch.

This was one of the prime thrills of Douglas's eleven-year-old life span.

Altogether, he counted twenty knives in the various squeaking drawers of the magic kitchen table from which Grandma, a kindly, gentle-faced, white-haired old witch, drew paraphernalia for her miracles.

Douglas was to be quiet. He could stand across the table from Grandmama, his freckled nose tucked over the edge, watching, but any loose boy-talk might interfere with the spell. It was a wonder when Grandma brandished silver shakers over the bird, supposedly sprinkling showers of mummy-dust and pulverized Indian bones, muttering mystical verses under her toothless breath.

"Grammy," said Douglas at last, breaking the silence, "am I like that inside?" He pointed at the chicken.

"Yes," said Grandma. "A little more orderly and presentable, but just about the same. . . ."

"And more *of* it!" added Douglas, proud of his guts.

"Yes," said Grandma. "More of it."

"Grandpa has lots more'n me. His sticks out in front so he can rest his elbows on it."

Grandma laughed and shook her head.

Douglas said, "And Lucie Williams, down the street, she . . ."

"Hush, child!" cried Grandma.

"But she's got . . ."

"Never you mind what she's got! That's different."

"But why is *she* different?"

The Man Upstairs

"A darning-needle dragon-fly is coming by some day and sew up your mouth," said Grandma firmly.

Douglas waited, then asked, "How do you know I've got insides like that, Grandma?"

"Oh, go 'way, now!"

The front doorbell rang.

Through the front-door glass as he ran down the hall, Douglas saw a straw hat. The bell jangled again and again. Douglas opened the door.

"Good morning, child, is the landlady at home?"

Cold gray eyes in a long, smooth, walnut-colored face gazed upon Douglas. The man was tall, thin, and carried a suitcase, a brief case, an umbrella under one bent arm, gloves rich and thick and gray on his thin fingers, and wore a horribly new straw hat.

Douglas backed up. "She's busy."

"I wish to rent her upstairs room, as advertised."

"We've got ten boarders, and it's already rented; go away!"

"Douglas!" Grandma was behind him suddenly. "How do you do?" she said to the stranger. "Never mind this child."

Unsmiling, the man stepped stiffly in. Douglas watched them ascend out of sight up the stairs, heard Grandma detailing the conveniences of the upstairs room. Soon she hurried down to pile linens from the linen closet on Douglas and send him scooting up with them.

Douglas paused at the room's threshhold. The room was changed oddly, simply because the stranger had been in it a moment. The straw hat lay brittle and terrible upon the bed, the umbrella leaned stiff against one wall like a dead bat with dark moist wings folded.

Douglas blinked at the umbrella.

The stranger stood in the center of the changed room, tall, tall.

"Here!" Douglas littered the bed with supplies. "We eat at noon sharp, and if you're late coming down the soup'll get cold. Grandma fixes it so it will, every time!"

The tall strange man counted out ten new copper pennies and tinkled them in Douglas' blouse pocket. "We shall be friends," he said, grimly.

It was funny, the man having nothing but pennies. Lots of them. No silver at all, no dimes, no quarters. Just new copper pennies.

Douglas thanked him glumly. "I'll drop these in my dime bank when I get them changed into a dime. I got six dollars and fifty cents in dimes all ready for my camp trip in August."

"I must wash now," said the tall strange man.

Once, at midnight, Douglas had wakened to hear a storm rumbling outside—the cold hard wind shaking the house, the rain driving against the window. And then a lightning bolt had landed outside the window with a silent, terrific concussion. He remembered that fear of looking about at his room, seeing it strange and awful in the instantaneous light.

So it was, now, in this room. He stood looking up at the stranger. This room was no longer the same, but changed indefinably because this man, quick as a lightning bolt, had shed his light about it. Douglas backed up slowly as the stranger advanced.

The door closed in his face.

The wooden fork went up with mashed potatoes, came down empty. Mr. Koberman, for that was his name, had brought the wooden fork and wooden knife and spoon with him when Grandma called lunch.

"Mrs. Spaulding," he had said, quietly, "my own cutlery; please use it. I will have lunch today, but from tomorrow on, only breakfast and supper."

Grandma bustled in and out, bearing steaming tureens of soup and beans and mashed potatoes to impress her new boarder, while Douglas sat rattling his silverware on his plate, because he had discovered it irritated Mr. Koberman.

"I know a trick," said Douglas. "Watch." He picked a fork-tine with his fingernail. He pointed at various sectors of the table, like a magician. Whenever he pointed, the sound of the vibrating fork-tine emerged, like a metal elfin voice. Simply done, of course. He pressed the fork handle on the table-top, secretly. The vibration came from the wood like a sounding board. It looked quite magical. "There, there, and *there!*" exclaimed Douglas, happily plucking the fork again. He pointed at Mr. Koberman's soup and the noise came from it.

Mr. Koberman's walnut-colored face became hard and firm and awful. He pushed the soup bowl away violently, his lips twisting. He fell back in his chair.

Grandma appeared. "Why, what's wrong, Mr. Koberman?"

"I cannot eat this soup."

"Why?"

"Because I am full and can eat no more. Thank you."

Mr. Koberman left the room, glaring.

"What did you do, just then?" asked Grandma at Douglas, sharply.

"Nothing. Grandma, why does he eat with *wooden* spoons?"

"Yours not to question! When do you go back to school, anyway?"
"Seven weeks."
"Oh, my land!" said Grandma.

Mr. Koberman worked nights. Each morning at eight he arrived mysteriously home, devoured a very small breakfast, and then slept soundlessly in his room all through the dreaming hot daytime, until the huge supper with all the other boarders at night.

Mr. Koberman's sleeping habits made it necessary for Douglas to be quiet. This was unbearable. So, whenever Grandma visited down the street, Douglas stomped up and down stairs beating a drum, bouncing golf balls, or just screaming for three minutes outside Mr. Koberman's door, or flushing the toilet seven times in succession.

Mr. Koberman never moved. His room was silent, dark. He did not complain. There was no sound. He slept on and on. It was very strange.

Douglas felt a pure white flame of hatred burn inside himself with a steady, unflickering beauty. Now that room was Koberman Land. Once it had been flowery bright when Miss Sadlowe lived there. Now it was stark, bare, cold, clean, everything in its place, alien and brittle.

Douglas climbed upstairs on the fourth morning.

Halfway to the second floor was a large sun-filled window, framed by six-inch panes of orange, purple, blue, red and burgundy glass. In the enchanted early mornings when the sun fell through to strike the landing and slide down the stair banister, Douglas stood entranced at this window peering at the world through the multicolored windows.

Now a blue world, a blue sky, blue people, blue streetcars and blue trotting dogs.

He shifted panes. Now—an amber world! Two lemonish women glided by, resembling the daughters of Fu Manchu! Douglas giggled. This pane made even the sunlight more purely golden.

It was eight A.M. Mr. Koberman strolled by below, on the sidewalk, returning from his night's work, his cane looped over his elbow, straw hat glued to his head with patent oil.

Douglas shifted panes again. Mr. Koberman was a red man walking through a red world with red trees and red flowers and—something else.

Something about—Mr. Koberman.

Douglas squinted.

The red glass *did* things to Mr. Koberman. His face, his suit, his hands. The clothes seemed to melt away. Douglas almost believed, for one terrible instant, that he could see *inside* Mr. Koberman. And what he saw made him lean wildly against the small red pane, blinking.

Mr. Koberman glanced up just then, saw Douglas, and raised his cane-umbrella angrily, as if to strike. He ran swiftly across the red lawn to the front door.

"Young man!" he cried, running up the stairs. "What were you doing?"

"Just looking," said Douglas, numbly.

"That's all, is it?" cried Mr. Koberman.

"Yes, sir. I look through all the glasses. All kinds of worlds. Blue ones, red ones, yellow ones. All different."

"All kinds of worlds, is it!" Mr. Koberman glanced at the little panes of glass, his face pale. He got hold of himself. He wiped his face with a handkerchief and pretended to laugh. "Yes. All kinds of worlds. All different." He walked to the door of his room. "Go right ahead; play," he said.

The door closed. The hall was empty. Mr. Koberman had gone in.

Douglas shrugged and found a new pane.

"Oh, everything's violet!"

Half an hour later, while playing in his sandbox behind the house, Douglas heard the crash and the shattering tinkle. He leaped up.

A moment later, Grandma appeared on the back porch, the old razor strop trembling in her hand.

"Douglas! I told you time and again never fling your basketball against the house! Oh, I could just cry!"

"I been sitting right here," he protested.

"Come see what you've done, you nasty boy!"

The great colored window panes lay shattered in a rainbow chaos on the upstairs landing. His basketball lay in the ruins.

Before he could even begin telling his innocence, Douglas was struck a dozen stinging blows upon his rump. Wherever he landed, screaming, the razor strop struck again.

Later, hiding his mind in the sandpile like an ostrich, Douglas nursed his dreadful pains. He knew who'd thrown that basketball. A man with a straw hat and a stiff umbrella and a cold, gray room. Yeah, yeah, yeah. He dribbled tears. Just wait. Just *wait*.

He heard Grandma sweeping up the broken glass. She brought it out and threw it in the trash bin. Blue, pink, yellow meteors of glass dropped brightly down.

When she was gone, Douglas dragged himself, whimpering, over to save out three pieces of the incredible glass. Mr. Koberman disliked the colored windows. These—he clinked them in his fingers—would be worth saving.

Grandfather arrived from his newspaper office each night, shortly ahead of the other boarders, at five o'clock. When a slow, heavy tread filled the hall, and a thick, mahogany cane thumped in the cane-case, Douglas ran to embrace the large stomach and sit on Grandpa's knee while he read the evening paper.

"Hi, Grandpa!"

"Hello, down there!"

"Grandma cut chickens again today. It's fun watching," said Douglas.

Grandpa kept reading. "That's twice this week, chickens. She's the chickenist woman. You like to watch her cut 'em, eh? Cold-blooded little pepper! Ho!"

"I'm just curious."

"You are," rumbled Grandpa, scowling. "Remember that day when that young lady was killed at the rail station. You just walked over and looked at her, blood and all." He laughed. "Queer duck. Stay that way. Fear nothing, ever in your life. I guess you get it from your father, him being a military man and all, and you so close to him before you came here to live last year." Grandpa returned to his paper.

A long pause. "Gramps?"

"Yes?"

"What if a man didn't have a heart or lungs or stomach but still walked around, alive?"

"That," rumbled Gramps, "would be a miracle."

"I don't mean a—a miracle. I mean, what if he was all *different* inside. Not like me."

"Well, he wouldn't be quite human then, would he, boy?"

"Guess not, Gramps. Gramps, you got a heart and lungs?"

Gramps chuckled. "Well, tell the truth, I don't *know*. Never seen them. Never had an X-ray, never been to a doctor. Might as well be potato-solid for all I know."

"Have *I* got a stomach?"

"You certainly have!" cried Grandma from the parlor entry. " 'Cause I feed it! And you've lungs, you scream loud enough to wake the crumblees. And you've dirty hands, go wash them! Dinner's ready. Grandpa, come on, Douglas, git!"

In the rush of boarders streaming downstairs, Grandpa, if he intended questioning Douglas further about the weird conversation, lost his opportunity. If dinner delayed an instant more, Grandma and the potatoes would develop simultaneous lumps.

The boarders, laughing and talking at the table—Mr. Koberman silent and sullen among them—were silenced when Grandfather cleared his throat. He talked politics a few minutes and then shifted over into the intriguing topic of the recent peculiar deaths in the town.

"It's enough to make an old newspaper editor pick up his ears," he said, eying them all. "That young Miss Larson, lived across the ravine, now. Found her dead three days ago for no reason, just funny kinds of tattoos all over her, and a facial expression that would make Dante cringe. And that other young lady, what was her name? Whitely? She disappeared and *never did* come back."

"Them things happen alla time," said Mr. Britz, the garage mechanic, chewing. "Ever peek inna Missing Peoples Bureau file? It's *that* long." He illustrated. "Can't tell *what* happens to most of 'em."

"Anyone want more dressing?" Grandma ladled liberal portions from the chicken's interior. Douglas watched, thinking about how that chicken had two kinds of guts—God-made and Man-made.

Well, how about *three* kinds of guts?

Eh?

Why not?

Conversation continued about the mysterious death of so-and-so, and, oh, yes, remember a week ago, Marion Barsumian died of heart failure, but maybe that didn't connect up? or did it? you're crazy! forget it, why talk about it at the dinner table? So.

"Never can tell," said Mr. Britz. "Maybe we got a vampire in town."

Mr. Koberman stopped eating.

"In the year 1927?" said Grandma. "A vampire? Oh, go on, now."

"Sure," said Mr. Britz. "Kill 'em with silver bullets. Anything silver for that matter. Vampires *hate* silver. I read it in a book somewhere, once. Sure, I did."

Douglas looked at Mr. Koberman who ate with wooden knives and forks and carried only new copper pennies in his pocket.

"It's poor judgment," said Grandpa, "to call anything by a name. We don't know what a hobgoblin or a vampire or a troll is. Could be lots of things. You can't heave them into categories with labels and say they'll act one way or another. That'd be silly. They're people. People who do things. Yes, that's the way to put it: people who *do* things."

"Excuse me," said Mr. Koberman, who got up and went out for his evening walk to work.

The stars, the moon, the wind, the clock ticking, and the chiming of the hours into dawn, the sun rising, and here it was another morning, another day, and Mr. Koberman coming along the sidewalk from his night's work. Douglas stood off like a small mechanism whirring and watching with carefully microscopic eyes.

At noon, Grandma went to the store to buy groceries.

As was his custom every day when Grandma was gone, Douglas yelled outside Mr. Koberman's door for a full three minutes. As usual, there was no response. The silence was horrible.

He ran downstairs, got the pass-key, a silver fork, and the three pieces of colored glass he had saved from the shattered window. He fitted the key to the lock and swung the door slowly open.

The room was in half light, the shades drawn. Mr. Koberman lay atop his bedcovers, in slumber clothes, breathing gently, up and down. He didn't move. His face was motionless.

"Hello, Mr. Koberman!"

The colorless walls echoed the man's regular breathing.

"Mr. Koberman, hello!"

Bouncing a golf ball, Douglas advanced. He yelled. Still no answer. "Mr. Koberman!"

Bending over Mr. Koberman, Douglas picked the tines of the silver fork in the sleeping man's face.

Mr. Koberman winced. He twisted. He groaned bitterly.

Response. Good. Swell.

Douglas drew a piece of blue glass from his pocket. Looking through the blue glass fragment he found himself in a blue room, in a blue world different from the world he knew. As different as was the red world. Blue furniture, blue bed, blue ceiling and walls, blue wooden eating utensils atop the blue bureau, and the sullen dark blue of Mr. Koberman's face and arms and his blue chest rising, falling. Also . . .

Mr. Koberman's eyes were wide, staring at him with a hungry darkness.

Douglas fell back, pulled the blue glass from his eyes.

Mr. Koberman's eyes were shut.

Blue glass again—open. Blue glass away—shut. Blue glass again—open. Away—shut. Funny. Douglas experimented, trembling. Through the glass the eyes seemed to peer hungrily, avidly through Mr. Koberman's closed lids. Without the blue glass they seemed tightly shut.

But it was the rest of Mr. Koberman's body....

Mr. Koberman's bedclothes dissolved off him. The blue glass had something to do with it. Or perhaps it was the clothes themselves, just being *on* Mr. Koberman. Douglas cried out.

He was looking through the wall of Mr. Koberman's stomach, right *inside* him!

Mr. Koberman was solid.

Or, nearly so, anyway.

There were strange shapes and sizes within him.

Douglas must have stood amazed for five minutes, thinking about the blue worlds, the red worlds, the yellow worlds side by side, living together like glass panes around the big white stair window. Side by side, the colored panes, the different worlds; Mr. Koberman had said so himself.

So this was why the colored window had been broken.

"Mr. Koberman, wake up!"

No answer.

"Mr. Koberman, where do you work at night? Mr. Koberman, where do you work?"

A little breeze stirred the blue window shade.

"In a red world or a green world or a yellow one, Mr. Koberman?"

Over everything was a blue glass silence.

"Wait there," said Douglas.

He walked down to the kitchen, pulled open the great squeaking drawer and picked out the sharpest, biggest knife.

Very calmly he walked into the hall, climbed back up the stairs again, opened the door to Mr. Koberman's room, went in, and closed it, holding the sharp knife in one hand.

Grandma was busy fingering a piecrust into a pan when Douglas entered the kitchen to place something on the table.

"Grandma, what's this?"

She glanced up briefly, over her glasses. "I don't know."

It was a square, like a box, and elastic. It was bright orange in color. It had four square tubes, colored blue, attached to it. It smelled funny.

"Ever see anything like it, Grandma?"

"No."

"That's what *I* thought."

Douglas left it there, went from the kitchen. Five minutes later he returned with something else. "How about *this?*"

He laid down a bright pink linked chain with a purple triangle at one end.

"Don't bother me," said Grandma. "It's only a chain."

Next time he turned with two hands full. A ring, a square, a triangle, a pyramid, a rectangle, and—other shapes. All of them were pliable, resilient, and looked as if they were made of gelatin. "This isn't all," said Douglas, putting them down. "There's more where this came from."

Grandma said, "Yes, yes," in a far-off tone, very busy.

"You were wrong, Grandma."

"About what?"

"About all people being the same inside."

"Stop talking nonsense."

"Where's my piggy-bank?"

"On the mantel, where you left it."

"Thanks."

He tromped into the parlor, reached up for his piggy-bank.

Grandpa came home from the office at five.

"Grandpa, come upstairs."

"Sure, son. Why?"

"Something to show you. It's not nice; but it's interesting."

Grandpa chuckled, followed his grandson's feet up to Mr. Koberman's room.

"Grandma mustn't know about this; she wouldn't like it," said Douglas. He pushed the door wide open. "There."

Grandpa gasped.

Douglas remembered the next few hours all the rest of his life. Standing over Mr. Koberman's naked body, the coroner and his assistants. Grandma, downstairs, asking somebody, "What's going on up there?" and Grandpa saying, shakily, "I'll take Douglas away on a long vacation so he can forget this whole ghastly affair. Ghastly, ghastly affair!"

Douglas said, "Why should it be bad? I don't see anything bad. I don't feel bad."

The coroner shivered and said, "Koberman's dead, all right."

His assistant sweated. "Did you see those *things* in the pans of water and in the wrapping paper?"

"Oh, my God, my God, yes, I saw them."

The coroner bent over Mr. Koberman's body again. "This better be kept secret, boys. It wasn't murder. It was a mercy the boy acted. God knows what might have happened if he hadn't."

"What was Koberman? A vampire? A monster?"

"Maybe. I don't know. Something—not human." The coroner moved his hands deftly over the suture.

Douglas was proud of his work. He'd gone to much trouble. He had watched Grandmother carefully and remembered. Needle and thread and all. All in all, Mr. Koberman was as neat a job as any chicken ever popped into hell by Grandma.

"I heard the boy say that Koberman lived even after all those *things* were taken out of him." The coroner looked at the triangles and chains and pyramids floating in the pans of water. "Kept on *living*. God."

"Did the boy say that?"

"He did."

"Then, what *did* kill Koberman?"

The coroner drew a few strands of sewing thread from their bedding. "This...." he said.

Sunlight blinked coldly off a half-revealed treasure trove; six dollars and seventy cents' worth of silver dimes inside Mr. Koberman's chest.

"I think Douglas made a wise investment," said the coroner, sewing the flesh back up over the "dressing" quickly.

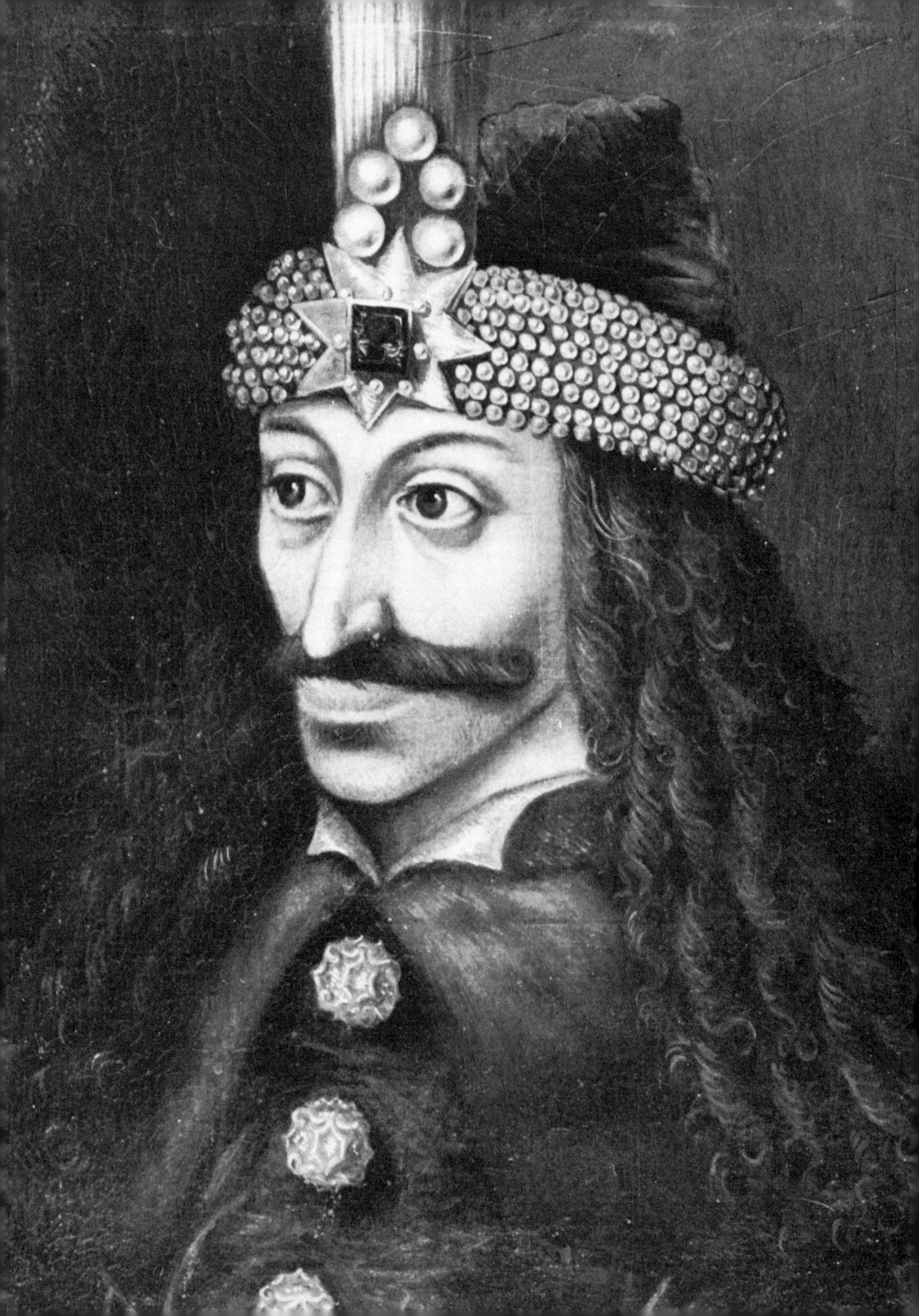

The Real Dracula

James F. Donohue

NEWTON, MASS. (AP)

Two Boston College historians set out four years ago to find the origins of the vampire stories of Dracula and found a flesh and blood Dracula whose real exploits of horror put the fictional vampire to shame.

That's according to the historians, Dr. Radu Florescu, professor of Romanian and Balkan history, and Dr. Raymond McNally, professor of Russian history, who tracked down the real Dracula, a 15th century Romanian prince.

For starters, they say, the real prince Dracula killed about 100,000 people during his lifetime, most of them in 1456-1462 when he ruled the Romanian province of Wallachia and parts of Transylvania.

His favorite mode of death was by impaling. He sat his victims on sharpened spikes.

In 1462 he stuck 20,000 Turks and Romanian nobles on spikes in one spot to discourage the invasion of Sultan Mohammed the Great, fresh from his conquest of Constantinople.

Another time he either impaled or burned to death the 20,000 persons who lived in a village where one of his enemies found sanctuary.

A madman? "Not really, although his terrorism was excessive even for his age," Florescu says.

"I would say that he occasionally became demented and had an obsession to impale people every once in a while."

The search for the real Dracula began some 15 years ago when McNally saw the 1931 Bela Lugosi movie classic about Count Dracula, the living corpse who roamed the dim, forested hills of Transylvania, sucking human blood by night and holing up in a casket by day.

McNally next read the 1897 Bram Stoker novel, "Dracula," the basis for the movie, and found "a great deal of true historical and geographical fact in the book.

"The book speaks of the towns of Cluj and Bistrita and of the Borgo Pass," McNally said.

"These places actually exist. So does Transylvania itself. It's one of three provinces of Romania even though most people think it's a mythical country dreamed up by Stoker.

"I said to myself," McNally said, "if the places are real, perhaps the person is real, too. Not, of course, as a vampire, but as an actual person who was portrayed in a poetic way in the Gothic novel."

McNally began checking Romanian, German, Slavic and Russian sources but made little headway until 1967 when he teamed up with Florescu.

They tramped all over Romania tracking down leads on the prince. They discovered Dracula's portrait in Castle Ambras near Innsbruck, Austria—"he's a bull-necked man with a fierce mustache and a jeweled turban"—and Castle Dracula atop a 300-foot precipice in Wallachia, just across the border from Transylvania.

Their efforts resulted in a book about Dracula. It was compiled mostly from folklore because documented, historical data about the prince are all but non-existent.

During their research, the two professors ran afoul of the "curse" of Dracula.

"I don't know what to say about the curse," Florescu says. "I am Romanian and naturally I am superstitious. I cannot say what I believe. But there is something there."

To play it safe, he has never spent a night in Castle Dracula.

The first time Florescu tried to climb the castle he didn't make it because his uncle, George Florescu, fell into a ravine and broke his hip.

The next time, Florescu made it to the castle, but immediately he became ill. "I don't think I was ill, exactly," he says. "I think I was just very, very tired.

"And nervous, too, I suppose. The people around the castle are very superstitious about it. When we asked for directions they said we must not go there, that the devil lives there guarding a treasure."

McNally, although presumably not affected by the family curse, became ill himself at one point and fainted, but not at Castle Dracula.

That was later when the professors found Dracula's portrait—in a place of honor in a chamber of horrors collected in 1591 by a Tyrolean prince.

Next to Dracula's portrait is one of the Wolfman of the Urals, a Russian nobleman with hair all over his face and funny ears. The Wolfman looks very much like Lon Chaney in the movie role.

"Dracula was put in the chamber of horrors," McNally said, "not because anybody thought he was a vampire but because of the awful things he had done."

The professors say there's more to the curse than fainting spells, illness and injurious falls. Dracula was buried in the chapel of an island monastery near Bucharest and, say McNally-Florescu, "the monastery suffered a series of misfortunes ever since his body was put there."

The monastery was turned into a prison in the 19th century and just as a group of chained prisoners were marching across a bridge to it, the bridge collapsed and the prisoners and their guards drowned.

McNally-Florescu found the grave of Dracula near the altar of the monastery chapel. The grave was empty, except for some prehistoric animal bones.

"Now, there are a couple of explanations for that," Florescu says with a grin.

"One is the vampire explanation. He's out wandering around someplace. The other is that the monks didn't want a man with Dracula's reputation so close to the altar.

"We accept the second explanation. We think the monks just moved the body."

McNally-Florescu believe Stoker learned about Prince Dracula from Arminium Vambery, a professor from the University of Bucharest who visited London in the 1890s.

They believe Vambery's tales of Dracula's exploits, coupled with the fact that the myth of vampires sprang up from Romania, led Stoker to his tale.

DRACULA
The BLOODY TERROR of TRANSYLVANIA
as the 'Count,' BELA LUGOSI
HELEN CHANDLER
Directed by TOD BROWNING
From a novel by ABRAHAM STOKER

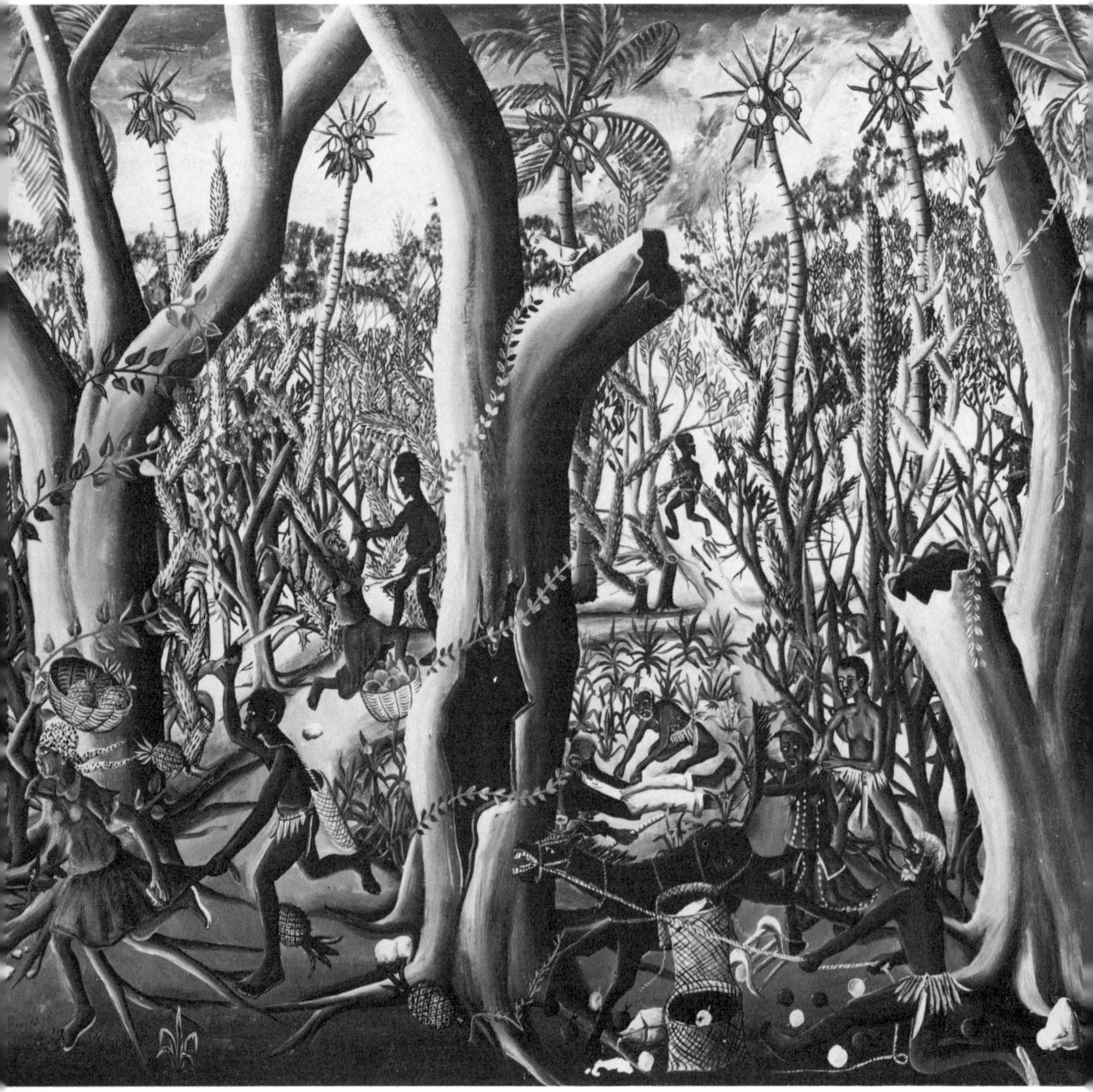

Dead Men Working in the Cane Fields
William Seabrook

Pretty mulatto Julie had taken baby Marianne to bed. Constant Polynice and I sat late before the doorway of his *caille,* talking of firehags, demons, werewolves and vampires, while a full moon, rising slowly, flooded his sloping cotton fields and the dark rolling hills beyond.

Polynice was a Haitian farmer, but he was no common jungle peasant. He lived on the island of La Gonave, where I shall return to him later on. He seldom went over to the Haitian mainland, but he knew what was going on in Port-au-Prince, and spoke sometimes of installing a radio.

A countryman, half peasant born and bred, he was familiar with every superstition of the mountains and the plain, yet too intelligent to believe them literally true—or at least so I gathered from his talk.

He was interested in helping me toward an understanding of the tangled Haitian folklore. It was only by chance that we came presently to a subject which—though I refused for a long time to admit it—lies in a baffling category on the ragged edge of things which are beyond either superstition or reason. He had been telling me of firehags who left their skins at home and set the cane fields blazing; of the vampire, a woman sometimes living, sometimes dead, who sucked the blood of children and who could be distinguished because her hair always turned an ugly red; of the werewolf—*chauché,* in creole—a man or woman who took the form of some animal, usually a dog, and went killing lambs, young goats, sometimes babies.

All this, I gathered, he considered to be pure superstition, as he told me with tolerant scorn how his friend and neighbor Osmann had one night seen a gray dog slinking with bloody jaws from his sheep pen, and who, after having shot and exorcized and buried it, was so convinced he had killed a certain girl named Liane who was generally reputed to be a *chauché* that when he met her two days later on the path to Grande Source, he believed she was a ghost come back for vengeance, and fled howling.

As Polynice talked on, I reflected that these tales ran closely parallel not only with those of the Negroes in Georgia and the Carolinas, but with the medieval folklore of white Europe. Werewolves, vampires and demons were certainly no novelty. But I recalled one creature I had been hearing about in Haiti, which sounded exclusively local—the *zombie*.

It seemed (or so I had been assured by Negroes more credulous than Polynice) that while the zombie came from the grave, it was neither a ghost, nor yet a person who had been raised like Lazarus from the dead. The zombie, they say, is a soulless human corpse, still dead, but taken from the grave and endowed by sorcery with a mechanical semblance of life—it is a dead body which is made to walk and act and move as if it were alive. People who have the power to do this go to a fresh grave, dig up the body before it has had time to rot, galvanize it into movement and then make of it a servant or slave, occasionally for the commission of some crime, more often simply as a drudge around the habitation or the farm, setting it dull heavy tasks, and beating it like a dumb beast if it slackens.

As this was revolving in my mind, I said to Polynice: "It seems to me that these werewolves and vampires are first cousins to those we have at home, but I have never, except in Haiti, heard of anything like zombies. Let us talk of them for a while. I wonder if you can tell me something of this zombie superstition. I should like to get at some idea of how it originated."

My rational friend Polynice was deeply astonished. He leaned over and put his hand in protest on my knee.

"Superstition? But I assure you that this of which you now speak is not a matter of superstition. Alas, these things—and other evil practices connected with the dead—exist. They exist to an extent that you whites do not dream of, though evidences are everywhere under your eyes.

"Why do you suppose that even the poorest peasants, when they can, bury their dead beneath solid tombs of masonry?

"Why do they bury them so often in their own yards, close to the doorway?

"Why, so often, do you see a tomb or grave set close beside a busy road or footpath where people are always passing?

"It is to assure the poor unhappy dead such protection as we can.

"I will take you in the morning to see the grave of my brother, who was killed in the way you know. It is over there on the little ridge which you can see clearly now in the moonlight, open space all round it, close beside the trail which everybody passes going to and from Grande Source. Through four nights we watched yonder, in the peristyle, Osmann and I, with shotguns—for at that time both my dead brother and I had bitter enemies—until we were sure the body had begun to rot.

"No, my friend, no, no. There are only too many true cases. At this very moment, in the moonlight, there are zombies working on this island, less than two hours' ride from my own habitation. We know about them, but we do not dare to interfere so long as our own dead are left unmolested. If you will ride with me tomorrow night, yes, I will show you dead men working in the cane fields. Close even to the cities, there are sometimes zombies. Perhaps you have already heard of those that were at Hasco...."

"What about Hasco?" I interrupted him, for in the whole of Haiti, Hasco is perhaps the last name anybody would think of connecting with either sorcery or superstition.

The word is American-commercial-synthetic, like Nabisco, Delco, Socony. It stands for the Haitian-American Sugar Company—an immense factory plant, dominated by a huge chimney, with clanging machinery, steam whistles, freight cars. It is like a chunk of Hoboken. It lies in the eastern suburbs of Port-au-Prince, and beyond it stretch the cane fields of the Cul-de-Sac. Hasco makes rum when the sugar market is off, pays low wages, twenty or thirty cents a day, and gives steady work. It is modern big business, and it sounds it, looks it, smells it.

Such, then, was the incongruous background for the weird tale Constant Polynice now told me.

The spring of 1918 was a big cane season, and the factory, which had its own plantations, offered a bonus on the wages of new workers. Soon heads of families and villages from the mountain and the plain came trailing their ragtag little armies, men, women, children, trooping to the registration bureau and thence into the fields.

One morning an old black headman, Ti Joseph of Colombier, appeared leading a band of ragged creatures who shuffled along behind him, staring dumbly, like people walking in a daze. As Joseph lined them up for registration, they still stared, vacant-eyed like cattle, and made no reply when asked to give their names.

Joseph said they were ignorant people from the slopes of Morne-au-Diable, a roadless mountain district near the Dominican border, and that they did not understand the creole of the plains. They were frightened, he said, by the din and smoke of the great factory, but under his direction they would work hard in the fields. The farther they were sent away from the factory, from the noise and bustle of the railroad yards, the better it would be.

Better indeed, for these were not living men and women but poor unhappy zombies whom Joseph and his wife Croyance had dragged from their peaceful graves to slave for him in the sun—and if by chance a brother or father of the dead should see and recognize them, Joseph knew that it would be a very bad affair for him.

So they were assigned to distant fields beyond the crossroads, and camped there, keeping to themselves like any proper family or village group; but in the evening when other little companies, encamped apart as they were, gathered each around its one big common pot of savory millet or plantains, generously seasoned with dried fish and garlic, Croyance would tend *two* pots upon the fire, for as everyone knows, the zombies must never be permitted to taste salt or meat. So the food prepared for them was tasteless and unseasoned.

As the zombies toiled day after day dumbly in the sun, Joseph sometimes beat them to make them move faster, but Croyance began to pity the poor dead creatures who should be at rest—and pitied them in the evenings when she dished out their flat, tasteless *bouillie*.

Each Saturday afternoon, Joseph went to collect the wages for them all, and what division he made was no concern of Hasco, so long as the work went forward. Sometimes Joseph alone, and sometimes Croyance alone, went to Croix de Bouquet for the Saturday night *bamboche* or the Sunday cockfight, but always one of them remained with the zombies to prepare their food and see that they did not stray away.

Through February this continued, until Fête Dieu approached, with a Saturday-Sunday-Monday holiday for all the workers. Joseph, with his pockets full of money, went to Port-au-Prince and left Croyance behind, cautioning her as usual; and she agreed to remain and tend the zombies, for he promised her that at the Mardi Gras she should visit the city.

But when Sunday morning dawned, it was lonely in the fields, and her kind old woman's heart was filled with pity for the zombies, and she thought, "Perhaps it will cheer them a little to see the gay crowds and the processions at Croix de Bouquet, and since all the Morne-au-Diable people will have gone back to the mountain to celebrate Fête Dieu at home, no one will recognize them, and no harm can come of it." And it is the truth that Croyance also wished to see the gay procession.

So she tied a new bright-colored handkerchief around her head, aroused the zombies from the sleep that was scarcely different from their waking, gave them their morning bowl of cold, unsalted plantains boiled in water, which they ate dumbly uncomplaining, and set out with them for the town, single file, as the country people always walk. Croyance, in her bright kerchief, leading the nine dead men and women behind her, past the railroad crossing, where she murmured a prayer to Legba, past the white-painted wooden Christ, who hung life-sized in the glaring sun, where she stopped to kneel and cross herself—but the poor zombies prayed neither to Papa Legba nor to Brother Jesus, for they were dead bodies walking, without souls or minds.

They followed her to the market square, before the church where hundreds of little thatched, open shelters, used on weekdays for buying and selling, were empty of trade, but crowded here and there by gossiping groups in the grateful shade.

To the shade of one of these market booths, which was still unoccupied, she led the zombies, and they sat like people asleep with their eyes open, staring, but seeing nothing, as the bells in the church began to ring, and the procession came from the priest's house—red-purple robes, golden crucifix held aloft, tinkling bells and swinging incense pots, followed by little black boys in white lace robes, little black girls in starched white dresses, white shoes and stockings, from the parish school, with colored ribbons in their kinky hair, a nun beneath a big umbrella leading them.

Croyance knelt with the throng as the procession passed, and wished she might follow it across the square to the church steps, but the zombies just sat and stared, seeing nothing.

When noontime came, women with baskets passed to and fro in the crowd, or sat selling bonbons (which were not candy but little sweet cakes), figs (which were not figs but sweet bananas), oranges, dried herring, biscuit, casava bread, and *clairin* poured from a bottle at a penny a glass.

As Croyance sat with her savory dried herring and biscuit baked with salt and soda, and provision of *clairin* in the tin cup by her side, she pitied the zombies who had worked so faithfully for Joseph in the cane fields, and who now had nothing, while all the other groups around were feasting, and as she pitied them, a woman passed, crying.

"*Tablettes! Tablettes pistaches! T'ois pour dix cobs!*"

Tablettes are a sort of candy, in shape and size like cookies, made of brown cane sugar (*rapadou*); sometimes with *pistaches*, which in Haiti are peanuts, or with coriander seed.

And Croyance thought, "These *tablettes* are not salted or seasoned, they are sweet, and can do no harm to the zombies just this once."

So she untied the corner of her kerchief, took out a coin, a *gourdon*, the quarter of a *gourde*, and bought some of the *tablettes*, which she broke in halves and divided among the zombies, who began sucking and mumbling them in their mouths.

But the baker of the *tablettes* had salted the *pistache* nuts before stirring them into the *rapadou,* and as the zombies tasted the salt, they knew that they were dead and made a dreadful outcry and arose and turned their faces toward the mountain.

No one dared stop them, for they were corpses walking in the sunlight, and they themselves and all the people knew that they were corpses. And they disappeared toward the mountain.

When later they drew near their own village on the slopes of Morne-au-Diable, these dead men and women walking single file in the twilight, with no soul leading them or daring to follow, the people of their village, who were also holding *bamboche* in the market place, saw them drawing closer, recognized among them fathers, brothers, wives and daughters whom they had buried months before.

Most of them knew at once the truth, that these were zombies who had been dragged from their graves, but others hoped that a blessed miracle had taken place on this Fête Dieu, and rushed forward to take them in their arms and welcome them.

But the zombies shuffled through the marketplace, recognizing neither father nor wife nor mother, and as they turned leftward up the path leading to the graveyard, a woman whose daughter was in the procession of the dead threw herself screaming before the girl's shuffling feet and begged her to stay; but the grave-cold feet of the daughter and the feet of the other dead shuffled over her and onward; and as they approached the graveyard, they began to shuffle faster and rushed among the graves, and each before his own empty grave began clawing at the stones and earth to enter it again; and as their cold hands touched the earth of their own graves, they fell and lay there, rotting carrion.

That night the fathers, sons and brothers of the zombies, after restoring the bodies to their graves, sent a messenger on muleback down the mountain, who returned next day with the name Ti Joseph and with a stolen shirt of Ti Joseph's which had been worn next his skin and was steeped in the grease-sweat of his body.

They collected silver in the village and went with the name of Ti Joseph and the shirt of Ti Joseph to a *bocor* beyond Trou Caiman, who made a deadly needle *ouanga,* a black bag *ouanga,* pierced all through with pins and needles, filled with dry goat dung, circled with cock's feathers dipped in blood.

And lest the needle *ouanga* be slow in working or be rendered weak by Joseph's counter magic, they sent men down to the plain, who lay in wait patiently for Joseph, and one night hacked off his head with a machete....

When Polynice had finished this recital, I said to him, after a moment of silence, "You are not a peasant like those of the Cul-de-Sac; you are a reasonable man, or at least it seems to me you are. Now how much of this story, honestly, do you believe?"

He replied earnestly: "I did not see these special things, but there were many witnesses, and why should I not believe them when I myself have also seen zombies? When you also have seen them, with their faces and their eyes in which there is no life, you will not only believe in these zombies who should be resting in their graves, you will pity them from the bottom of your heart."

Before finally taking leave of La Gonave, I did see these "walking dead men," and I did, in a sense, believe in them and pitied them, indeed, from the bottom of my heart. It was not the next night, though Polynice, true to his promise, rode with me across the Plaine Mapou to the deserted, silent cane fields where he had hoped to show me zombies laboring. It was not on any night. It was in broad daylight one afternoon, when we passed that way again, on the lower trail to Picmy. Polynice reined in his horse and pointed to a rough, stony, terraced slope—on which four laborers, three men and a woman, were chopping the earth with machetes, among straggling cotton stalks, a hundred yards distant from the trail.

"Wait while I go up there," he said, excited because a chance had come to fulfill his promise. "I think it is Lamercie with the zombies. If I wave to you, leave your horse and come." Starting up the slope, he shouted to the woman, "It is I, Polynice," and when he waved later, I followed.

As I clambered up, Polynice was talking to the woman. She had stopped work—a big-boned, hard-faced black girl, who regarded us with surly unfriendliness. My first impression of the three supposed zombies, who continued dumbly at work, was that there was something about them unnatural and strange. They were plodding like brutes, like automatons. Without stooping down, I could not fully see their faces, which were bent expressionless over their work. Polynice touched one of them on the shoulder, motioned him to get up. Obediently, like an animal, he slowly stood erect—and what I saw then, coupled with what I had heard previously, or despite it, came as a rather sickening shock. The eyes were the worst. It was not my imagination. They were in truth like the eyes of a dead man, not blind, but staring, unfocused, unseeing. The whole face, for that matter, was bad enough. It was vacant, as if there was nothing behind it. It seemed not only expressionless, but incapable of expression. I had seen so much previously in Haiti that was outside ordinary normal experience that for the flash of a second I had a sickening, almost panicky lapse in which I thought, or rather felt, Great God, maybe this stuff is really true, and if it is true, it is rather awful, for it upsets everything. By "everything" I meant the natural fixed laws and processes on which all modern human thought and actions are based. Then suddenly I remembered—and my mind seized the memory as a man sinking in water clutches a solid plank—the face of a dog I had once seen in the histological laboratory at Columbia. Its entire front brain had been removed in an experimental operation weeks before; it moved about, it was alive, but its eyes were like the eyes I now saw staring.

I recovered from my mental panic. I reached out and grasped one of the dangling hands. It was calloused, solid, human. Holding it, I said, *"Bonjour, compère."* The zombie stared without responding. The black wench, Lamercie, who was their keeper, now more sullen than ever, pushed me away—*"Z'affai' nèg' pas z'affai' blanc"* (Negroes' affairs are not for whites). But I had seen enough. "Keeper" was the key to it. "Keeper" was the word that had leapt naturally into my mind as she protested, and just as naturally the zombies were nothing but poor, ordinary demented human beings, idiots, forced to toil in the fields.

It was a good rational explanation, but it is far from being the end of this story. It satisfied me then, and I said as much to Polynice as we went down the slope. At first he did not contradict me, even said doubtfully, "Perhaps"; but as we reached the horses, before mounting, he stopped and said, "Look here, I respect your distrust of what you call superstition and your desire to find out the truth, but if what you were saying now were the whole truth, how could it be that over and over again, people who have stood by and seen their own relatives buried have, sometimes soon, sometimes months or years afterward, found those relatives working as zombies, and have sometimes killed the man who held them in servitude?"

"Polynice," I said, "that's just the part of it that I can't believe. The zombies in such cases may have resembled the dead persons, or even been 'doubles'—you know what doubles are, how two people resemble each other to a startling degree. But it is a fixed rule of reasoning in America that we will never accept the possibility of a thing's being 'supernatural' so long as any natural explanation, even farfetched, seems adequate."

"Well," said he, "if you spent many years in Haiti, you would have a very hard time to fit this American reasoning into some of the things you encountered here."

As I have said, there is more to this story—and I think it is best to tell it very simply.

In all Haiti, there is no clearer scientifically trained mind, no sounder pragmatic rationalist, than Dr. Antoine Villiers. When I sat later with him in his study, surrounded by hundreds of scientific books in French, German and English, and told him of what I had seen and of my conversations with Polynice, he said:

"My dear sir, I do not believe in miracles nor in supernatural events, and I do not want to shock your Anglo-Saxon intelligence, but this Polynice of yours, with all his superstition, may have been closer to the partial truth than you were. Understand me clearly. I do not believe that anyone has ever been raised literally from the dead—neither Lazarus, nor the daughter of Jairus, nor Jesus Christ himself—yet I am not sure, paradoxical as it may sound, that there is not something frightful, something in the nature of criminal sorcery if you like, in some cases at least, in this matter of zombies. I am by no means sure that some of them who now toil in the fields were not dragged from the actual graves in which they lay in their coffins, buried by their mourning families!"

"It is then something like suspended animation?" I asked.

"I will show you," he replied, "a thing which may supply the key to what you are seeking," and standing on a chair, he pulled down a paperbound book from a top shelf. It was nothing mysterious or esoteric. It was the current official *Code Pénal* (Criminal Code) of the Republic of Haiti. He thumbed through it and pointed to a paragraph which read:

> "*Article* 249. Also shall be qualified as attempted murder the employment which may be made against any person of substances which, without causing actual death, produce a lethargic coma more or less prolonged. If, after the administering of such substances, the person has been buried, the act shall be considered murder no matter what result follows."

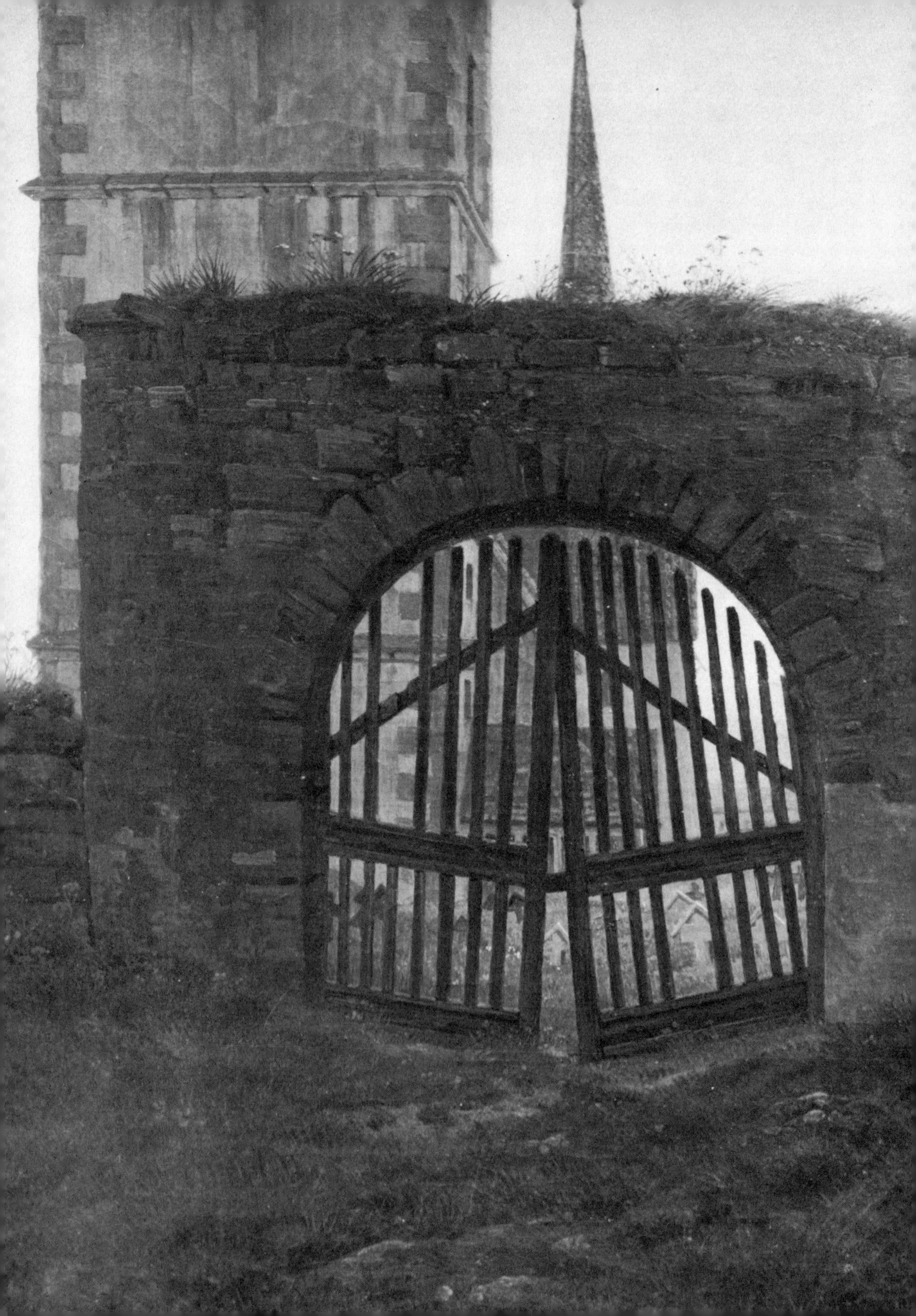

In the Vault

H. P. Lovecraft

There is nothing more absurd, as I view it, than that conventional association of the homely and the wholesome which seems to pervade the psychology of the multitude. Mention a bucolic Yankee setting, a bungling and thick-fibered village undertaker, and a careless mishap in a tomb, and no average reader can be brought to expect more than a hearty albeit grotesque phase of comedy. God knows, though, that the prosy tale which George Birch's death permits me to tell has in it aspects beside which some of our darkest tragedies are light.

Birch acquired a limitation and changed his business in 1881, yet never discussed the case when he could avoid it. Neither did his old physician, Dr. Davis, who died years ago. It was generally stated that the affliction and shock were results of an unlucky slip whereby Birch had locked himself for nine hours in the receiving-tomb of Peck Valley Cemetery, escaping only by crude and disastrous mechanical means; but while this much was undoubtedly true, there were other and blacker things which the man used to whisper to me in his drunken delirium toward the last. He confided in me because I was his doctor, and because he probably felt the need of confiding in some one else after Davis died. He was a bachelor, wholly without relatives.

Birch, before 1881, had been the village undertaker of Peck Valley, and was a very calloused and primitive specimen even as such specimens go. The practices I heard attributed to him would be unbelievable today, at least in a city; and even Peck Valley would have shuddered a bit had it known the easy ethics of its mortuary artist in such matters as the ownership of costly "laying-out" apparel invisible beneath the casket's lid, and the degrees of dignity to be maintained in posing and adapting the unseen members of lifeless tenants to containers not always calculated with sublimest accuracy. Most distinctly Birch was lax, insensitive, and professionally undesirable; yet I still think he was not an evil man. He was merely crass of fiber and function—thoughtless, careless, and liquorish, as his easily avoidable accident proves, and without that modicum of imagination which holds the average citizen within certain limits fixed by taste.

In the Vault

Just where to begin Birch's story I can hardly decide, since I am no practiced teller of tales. I suppose one should start in the cold December of 1880, when the ground froze and the cemetery delvers found they could dig no more graves till spring. Fortunately the village was small and the death rate low, so that it was possible to give all of Birch's inanimate charges a temporary haven in the single antiquated receiving-tomb. The undertaker grew doubly lethargic in the bitter weather, and seemed to outdo even himself in carelessness. Never did he knock together flimsier and ungainlier caskets, nor disregard more flagrantly the needs of the rusty lock on the tomb door which he slammed open and shut with such nonchalant abandon.

At last the spring thaw came, and graves were laboriously prepared for the nine silent harvests of the grim reaper which waited in the tomb. Birch, though dreading the bother of removal and interment, began his task of transference one disagreeable April morning, but ceased before noon because of a heavy rain that seemed to irritate his horse, after having laid but one body to its permanent rest. That was Darius Peck, the nonagenarian, whose grave was not far from the tomb. Birch decided that he would begin the next day with little old Matthew Fenner, whose grave was also near by; but actually postponed the matter for three days, not getting to work until Good Friday, the fifteenth. Being without superstition, he did not heed the day at all; though ever afterward he refused to do anything of importance on that fateful sixth day of the week. Certainly, the events of that evening greatly changed George Birch.

On the afternoon of Friday, April fifteenth, then, Birch set out for the tomb with horse and wagon to transfer the body of Matthew Fenner. That he was not perfectly sober, he subsequently admitted; though he had not then taken to the wholesale drinking by which he later tried to forget certain things. He was just dizzy and careless enough to annoy his sensitive horse, which as he drew it viciously up at the tomb neighed and pawed and tossed its head, much as on that former occasion when the rain had seemingly vexed it. The day was clear, but a high wind had sprung up; and Birch was glad to get to shelter, as he unlocked the iron door and entered the side-hill vault. Another might not have relished the damp, odorous chamber with the eight carelessly placed coffins; but Birch in those days was insensitive, and was concerned only in getting the right coffin for the right grave. He had not forgotten the criticism aroused when Hannah Bixby's relatives, wishing to transport her body to the cemetery in the city whither they had moved, found the casket of Judge Capwell beneath her headstone.

The light was dim, but Birch's sight was good, and he did not get Asaph Sawyer's coffin by mistake, although it was very similar. He had, indeed, made that coffin for Matthew Fenner; but had cast it aside at last as too awkward and flimsy, in a fit of curious sentimentality aroused by recalling how kindly and generous the little old man had been to him during his bankruptcy five years before. He gave old Matt the very best his skill could produce, but was thrifty enough to save the rejected specimen, and to use it when Asaph Sawyer died of a malignant fever. Sawyer was not a lovable man, and many stories were told of his almost inhuman vindictiveness and tenacious memory for wrongs real or fancied. To him Birch had felt no compunction in assigning the carelessly made coffin which he now pushed out of the way in his quest for the Fenner casket.

It was just as he had recognized old Matt's coffin that the door slammed to in the wind, leaving him in a dusk even deeper than before. The narrow transom admitted only the feeblest rays, and the overhead ventilation funnel virtually none at all; so that he was reduced to a profane fumbling as he made his halting way among the long boxes toward the latch. In this funereal twilight he rattled the rusty handles, pushed at the iron panels, and wondered why the massive portal had grown so suddenly recalcitrant. In this twilight, too, he began to realize the truth and to shout loudly as if his horse outside could do more than neigh an unsympathetic reply. For the long-neglected latch was obviously broken, leaving the careless undertaker trapped in the vault, a victim of his own oversight.

The thing must have happened at about three-thirty in the afternoon. Birch, being by temperament phlegmatic and practical, did not shout long; but proceeded to grope about for some tools which he recalled seeing in a corner of the tomb. It is doubtful whether he was touched at all by the horror and exquisite weirdness of his position, but the bald fact of imprisonment so far from the daily paths of men was enough to exasperate him thoroughly. His day's work was sadly interrupted, and unless chance presently brought some rambler hither, he might have to remain all night or longer. The pile of tools soon reached, and a hammer and chisel selected, Birch returned over the coffins to the door. The air had begun to be exceedingly unwholesome, but to this detail he paid no attention as he toiled, half by feeling, at the heavy and corroded metal of the latch. He would have given much for a lantern or bit of candle; but, lacking these, bungled semi-sightlessly as best he might.

When he perceived that the latch was hopelessly unyielding, at least to such meager tools and under such tenebrous conditions as these, Birch

In the Vault

glanced about for other possible points of escape. The vault had been dug from a sidehill, so that the narrow ventilation funnel in the top ran through several feet of earth, making this direction utterly useless to consider. Over the door, however, the high, slit-like transom in the brick façade gave promise of possible enlargement to a diligent worker; hence upon this his eyes long rested as he racked his brains for means to reach it. There was nothing like a ladder in the tomb, and the coffin niches on the sides and rear, which Birch seldom took the trouble to use, afforded no ascent to the space above the door. Only the coffins themselves remained as potential stepping-stones, and as he considered these he speculated on the best mode of arranging them. Three coffin-heights, he reckoned, would permit him to reach the transom; but he could do better with four. The boxes were fairly even, and could be piled up like blocks; so he began to compute how he might most stably use the eight to rear a scalable platform four deep. As he planned, he could not but wish that the units of his contemplated staircase had been more securely made. Whether he had imagination enough to wish they were empty, is strongly to be doubted.

Finally he decided to lay a base of three parallel with the wall, to place upon this two layers of two each, and upon these a single box to serve as the platform. This arrangement could be ascended with a minimum of awkwardness, and would furnish the desired height. Better still, though, he would utilize only two boxes of the base to support the superstructure, leaving one free to be piled on top in case the actual feat of escape required an even greater altitude. And so the prisoner toiled in the twilight, heaving the unresponsive remnants of mortality with little ceremony as his miniature Tower of Babel rose course by course. Several of the coffins began to split under the stress of handling, and he planned to save the stoutly built casket of little Matthew Fenner for the top, in order that his feet might have as certain a surface as possible. In the semi-gloom he trusted mostly to touch to select the right one, and indeed came upon it almost by accident, since it tumbled into his hands as if through some odd volition—after he had unwittingly placed it beside another on the third layer.

The tower at length finished, and his aching arms rested by a pause during which he sat on the bottom step of his grim device, Birch cautiously ascended with his tools and stood abreast of the narrow transom. The borders of the space were entirely of brick, and there seemed little doubt that he could shortly chisel away enough to allow his body to pass. As his hammer blows began to fall, the horse outside whinnied in a tone which may have been encouraging and may have been mocking. In either case, it would have been appropriate, for the unexpected tenacity of the easy-looking brickwork was surely a sardonic commentary on the vanity of mortal hopes, and the source of a task whose performance deserved every possible stimulus.

Dusk fell and found Birch still toiling. He worked largely by feeling now, since newly-gathered clouds hid the moon; and though progress was still slow, he felt heartened at the extent of his encroachments on the top and bottom of the aperture. He could, he was sure, get out by midnight; though it is characteristic of him that this thought was untinged with eery implications. Undisturbed by oppressive reflections on the time, the place, and the company beneath his feet, he philosophically chipped away the stony brickwork, cursing when a fragment hit him in the face, and laughing when one struck the increasingly excited horse that pawed near the cypress tree. In time the hole grew so large that he ventured to try his body in it now and then, shifting about so that the coffins beneath him rocked and creaked. He would not, he found, have to pile another on his platform to make the proper height, for the hole was on exactly the right level to use as soon as its size would permit.

It must have been midnight at least when Birch decided he could get through the transom. Tired and perspiring despite many rests, he descended to the floor and sat a while on the bottom box to gather strength for the final wriggle and leap to the ground outside. The hungry horse was neighing repeatedly and almost uncannily, and he vaguely wished it would stop. He was curiously unelated over his impending escape, and almost dreaded the exertion, for his form had the indolent stoutness of early middle age. As he remounted the splitting coffins he felt his weight very poignantly; especially when, upon reaching the topmost one, he heard that aggravated crackle which bespeaks the wholesale rending of wood. He had, it seems, planned in vain when choosing the stoutest coffin for the platform; for no sooner was his full bulk again upon it than the rotting lid gave way, jouncing him two feet down on a surface which even he did not care to imagine. Maddened by the sound, or by the stench which billowed forth even to the open air, the waiting horse gave a scream that was too frantic for a neigh, and plunged madly off through the night, the wagon rattling crazily behind it.

Birch, in his ghastly situation, was now too low for an easy scramble out of the enlarged transom, but gathered his energies for a determined try. Clutching the edges of the aperture, he sought to pull himself up, when he noticed a queer retardation in the form of an apparent drag on

In the Vault

both his ankles. In another moment he knew the fear for the first time that night; for struggle as he would, he could not shake clear of the unknown grasp which held his feet in relentless captivity. Horrible pains, as of savage wounds, shot through his calves; and in his mind was a vortex of fright mixed with an unquenchable materialism that suggested splinters, loose nails, or some other attribute of a breaking wooden box. Perhaps he screamed. At any rate, he kicked and squirmed frantically and automatically whilst his consciousness was almost eclipsed in a half-swoon.

Instinct guided him in his wriggle through the transom, and in the crawl which followed his jarring thud on the damp ground. He could not walk, it appeared, and the emerging moon must have witnessed a horrible sight as he dragged his bleeding ankles toward the cemetery lodge, his fingers clawing the black mold in brainless haste, and his body responding with that maddening slowness from which one suffers when chased by the phantoms of nightmare. There was evidently, however, no pursuer; for he was alone and alive when Armington, the lodge-keeper, responded to his feeble clawing at the door.

Armington helped Birch to the outside of a spare bed and sent his little son Edwin for Dr. Davis. The afflicted man was fully conscious, but would say nothing of any consequence, merely muttering such things as "Oh, my ankles!", "Let go!", or ". . . shut in the tomb." Then the doctor came with his medicine-case and asked crisp questions, and removed the patient's outer clothing, shoes and socks. The wounds—for both ankles were frightfully lacerated about the Achilles tendons—seemed to puzzle the old physician greatly, and finally almost to frighten him. His questioning grew more than medically tense, and his hands shook as he dressed the mangled members, binding them as if he wished to get the wounds out of sight as quickly as possible.

For an impersonal doctor, Davis's ominous and awe-struck cross-examination became very strange indeed, as he sought to drain from the weakened undertaker every last detail of his horrible experience. He was oddly anxious to know if Birch were sure—absolutely sure—of the identity of the top coffin of the pile, how he had chosen it, how he had been certain of it as the Fenner coffin in the dark, and how he had distinguished it from the inferior duplicate coffin of vicious Asaph Sawyer. Would the firm Fenner casket have caved in so readily? Davis, an old-time village practitioner, had of course seen both of the respective funerals, as indeed he had attended both Fenner and Sawyer in their last illnesses. He had even wondered, at Sawyer's funeral, how the vindictive farmer had managed to lie straight in a box so closely akin to that of the diminutive Fenner.

After a full two hours Dr. Davis left, urging Birch to insist at all times that his wounds were due entirely to loose nails and splintering wood. What else, he added, could ever in any case be proved or believed? But it would be well to say as little as could be said, and to let no other doctor treat the wounds. Birch heeded this advice all the rest of his life until he told me his story, and when I saw the scars—ancient and whitened as they then were—I agreed that he was wise in so doing. He always remained lame, for the great tendons had been severed; but I think the greatest lameness was in his soul. His thinking processes, once so phlegmatic and logical, had become ineffaceably scarred, and it was pitiful to note his reaction to certain chance allusions such as "Friday," "tomb," "coffin," and words of less obvious concatenation. His frightened horse had gone home, but his frightened wits never quite did that. He changed his business, but something always preyed upon him. It may have been fear, and it may have been fear mixed with a queer belated sort of remorse for bygone crudities. His drinking, of course, only aggravated what he sought to alleviate.

When Dr. Davis left Birch that night, he had taken a lantern and gone to the old receiving-tomb. The moon was shining on the scattered brick fragments and marred facade, and the latch of the great door yielded readily to a touch from the outside. Steeled by old ordeals in dissecting-rooms, the doctor entered and looked about, stifling the nausea of mind and body that everything in sight and smell induced. He cried aloud once, and a little later gave a gasp that was more terrible than a cry. Then he fled back to the lodge and broke all the rules of his calling by rousing and shaking his patient, and hurling at him a succession of shuddering whispers that seared into the bewildered ears like the hissing of vitriol.

"It was Asaph's coffin, Birch, just as I thought! I knew his teeth, with the front ones missing on the upper jaw—never, for God's sake, show those wounds! The body was pretty badly gone, but if ever I saw vindictiveness on any face—or former face! . . . You know what a fiend he was for revenge—how he ruined old Raymond thirty years after their boundary suit, and how he stepped on that puppy that snapped at him a year ago last August. . . . He was the devil incarnate, Birch, and I believe his eye-for-an-eye fury could beat time and death! God, his rage—I'd hate to have it aimed at me!

"Why did you do it, Birch? He was a scoundrel, and I don't blame you for giving him a cast-aside coffin, but you always did go too damned far!

Well enough to skimp on the thing in some way, but you knew what a little man old Fenner was.

"I'll never get the picture out of my head as long as I live. You kicked hard, for Asaph's coffin was on the floor. His head was broken in, and everything was tumbled about. I've seen sights before, but there was one thing too much here. An eye for an eye! Great heavens, Birch, but you got what you deserved! The skull turned my stomach, but the other was worse—*those ankles cut neatly off to fit Matt Fenner's cast-aside coffin!*"

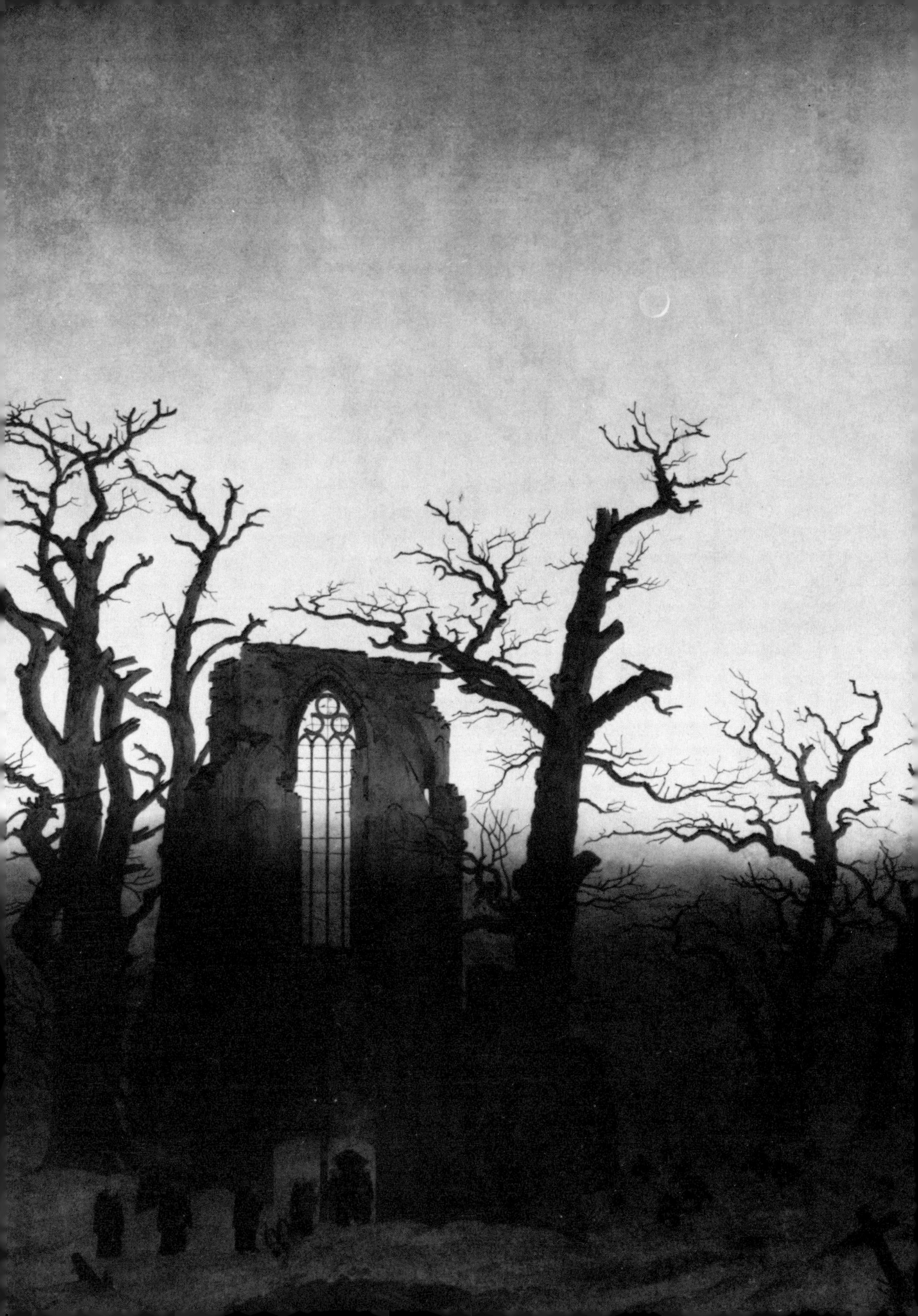

The Considerate Hosts

Thorp McClusky

Midnight.

It was raining, abysmally. Not the kind of rain in which people sometimes fondly say they like to walk, but rain that was heavy and pitiless, like the rain that fell in France during the war. The road, unrolling slowly beneath Marvin's headlights, glistened like the flank of a great blacksnake; almost Marvin expected it to writhe out from beneath the wheels of his car. Marvin's small coupé was the only man-made thing that moved through the seething night.

Within the car, however, it was like a snug little cave. Marvin might almost have been in a theater, unconcernedly watching some somber drama in which he could revel without really being touched. His sensation was almost one of creepiness; it was incredible that he could be so close to the rain and still so warm and dry. He hoped devoutly that he would have not have a flat tire on a night like this!

Ahead a tiny red pinpoint appeared at the side of the road, grew swiftly, then faded in the car's glare to the bull's-eye of a lantern, swinging in the gloved fist of a big man in a streaming rubber coat. Marvin automatically braked the car and rolled the right-hand window down a little way as he saw the big man come splashing toward him.

"Bridge's washed away," the big man said. "Where you going, Mister?"

"Felders, damn it!"

"You'll have to go around by Little Rock Falls. Take your left up that road. It's a country road, but it's passable. Take your right after you cross Little Rock Falls bridge. It'll bring you into Felders."

Marvin swore. The trooper's face, black behind the ribbons of water dripping from his hat, laughed.

"It's a bad night, Mister."

"Gosh, yes! Isn't it!"

Well, if he must detour, he must detour. What a night to crawl for miles along a rutty back road!

Rutty was no word for it. Every few feet Marvin's car plunged into water-filled holes, gouged out from beneath by the settling of the light roadbed. The sharp, cutting sound of loose stone against the tires was audible even above the hiss of the rain.

Four miles, and Marvin's motor began to sputter and cough. Another mile, and it surrendered entirely. The ignition was soaked; the car would not budge.

Marvin peered through the moisture-streaked windows, and, vaguely, like blacker masses beyond the road, he sensed the presence of thickly clustered trees. The car stopped in the middle of a little patch of woods. "Judas!" Marvin thought disgustedly. "What a swell place to get stalled!" He switched off the lights to save the battery.

He saw the glimmer then, through the intervening trees, indistinct in the depths of rain.

Where there was a light there was certainly a house, and perhaps a telephone. Marvin pulled his hat tightly down upon his head, clasped his coat collar up around his ears, got out of the car, pushed the small coupé over on the shoulder of the road, and ran for the light.

The house stood perhaps twenty feet back from the road, and the light shone from a front-room window. As he plowed through the muddy yard—there was no sidewalk—Marvin noticed a second stalled car—a big sedan—standing black and deserted a little way down the road.

The rain was beating him, soaking him to the skin; he pounded on the house door like an impatient sheriff. Almost instantly the door swung open, and Marvin saw a man and a woman standing just inside, in a little hallway that led directly into a well-lighted living-room.

The hallway itself was quite dark. And the man and woman were standing close together, almost as though they might be endeavoring to hide something behind them. But Marvin, wholly preoccupied with his own plight, failed to observe how unusual it must be for these two rural people to be up and about, fully dressed, long after midnight.

Partly shielded from the rain by the little overhang above the door, Marvin took off his dripping hat and urgently explained his plight.

"My car. Won't go. Wires wet, I guess. I wonder if you'd let me use your phone? I might be able to get somebody to come out from Little Rock Falls. I'm sorry that I had to—"

"That's all right," the man said. "Come inside. When you knocked at the door you startled us. We—we really hadn't—well, you know how it is, in the middle of the night and all. But come in."

"We'll have to think this out differently, John," the woman said suddenly.

Think what out differently? thought Marvin absently.

The Considerate Hosts

Marvin muttered something about you never can be too careful about strangers, what with so many hold-ups and all. And, oddly, he sensed that in the half darkness the man and woman smiled briefly at each other, as though they shared some secret that made any conception of physical danger to themselves quietly, mildly amusing.

"We weren't thinking of you in that way," the man reassured Marvin. "Come into the living-room."

The living-room of that house was—just ordinary. Two overstuffed chairs, a davenport, a bookcase. Nothing particularly modern about the room. Not elaborate, but adequate.

In the brighter light Marvin looked at his hosts. The man was around forty years of age, the woman considerably younger, twenty-eight, or perhaps thirty. And there was something definitely attractive about them. It was not their appearance so much, for in appearance they were merely ordinary people; the woman was almost painfully plain. But they moved and talked with a curious singleness of purpose. They reminded Marvin of a pair of gray doves.

Marvin looked around the room until he saw the telephone in a corner, and noticed with some surprise that it was one of the old-style, coffee-grinder affairs. The man was watching him with peculiar intentness.

"We haven't tried to use the telephone tonight," he told Marvin abruptly, "but I'm afraid it won't work."

"I don't see how it *can* work," the woman added.

Marvin took the receiver off the hook and rotated the little crank. No answer from Central. He tried again, several times, but the line remained dead.

The man nodded his head slowly. "I didn't think it would work," he said, then.

"Wires down or something, I suppose," Marvin hazarded. "Funny thing, I haven't seen one of those old-style phones in years. Didn't think they used 'em any more."

"You're out in the sticks now," the man laughed. He glanced from the window at the almost opaque sheets of rain falling outside.

"You might as well stay here a little while. While you're with us you'll have the illusion, at least, that you're in a comfortable house."

What on earth is he talking about? Marvin asked himself. Is he just a little bit off, maybe? That last sounded like nonsense.

Suddenly the woman spoke.

"He'd better go, John. He can't stay here too long, you know. It would be horrible if someone took his license number and people—jumped to conclusions afterward. No one should know that he stopped here."

The man looked thoughtfully at Marvin.

"Yes, dear, you're right. I hadn't thought that far ahead. I'm afraid, sir, that you'll have to leave," he told Marvin. "Something extremely strange—"

Marvin bristled angrily, and buttoned his coat with an air of affronted dignity.

"I'll go," he said shortly. "I realize perfectly that I'm an intruder. You should not have let me in. After you let me in I began to expect ordinary human courtesy from you. I was mistaken. Good night."

The man stopped him. He seemed very much distressed.

"Just a moment. Don't go until we explain. We have never been considered discourteous before. But tonight—tonight . . .

"I must introduce myself. I am John Reed, and this is my wife, Grace."

He paused significantly, as though that explained everything, but Marvin merely shook his head. "My name's Marvin Phelps, but that's nothing to you. All this talk seems pretty needless."

The man coughed nervously. "Please understand. We're only asking you to go for your own good."

"Oh, sure," Marvin said. "Sure. I understand perfectly. Good night."

The man hesitated. "You see," he said slowly, "things aren't as they seem. We're really ghosts."

"You don't say!"

"My husband is quite right," the woman said loyally. "We've been dead twenty-one years."

"Twenty-two years next October," the man added, after a moment's calculation. "It's a long time."

"Well, I never heard such hooey!" Marvin babbled. "Kindly step away from the door, Mister, and let me out of here before I swing from the heels."

"I know it sounds odd," the man admitted, without moving, "and I hope that you will realize that it's from no choosing of mine that I have to explain. Nevertheless, I was electrocuted, twenty-one years ago, for the murder of the Chairman of the School Board, over in Little Rock Falls. Notice how my head is shaved, and my split trouser-leg? The fact is, that whenever we materialize we have to appear exactly as we were in our last moment of life. It's a restriction on us."

Screwy, certainly screwy. And yet Marvin hazily remembered that School Board affair. Yes, the murderer *had* been a fellow named Reed. The wife had committed suicide a few days after burial of her husband's body.

It was such an odd insanity. Why, they *both* believed it. They even dressed the part. That odd dress the woman was wearing. 'Way out of date. And the man's slit trouser-leg. The screwy cluck had even shaved a little patch on his head, too, and his shirt was open at the throat.

They didn't look dangerous, but you never can tell. Better humor them, and get out of here as quick as I can.

Marvin cleared his throat.

"If I were you—why, say, I'd have lots of fun materializing. I'd be at it every night. Build up a reputation for myself."

The man looked disgusted. "I should kick you out of doors," he remarked bitterly. "I'm trying to give you a decent explanation, and you keep making fun of me."

"Don't bother with him, John," the wife exclaimed. "It's getting late."

"Mr. Phelps," the self-styled ghost doggedly persisted, ignoring the woman's interruption, "perhaps you noticed a car stalled on the side of the road as you came in our yard. Well, that car, Mr. Phelps, belongs to Lieutenant-Governor Lyons, of Felders, who prosecuted me for that murder and won a conviction, although he knew that I was innocent. Of course he wasn't Lieutenant-Governor then; he was only County Prosecutor. . . .

"That was a political murder, and Lyons knew it. But at that time he still had his way to make in the world—and circumstances pointed toward me. For example, the body of the slain man was found in the ditch just beyond my house. The body had been robbed. The murderer had thrown the victim's pocketbook and watch under our front steps. Lyons said that I had *hidden* them there—though obviously I'd never have done a suicidal thing like that, had I really been the murderer. Lyons knew that, too—but he had to burn somebody.

"What really convicted me was the fact that my contract to teach had not been renewed that spring. It gave Lyons a readymade motive to pin on me.

"So he framed me. They tried, sentenced, and electrocuted me, all very neatly and legally. Three days after I was buried, my wife committed suicide."

Though Marvin was a trifle afraid, he was nevertheless beginning to enjoy himself. Boy, what a story to tell the gang! If only they'd believe him!

"I can't understand," he pointed out slyly, "how you can be so free with this house if, as you say, you've been dead twenty-one years or so.

Don't the present owners or occupants object? If I lived here I certainly wouldn't turn the place over to a couple of ghosts—especially on a night like this!"

The man answered readily, "I told you that things are not as they seem. This house has not been lived in since Grace died. It's not a very modern house, anyway—and people have natural prejudices. At this very moment you are standing in an empty room. Those windows are broken. The wallpaper has peeled away, and half the plaster has fallen off the walls. There is really no light in the house. If things appear to you as they really are you could not see your hand in front of your face."

Marvin felt in his pocket for his cigarettes. "Well," he said, "you seem to know all the answers. Have a cigarette. Or don't ghosts smoke?"

The man extended his hand. "Thanks," he replied. "This is an unexpected pleasure. You'll notice that although there are ash-trays about the room there are no cigarettes or tobacco. Grace never smoked, and when they took me to jail she brought all my tobacco there to me. Of course, as I pointed out before, you see this room exactly as it was at the time she killed herself. She's wearing the same dress, for example. There's a certain form about these things, you know."

Marvin lit the cigarettes. "Well!" he exclaimed. "Brother, you certainly seem to think of everything! Though I can't understand, even yet, why you want me to get out of here. I should think that after you've gone to all this trouble, arranging your effects and so on, you'd want somebody to haunt."

The woman laughed dryly.

"Oh, you're not the man we want to haunt, Mr. Phelps. You came along quite by accident; we hadn't counted on you at all. No, Mr. Lyons is the man we're interested in."

"He's out in the hall now," the man said suddenly. He jerked his head toward the door through which Marvin had come. And all at once all this didn't seem half so funny to Marvin as it had seemed a moment before.

"You see," the woman went on quickly, "this house of ours is on a back road. Nobody ever travels this way. We've been trying for years to—to haunt Mr. Lyons, but we've had very little success. He lives in Felders, and we're pitifully weak when we go to Felders. We're strongest when we're in this house, perhaps because we lived here so long.

"But tonight, when the bridge went out, we knew that our opportunity had arrived. We knew that Mr. Lyons was not in Felders, and we knew

The Considerate Hosts

that he would have to take this detour in order to get home.

"We felt very strongly that Mr. Lyons would be unable to pass this house tonight.

"It turned out as we had hoped. Mr. Lyons had trouble with his car, exactly as you did, and he came straight to this house to ask if he might use the telephone. Perhaps he had forgotten us, years ago—twenty-one years is a long time. Perhaps he was confused by the rain, and didn't know exactly where he was.

"He fainted, Mr. Phelps, the instant he recognized us. We have known for a long time that his heart is weak, and we had hoped that seeing us would frighten him to death, but he is still alive. Of course while he is unconscious we can do nothing more. Actually, we're almost impalpable. If you weren't so convinced that we are real you could pass your hand right through us.

"We decided to wait until Mr. Lyons regained consciousness and then frighten him again. We even discussed beating him to death with one of those non-existing chairs you think you see. You understand, his body would be unmarked; he would really die of terror. We were still discussing what to do when you came along.

"We realized at once how embarrassing it might prove for you if Mr. Lyons' body were found in this house tomorrow and the police learned that you were also in the house. That's why we want you to go."

"Well," Marvin said bluntly, "I don't see how I can get my car away from here. It won't run, and if I walk to Little Rock Falls and get somebody to come back here with me the damage'll be done."

"Yes," the man admitted thoughtfully. "It's a problem."

For several minutes they stood like a tableau, without speaking. Marvin was uneasily wondering: Did these people really have old Lyons tied up in the hallway; were they really planning to murder the man? The big car standing out beside the road belonged to *somebody*. . . .

Marvin coughed discreetly.

"Well, it seems to me, my dear shades," he said, "that unless you are perfectly willing to put me into what might turn out to be a very unpleasant position you'll have to let your vengeance ride, for tonight, anyway."

"There'll never be another opportunity like this," the man pointed out. "That bridge won't go again in ten lifetimes."

"We don't want the young man to suffer though, John."

"It seems to me," Marvin suggested, "as though this revenge idea of yours is overdone, anyway. Murdering Lyons won't really do you any good, you know."

"It's the customary thing when a wrong has been done," the man protested.

"Well, maybe," Marvin argued, and all the time he was wondering whether he were really facing a madman who might be dangerous or whether he were at home dreaming in bed; "but I'm not so sure about that. Hauntings are pretty infrequent, you must admit. I'd say that shows that a lot of ghosts really don't care much about the vengeance angle, despite all you say. I think that if you check on it carefully you'll find that a great many ghosts realize that revenge isn't so much. It's really the thinking about revenge, and the planning it, that's all the fun. Now, for the sake of argument, what good would it do you to put old Lyons away? Why, you'd hardly have any incentive to be ghosts any more. But if you let him go, why, say, any time you wanted to, you could start to scheme up a good scare for him, and begin to calculate how it would work, and time would fly like everything. And on top of all that, if anything happened to me on account of tonight, it would be just too bad for you. *You'd* be haunted, really. It's a bad rule that doesn't work two ways."

The woman looked at her husband. "He's right, John," she said tremulously. "We'd better let Lyons go."

The man nodded. He looked worried.

He spoke very stiffly to Marvin. "I don't agree entirely with all you've said," he pointed out, "but I admit that in order to protect you we'll have to let Lyons go. If you'll give me a hand we'll carry him out and put him in his car."

"Actually, I suppose, I'll be doing all the work."

"Yes," the man agreed, "you will."

They went into the little hall, and there, to Marvin's complete astonishment, crumpled on the floor lay old Lyons. Marvin recognized him easily from the newspaper photographs he had seen.

"Hard-looking duffer, isn't he?" Marvin said, trying to stifle a tremor in his voice.

The man nodded without speaking.

Together, Marvin watching the man narrowly, they carried the lax body out through the rain and put it into the big sedan. When the job was done the man stood silently for a moment, looking up into the black invisible clouds.

"It's clearing," he said matter-of-factly. "In an hour it'll be over."

"My wife'll kill me when I get home," Marvin said.

The man made a little clucking sound. "Maybe if you wiped your ignition now your car'd start. It's had a chance to dry a little."

"I'll try it," Marvin said. He opened the hood and wiped the distributor cap and points and around the spark plugs with his handkerchief. He got in the car and stepped on the starter, and the motor caught almost immediately.

The man stepped toward the door, and Marvin doubled his right fist, ready for anything. But then the man stopped.

"Well, I suppose you'd better be going along," he said. "Good night."

"Good night," Marvin said. "And thanks. I'll stop by one of these days and say hello."

"You wouldn't find us in," the man said simply.

By Heaven, he *is* nuts, Marvin thought. "Listen, brother," he said earnestly, "you aren't going to do anything funny to old Lyons after I'm gone?"

The other shook his head. "No. Don't worry."

Marvin let in the clutch and stepped on the gas. He wanted to get out of there as quickly as possible.

In Little Rock Falls he went into an all-night lunch and telephoned the police that there was an unconscious man sitting in a car three or four miles back on the detour. Then he drove home.

Early the next morning, on his way to work, he drove back over the detour.

He kept watching for the little house, and when it came in sight he recognized it easily from the contour of the rooms and the spacing of the windows and the little overhang above the door.

But as he came closer he saw that it was deserted. The windows were out, the steps had fallen in. The clapboards were gray and weather-beaten, and naked rafters showed through holes in the roof.

Marvin stopped his car and sat there beside the road for a little while, his face oddly pale. Finally he got out of the car and walked over to the house and went inside.

There was not one single stick of furniture in the rooms. Jagged scars showed in the ceiling where the electric fixtures had been torn away. The house had been wrecked years before by vandals, by neglect, by the merciless wearing of the sun and the rain.

In shape alone were the hallway and living-room as Marvin remembered them. *"There,"* he thought, "is where the bookcases were. The table was *there*—the davenport *there*."

Suddenly he stopped, and stared at the dusty boards and underfoot.

On the naked floor lay the butt of a cigarette. And, a half-dozen feet away, lay another cigarette that had not been smoked—that had not even been lighted!

Marvin turned around blindly, and, like an automaton, walked out of that house.

Three days later he read in the newspapers that Lieutenant-Governor Lyons was dead. The Lieutenant-Governor had collapsed, the item continued, while driving his own car home from the state capital the night the Felders bridge was washed out. The death was attributed to heart disease....

After all, Lyons was not a young man.

So Marvin Phelps knew that, even though his considerate ghostly hosts had voluntarily relinquished their vengeance, blind, impartial nature had meted out justice. And, in a strange way, he felt glad that that was so, glad that Grace and John Reed had left to Fate the punishment they had planned to impose with their own ghostly hands....

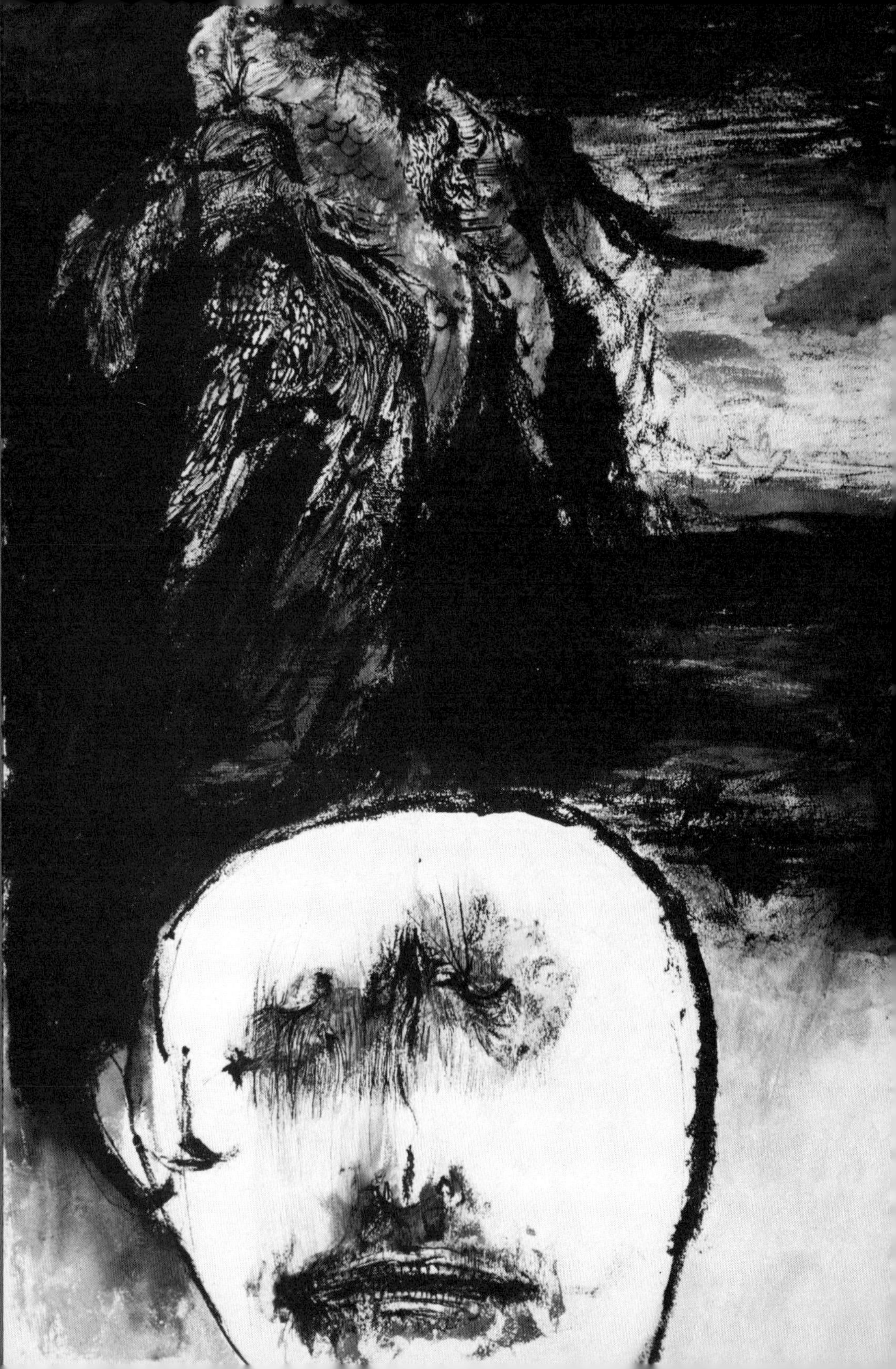

The Haunted and the Haunters

Edward Bulwer-Lytton

A friend of mine, who is a man of letters and a philosopher, said to me one day, as if between jest and earnest, "Fancy! since we last met, I have discovered a haunted house in the midst of London."

"Really haunted?—and by what? ghosts?"

"Well, I can't answer that question: all I know is this—six weeks ago my wife and I were in search of a furnished apartment. Passing a quiet street, we saw on the window of one of the houses a bill, 'Apartments Furnished.' The situation suited us; we entered the house—liked the rooms—engaged them by the week—and left them the third day. No power on earth could have reconciled my wife to stay longer; and I don't wonder at it."

"What did you see?"

"Excuse me—I have no desire to be ridiculed as a superstitious dreamer—nor, on the other hand, could I ask you to accept on my affirmation what you would hold to be incredible without the evidence of your own senses. Let me only say this, it was not so much what we saw or heard (in which you might fairly suppose that we were the dupes of our own excited fancy, or the victims of imposture in others) that drove us away, as it was an undefinable terror which seized both of us whenever we passed by the door of a certain unfurnished room, in which we neither saw nor heard anything. And the strangest marvel of all was, that for once in my life I agreed with my wife, silly woman though she be—and allowed, after the third night, that it was impossible to stay a fourth in that house. Accordingly, on the fourth morning I summoned the woman who kept the house and attended on us, and told her that the rooms did not quite suit us, and we would not stay out our week. She said, dryly, 'I know why: you have stayed longer than any other lodger. Few ever stay a second night; none before you a third. But I take it they have been very kind to you.'

" 'They—who?' I asked, affecting to smile.

" 'Why, they who haunt the house, whoever they are. I don't mind them; I remember them from many years ago, when I lived in this house, not as a servant; but I know they will be the death of me some day. I don't care—I'm old, and must die soon anyhow; and then I shall be with them, and in this house still.' The woman spoke with so dreary a calmness, that really it was a sort of awe that prevented my conversing with her further. I paid for my week, and too happy were my wife and I to get off so cheaply."

"You excite my curiosity," said I; "nothing I should like better than to sleep in a haunted house. Pray give me the address of the one which you left so ignominiously."

My friend gave me the address; and when we parted, I walked straight towards the house thus indicated.

It is situated on the north side of Oxford Street (in a dull but respectable thoroughfare). I found the house shut up—no bill at the window, and no response to my knock. As I was turning away, a beer-boy, collecting pewter pots at the neighboring areas, said to me, "Do you want any one at that house, sir?"

"Yes, I heard it was to be let."

"Let!—why, the woman who kept it is dead—has been dead these three weeks, and no one can be found to stay there, though Mr. J—— offered ever so much. He offered Mother, who chars for him, £1 a week just to open and shut the windows, and she would not."

"Would not!—and why?"

"The house is haunted; and the old woman who kept it was found dead in her bed, with her eyes wide open. They say the devil strangled her."

"Pooh!—you speak of Mr. J——. Is he the owner of the house?"

"Yes."

"Where does he live?"

"What is he—in any business?"

"No, sir—nothing particular; a single gentleman."

I gave the pot-boy the gratuity earned by his liberal information, and proceeded to Mr. J——, in G—— Street, which was close by the street that boasted the haunted house. I was lucky enough to find Mr. J—— at home, an elderly man, with intelligent countenance and prepossessing manners.

I communicated my name and my business frankly. I said I heard the house was considered to be haunted—that I had a strong desire to examine a house with so equivocal a reputation—that I should be greatly obliged if he would allow me to hire it, though only for a night. I was willing to pay for that privilege whatever he might be inclined to ask.

"Sir," said Mr. J——, with great courtesy, "the house is at your service, for as short or as long a time as you please. Rent is out of the question—the obligation will be on my side should you be able to discover the cause of the strange phenomena which at present deprive it of all value. I cannot let it, for I cannot even get a servant to keep it in order or answer the door. Unluckily the house is haunted, if I may use that expression, not only by night, but by day; though at night the disturbances are of a more unpleasant and sometimes of a more alarming character. The poor old woman who died in it three weeks ago was a pauper whom I took out of a workhouse, for in her childhood she had been known to some of my family, and had once been in such good circumstances that she had rented that house of my uncle. She was a woman of superior education and strong mind, and was the only person I could ever induce to remain in the house. Indeed, since her death, which was sudden, and the coroner's inquest, which gave it a notoriety in the neighborhood, I have so despaired of finding any person to take charge of the house, much more a tenant, that I would willingly let it rent-free for a year to any one who would pay its rates and taxes."

"How long is it since the house acquired this sinister character?"

"That I can scarcely tell you, but very many years since. The old woman I spoke of said it was haunted when she rented it between thirty and forty years ago. The fact is, that my life has been spent in the East Indies, and in the civil service of the Company. I returned to England last year, on inheriting the fortune of an uncle, among whose possessions was the house in question. I found it shut up and uninhabited. I was told that it was haunted, that no one would inhabit it. I smiled at what seemed to be so idle a story. I spent some money in repairing it—added to its old-fashioned furniture a few modern articles—advertised it, and obtained a lodger for a year. He was a colonel retired on half-pay. He came in with his family, a son and a daughter, and four or five servants: they all left the house the next day; and, although each of them declared that he had seen something different from that which had scared the others, a something still was equally terrible to all. I really could not in conscience sue, nor even blame, the colonel for breach of agreement. Then I put in the old woman I have spoken of, and she was empowered to let the house in apartments. I never had one lodger who stayed more than three days. I do not tell you their stories—to no two lodgers have there been exactly the same phenomena repeated. It is better that you should judge for yourself, than enter the house with an imagination influenced by previous narratives; only be prepared to see and to hear something or other, and take whatever precautions you yourself please."

"Have you never had a curiosity yourself to pass a night in that house?"

"Yes. I passed not a night, but three hours in broad daylight alone in that house. My curiosity is not satisfied but it is quenched. I have no desire to renew the experiment. You cannot complain, you see, sir, that I am not sufficiently candid; and unless your interest be exceedingly eager and your nerves unusually strong, I honestly add, that I advise you not to pass a night in that house."

"My interest *is* exceedingly keen," said I, "and though only a coward will boast of his nerves in situations wholly unfamiliar to him, yet my nerves have been seasoned in such variety of danger that I have the right to rely on them—even in a haunted house."

Mr. J—— said very little more; he took the keys of the house out of his bureau, gave them to me—and, thanking him cordially for his frankness, and his urbane concession to my wish, I carried off my prize.

Impatient for the experiment, as soon as I reached home, I summoned my confident servant—a young man of gay spirits, fearless temper, and as free from superstitious prejudices as any one I could think of.

"F——," said I, "you remember in Germany how disappointed we were at not finding a ghost in that old castle, which was said to be haunted by a headless apparition? Well, I have heard of a house in London which, I have reason to hope, is decidedly haunted. I mean to sleep there tonight. From what I hear, there is no doubt that something will allow itself to be seen or to be heard—something, perhaps, excessively horrible. Do you think if I take you with me, I may rely on your presence of mind, whatever may happen?"

"Oh, sir! pray trust me," answered F——, grinning with delight.

"Very well; then here are the keys of the house—this is the address. Go now—select for me any bedroom you please; and since the house has not been inhabited for weeks, make up a good fire—air the bed well—see, of course, that there are candles as well as fuel. Take with you my revolver and my dagger—so much for my weapons—arm yourself equally well; and if we are not a match for a dozen ghosts, we shall be but a sorry couple of Englishmen."

I was engaged for the rest of the day on business so urgent that I had not leisure to think much on the nocturnal adventure to which I had plighted my honor. I dined alone, and very late, and while dining, read, as is my habit. I selected one of the volumes of Macaulay's *Essays*. I thought to myself that I would take the book with me; there was so much of the healthfulness in the style, and practical life in the subjects, that it would serve as an antidote against the influence of superstitious fancy.

Accordingly, about half-past nine, I put the book into my pocket, and strolled leisurely towards the haunted house. I took with me a favorite dog—an exceedingly sharp, bold and vigilant bull-terrier—a dog fond of prowling about strange ghostly corners and passages at night in search of rats—a dog of dogs for a ghost.

It was a summer night, but chilly, the sky somewhat gloomy and overcast. Still there was a moon—faintly and sickly, but still a moon—and if the clouds permitted, after midnight it would be brighter.

I reached the house, knocked, and my servant opened with a cheerful smile.

"All right, sir, and very comfortable."

"Oh!" said I, rather disappointed; "have you not seen nor heard anything remarkable?"

"Well, sir, I must own I have heard something queer."

"What—what?"

"The sound of feet pattering behind me; and once or twice small noises like whispers close at my ear—nothing more."

"You are not at all frightened?"

"I! not a bit of it, sir," and the man's bold look reassured me on one point—viz., that happen what might, he would not desert me.

We were in the hall, the street-door closed, and my attention was now drawn to my dog. He had at first run in eagerly enough, but had sneaked back to the door, and was scratching and whining to get out. After patting him on the head, and encouraging him gently, the dog seemed to reconcile himself to the situation, and followed me and F—— through the house, but keeping close at my heels instead of hurrying inquisitively in advance, which was his usual and normal habit in all strange places. We first visited the subterranean apartments, the kitchen and other offices, and especially the cellars, in which last there were two or three bottles of wine still left in a bin, covered with cobwebs, and evidently, by their appearance, undisturbed for many years. It was clear that the ghosts were not wine-bibbers. For the rest we discovered nothing of interest. There was a gloomy little backyard with very high walls. The stones of this yard were very damp; and what with the damp, and what with the dust and smoke-grime on the pavement, our feet left a slight impression where we passed.

And now appeared the first strange phenomenon witnessed by myself in this strange abode. I saw, just before me, the print of a foot suddenly form itself, as it were. I stopped, caught hold of my servant, and pointed to it. In advance of that footprint as suddenly dropped another. We both saw it. I advanced quickly to the place; the footprint kept advancing before me, a small footprint—the foot of a child; the impression was too faint thoroughly to distinguish the shape, but it seemed to us both that it was the print of a naked foot. This phenomenon ceased when we arrived at the opposite wall, nor did it repeat itself on returning. We remounted the stairs, and entered the rooms on the ground floor, a dining parlor, a small back parlor, and a still smaller third room that had been probably appropriated to a footman—all still as death. We then visited the drawing-rooms, which seemed fresh and new. In the front room I seated myself in an armchair. F—— placed on the table the candlestick with which he had lighted us. I told him to shut the door. As he had turned to do so, a chair opposite to me moved from the wall quickly and noiselessly, and dropped itself about a yard from my own chair, immediately fronting it.

"Why, this is better than the turning tables," said I, with a half laugh; and as I laughed, my dog put back his head and howled.

F——, coming back, had not observed the movement of the chair. He employed himself now in stilling the dog. I continued to gaze on the chair, and fancied I saw on it a pale blue misty outline of a human figure, but an outline so indistinct that I could only distrust my own vision. The dog now was quiet.

"Put back that chair opposite me," said I to F——; "put it back to the wall."

F—— obeyed. "Was that you, sir?" said he, turning abruptly.

"I!—what?"

"Why, something struck me. I felt it sharply on the shoulder—just here."

"No," said I. "But we have jugglers present, and though we may not discover their tricks, we shall catch *them* before they frighten *us*."

We did not stay long in the drawing rooms—in fact, they felt so damp and so chilly that I was glad to get to the fire upstairs. We locked the doors of the drawing rooms—a precaution which, I should observe, we had taken with all the rooms we had searched below. The bedroom my servant had selected for me was the best on the floor—a large one, with two windows fronting the street. The four-posted bed, which took up no inconsiderable space, was opposite to the fire, which burned clear and bright; a door in the wall to the left, between the bed and the window, communicated with the room which my servant appropriated to himself. This last was a small room with a sofa bed, and had no communication with the landing-place—no other door but that which conducted to the bedroom I was to occupy. On either side of my fireplace was a cupboard, without locks, flush with the wall and covered with the same dull-brown paper. We examined these cupboards—only hooks to suspend female dresses—nothing else; we sounded the walls—evidently solid—the outer walls of the building. Having finished the survey of these apartments, warmed myself a few moments, and lighted my cigar, I then, still accompanied by F——, went forth to complete my reconnoiter. In the landing-place there was another door; it was closed firmly. "Sir," said my servant, in surprise, "I unlocked this door with all the others when I first came; it cannot have got locked from the inside, for—"

Before he had finished his sentence, the door, which neither of us then was touching, opened quietly of itself. We looked at each other a single instant. The same thought seized both—some human agency might be detected here. I rushed in first, my servant followed. A small blank dreary room without furniture—few empty boxes and hampers in a corner —a small window—the shutters closed—not even a fireplace—no other door than that by which we had entered—no carpet on the floor, and the floor seemed very old, uneven, worm-eaten, mended here and there, as was shown by the whiter patches on the wood; but no living being, and no visible place in which a living being could have hidden. As we stood gazing round, the door by which we had entered closed as quietly as it had before opened: we were imprisoned.

For the first time I felt a creep of undefinable horror. Not so my servant. "Why, they don't think to trap us, sir; I could break the trumpery door with a kick of my foot."

"Try first if it will open to your hand," said I, shaking off the vague apprehension that had seized me, "while I unclose the shutters and see what is without."

I unbarred the shutters—the window looked on the little back yard I have before described; there was no ledge without—nothing to break the sheer descent of the wall. No man getting out of that window would have found any footing till he had fallen on the stones below.

F——, meanwhile, was vainly attempting to open the door. He now turned round to me and asked my permission to use force. And I should here state, in justice to the servant, that, far from evincing any superstitious terrors, his nerve, composure, and even gayety amidst circumstances so extraordinary, compelled my admiration, and made me congratulate myself on having secured a companion in every way fitted to the occasion. I willingly gave him the permission he required. But though he was a remarkably strong man, his force was as idle as his milder efforts; the door did not even shake to his stoutest kick. Breathless and panting, he desisted. I then tried the door myself, equally in vain. As I ceased from the effort, again that creep of horror came over me; but this time it was more cold and stubborn. I felt as if some strange and ghastly exhalation were rising up from the chinks of that rugged floor, and filling the atmosphere with a venomous influence hostile to human life. The door now very slowly and quietly opened as of its own accord. We precipitated ourselves into the landing-place. We both saw a large pale light—as large as the human figure but shapeless and unsubstantial—move before us, and ascend the stairs that led from the landing into the attics. I followed the light, and my servant followed me. It entered, to the right of the landing, a small garret, of which the door stood open. I entered in the same instant. The light then collapsed into a small globule, exceedingly brilliant and vivid; rested a moment on a bed in the corner, quivered, and vanished.

We approached the bed and examined it—a half-tester, such as is commonly found in attics devoted to servants. On the drawers that stood near it we perceived an old faded silk kerchief, with the needle still left in a rent half repaired. The kerchief was covered with dust; probably it had belonged to the old woman who had died in that house, and this might have been her sleeping room. I had sufficient curiosity to open the drawers: there were a few odds and ends of female dress, and two letters tied round with a narrow ribbon of faded yellow. I took the liberty to possess myself of the letters. We found nothing else in the room worth noticing—nor did the light reappear; but we distinctly heard, as we turned to go, a pattering footfall on the floor—just before us. We went through the other attics (in all four), the footfall still preceding us. Nothing to be seen—nothing but the footfall heard. I had the letters in my hand: just as I was descending the stairs I distinctly felt my wrist seized, and a faint soft effort made to draw the letters from my clasp. I only held them the more tightly, and the effort ceased.

We regained the bedchamber appropriated to myself, and I then remarked that my dog had not followed us when we had left it. He was thrusting himself close to the fire, and trembling. I was impatient to examine the letters; and while I read them, my servant opened a little box in which he had deposited the weapons I had ordered him to bring; took them out, placed them on a table close at my bed-head, and then occupied himself in soothing the dog, who, however, seemed to heed him very little.

The letters were short—they were dated; the dates exactly thirty-five years ago. They were evidently from a lover to his mistress, or a husband to some young wife. Not only the terms of expression, but a distinct reference to a former voyage, indicated the writer to have been a seafarer. The spelling and handwriting were those of a man imperfectly educated, but still the language itself was forcible. In the expressions of endearment there was a kind of rough wild love; but here and there were dark and unintelligible hints at some secret not of love—some secret that seemed of crime. "We ought to love each other," was one of the sentences I remember, "for how every one else would execrate us if all was known." Again: "Don't let any one be in the same room with you at night—you talk in your sleep." And again: "What's done can't be undone; and I tell you there's nothing against us unless the dead could come to life." Here there was underlined in a better handwriting (a female's), "They do!" At the end of the letter latest in date the same female hand had written these words: "Lost at sea the 4th of June, the same day as———."

I put down the letters, and began to muse over their contents.

Fearing, however, that the train of thought into which I fell might unsteady my nerves, I fully determined to keep my mind in a fit state to cope with whatever of the marvelous the advancing night might bring forth. I roused myself—laid the letters on the table—stirred up the fire, which was still bright and cheering—and opened my volume of Macaulay. I read quietly enough till about half-past eleven. I then threw myself dressed upon the bed, and told my servant he might retire to his own room, but must keep himself awake. I bade him leave open the doors between the two rooms. Thus alone, I kept two candles burning on the table by my bed-head. I placed my watch beside the weapons, and calmly resumed my Macaulay. Opposite to me the fire burned clear; and on the hearthrug, seemingly asleep, lay the dog. In about twenty minutes I felt an exceedingly cold air pass by my cheek, like a sudden draught. I fancied the door to my right, communicating with the landing-place, must have got open; but no—it was closed. I then turned my glance to my left, and saw the flame of the candles violently swayed as by a wind. At the same moment the watch beside the revolver softly slid from the table—softly, softly—no visible hand—it was gone. I sprang up, seizing the revolver with the one hand, the dagger with the other: I was not willing that my weapons should share the fate of the watch. Thus armed, I looked round the floor—no sign of the watch. Three slow, loud, distinct knocks were now heard at the bed-head; my servant called out, "Is that you, sir?"

"No; be on your guard."

The dog now roused himself and sat on his haunches, his ears moving quickly backwards and forwards. He kept his eyes fixed on me with a look so strange that he concentered all my attention on himself. Slowly he rose up, all his hair bristling, and stood perfectly rigid, and with the same wild stare. I had no time, however, to examine the dog. Presently my servant emerged from his room; and if ever I saw horror in the human face, it was then. I should not have recognized him had we met in the street, so altered was every lineament. He passed by me quickly, saying in a whisper that seemed scarcely to come from his lips, "Run—run! it is after me!" He gained the door to the landing, pulled it open, and rushed forth. I followed him into the landing involuntarily, calling him to stop; but, without heeding me, he bounded down the stairs, clinging to the balusters, and taking several steps at a time. I heard, where I stood, the street-door open—heard it again clap to. I was left alone in the haunted house.

It was but for a moment that I remained undecided whether or not to follow my servant; pride and curiosity alike forbade so dastardly a flight. I re-entered my room, closing the door after me, and proceeded cautiously into the interior chamber. I encountered nothing to justify my servant's terror. I again carefully examined the walls, to see if there were any concealed door. I could find no trace of one—not even a seam in the dull-brown paper with which the room was hung. How, then, had the THING, whatever it was, which had so scared him, obtained ingress except through my own chamber?

I returned to my room, shut and locked the door that opened upon the interior one, and stood on the hearth, expectant and prepared. I now perceived that the dog had slunk into an angle of the wall, and was pressing himself close against it, as if literally striving to force his way into it. I approached the animal and spoke to it; the poor brute was evidently beside itself with terror. It showed all its teeth, the slaver dropping from its jaws, and would certainly have bitten me if I had touched it. It did not seem to recognize me. Whoever has seen at the Zoological Gardens a rabbit fascinated by a serpent, cowering in a corner, may form some idea of the anguish which the dog exhibited. Finding all efforts to soothe the animal in vain, and fearing that his bite might be as venomous in that state as in the madness of hydrophobia, I left him alone, placed my weapons on the table beside the fire, seated myself, and recommenced my Macaulay.

Perhaps, in order not to appear seeking credit for a courage, or rather a coolness, which the reader may conceive I exaggerate, I may be pardoned if I pause to indulge in one or two egotistical remarks.

As I hold presence of mind, or what is called courage, to be precisely proportioned to familiarity with the circumstances that lead to it, so I should say that I had been long sufficiently familiar with all experiments that appertain to the Marvelous. I had witnessed many very extraordinary phenomena in various parts of the world—phenomena that would be either totally disbelieved if I stated them, or ascribed to supernatural agencies. Now, my theory is that the Supernatural is the Impossible, and that what is called supernatural is only a something in the laws of nature of which we have been hitherto ignorant. Therefore, if a ghost rise before me, I have not the right to say, "So, then, the supernatural is possible," but rather, "So, then, the apparition of a ghost is, contrary to received opinion, within the laws of nature—*i.e.*, not supernatural."

Now, in all that I had hitherto witnessed, and indeed in all the wonders which the amateurs of mystery in our age record as facts, a material living agency is always required. On the continent you will still find magicians who assert that they can raise spirits. Assume for the moment that they assert truly, still the living material form of the magician is present; and he is the material agency by which, from some constitutional peculiarities, certain strange phenomena are represented to your natural senses.

Accept, again, as truthful, the tales of spirit manifestation in America —musical or other sounds—writings on paper, produced by no discernible hand—articles of furniture moved without apparent human agency—or the actual sight and touch of hands, to which no bodies seem to belong —still there must be found the MEDIUM or living being, with constitutional peculiarities capable of obtaining these signs. In fine, in all such marvels, supposing even that there is no imposture, there must be a human being like ourselves by whom, or through whom, the effects presented to human beings are produced. It is so with the now familiar phenomena of mesmerism or electro-biology; the mind of the person operated on is affected through a material living agent. Nor, supposing it true that a mesmerized patient can respond to the will or passes of a mesmerizer a hundred miles distant, is the response less occasioned by a material fluid —call it Electric, call it Odic, call it what you will—which has the power of traversing space and passing obstacles, that the material effect is communicated from one to the other. Hence all that I had hitherto witnessed, or expected to witness, in this strange house, I believed to be occasioned through some agency or medium as mortal as myself: and this idea necessarily prevented the awe with which those who regard as supernatural things that are not within the ordinary operations of nature might have been impressed by the adventures of that memorable night.

As, then, it was my conjecture that all that was presented, or would be presented to my senses, must originate in some human being gifted by constitution with the power so to present them, and having some motive so to do, I felt an interest in my theory which, in its way, was rather philosophical than superstitious. And I can sincerely say that I was in as tranquil a temper for observation as any practical experimentalist could be in awaiting the effect of some rare, though perhaps perilous, chemical combination. Of course, the more I kept my mind detached from fancy, the more the temper fitted for observation would be obtained; and I therefore riveted eye and thought on the strong daylight sense in the page of my Macaulay.

I now became aware that something interposed between the page and the light—the page was overshadowed: I looked up, and I saw what I shall find very difficult, perhaps impossible, to describe.

It was a Darkness shaping itself forth from the air in very undefined outline. I cannot say it was of a human form, and yet it had more resemblance to a human form, or rather shadow, than to anything else. As it stood, wholly apart and distinct from the air and the light around it, its dimensions seemed gigantic, the summit nearly touching the ceiling. While I gazed, a feeling of intense cold seized me. An iceberg before me could not more have chilled me; nor could the cold of an iceberg have been more purely physical. I feel convinced that it was not the cold caused by fear. As I continued to gaze, I thought—but this I cannot say with precision—that I distinguished two eyes looking down on me from the height. One moment I fancied that I distinguished them clearly, the next they seemed gone; but still two rays of a pale-blue light frequently shot through the darkness, as from the height on which I half believed, half doubted, that I had encountered the eyes.

I strove to speak—my voice utterly failed me; I could only think to myself, "Is this fear? it is *not* fear!" I strove to rise—in vain; I felt as if weighed down by an irresistible force. Indeed, my impression was that of an immense and overwhelming Power opposed to any volition—that sense of utter inadequacy to cope with a force beyond man's, which one may feel *physically* in a storm at sea, in a conflagration, or when confronting some terrible wild beast, or rather, perhaps, the shark of the ocean, I felt *morally*. Opposed to my will was another will, as far superior to its strength as storm, fire, and shark are superior in material force to the force of man.

And now, as this impression grew on me—now came, at last, horror—

horror to a degree that no words can convey. Still I retained pride, if not courage; and in my own mind I said, "This is horror, but it is not fear; unless I fear I cannot be harmed; my reason rejects this thing, it is an illusion—I do not fear." With a violent effort I succeeded at last in stretching out my hand towards the weapon on the table; as I did so, on the arm and shoulder I received a strange shock, and my arm fell to my side powerless. And now, to add to my horror, the light began slowly to wane from the candles; they were not, as it were, extinguished, but their flame seemed very gradually withdrawn; it was the same with the fire—the light was extracted from the fuel; in a few minutes the room was in utter darkness.

The dread that came over me, to be thus in the dark with that dark Thing, whose power was so intensely felt, brought a reaction of nerve. In fact, terror had reached that climax, that either my senses must have deserted me, or I must have burst through the spell. I did burst through it. I found voice, though the voice was a shriek. I remember that I broke forth with words like these—"I do not fear, my soul does not fear"; and at the same time I found strength to rise. Still in that profound gloom I rushed to one of the windows—tore aside the curtain—flung open the shutters; my first thought was—LIGHT. And when I saw the moon high, clear, and calm, I felt a joy that almost compensated for the previous terror. There was the moon, there was also the light from the gas lamps in the deserted slumberous street. I turned to look back into the room; the moon penetrated its shadow very palely and partially—but still there was light. The dark Thing, whatever it might be, was gone—except that I could yet see a dim shadow, which seemed the shadow of that shade, against the opposite wall.

My eye now rested on the table, and from under the table (which was without cloth or cover—an old mahogany round table) there rose a hand, visible as far as the wrist. It was a hand, seemingly, as much of flesh and blood as my own, but the hand of an aged person—lean, wrinkled, small, too—a woman's hand. That hand very softly closed on the two letters that lay on the table: hand and letters both vanished. There then came the same three loud measured knocks I heard at the bed-head before this extraordinary drama had commenced.

As those sounds slowly ceased, I felt the whole room vibrate sensibly; and at the far end there rose, as from the floor, sparks or globules like bubbles of light, many-colored—green, yellow, fire-red, azure. Up and down, to and fro, hither, thither, as tiny Will-o'-the-Wisps the sparks moved slow or swift, each at his own caprice. A chair (as in the drawing-room below) was now advanced from the wall without apparent agency, and placed at the opposite side of the table. Suddenly as forth from the chair, there grew a shape—a woman's shape. It was distinct as a shape of life—ghastly as a shape of death. The face was that of youth, with a strange mournful beauty: the throat and shoulders were bare, the rest of the form in a loose robe of cloudy white. It began sleeking its long yellow hair, which fell over its shoulders; its eyes were not turned towards me, but to the door; it seemed listening, watching, waiting. The shadow of the shade in the background grew darker; and again I thought I beheld the eyes gleaming out from the summit of the shadow—eyes fixed upon that shape.

As if from the door, though it did not open, there grew out another shape, equally distinct, equally ghastly—a man's shape —a young man's. It was in the dress of the last century, or rather in a likeness of such dress (for both the male shape and the female, though defined, were evidently unsubstantial, impalpable—simulacra—phantasms); and there was something incongruous, grotesque, yet fearful, in the contrast between the elaborate finery, the courtly precision of that old-fashioned garb, with its ruffles and lace and buckles, and the corpse-like aspect and ghost-like stillness of the flitting wearer. Just as the male shape approached the female, the dark shadow started from the wall, all three for a moment wrapped in darkness. When the pale light returned, the two phantoms were as in the grasp of the shadow that towered between them; and there was a bloodstain on the breast of the female; and the phantom male was leaning on its phantom sword, and blood seemed trickling fast from the ruffles, from the lace; and the darkness of the intermediate Shadow swallowed them up—they were gone. And again the bubbles of light shot, and sailed, and undulated, growing thicker and thicker and more wildly confused in their movements.

The closet door to the right of the fireplace now opened, and from the aperture there came the form of an aged woman. In her hand she held letters—the very letters over which I had seen *the* Hand close; and behind her I heard a footstep. She turned round as if to listen, and then she opened the letters and seemed to read; and over her shoulder I saw a livid face, the face as of a man long drowned—bloated, bleached, sea-weed tangled in its dripping hair; and at her feet lay a form as of a corpse, and beside the corpse there cowered a child, a miserable squalid child, with famine in its cheeks and fear in its eyes. And as I looked in the old woman's face, the wrinkles and lines vanished and it became a face of youth—hard-eyed, stony, but still youth; and the Shadow darted forth, and darkened over these phantoms as it had darkened over the last.

Nothing now was left but the Shadow, and on that my eyes were intently fixed, till again eyes grew out of the Shadow—malignant, serpent eyes. And the bubbles of light again rose and fell, and in their disorder, irregular, turbulent maze, mingled with the wan moonlight. And now from these globules themselves, as from the shell of an egg, monstrous things burst out; the air grew filled with them; larvae so bloodless and so hideous that I can in no way describe them except to remind the reader of the swarming life which the solar microscope brings before his eyes in a drop of water—things transparent, supple, agile, chasing each other, devouring each other—forms like nought ever beheld by the naked eye. As the shapes were without symmetry, so their movements were without order. In their very vagrancies there was no sport; they came round me and round, thicker and faster and swifter, swarming over my head, crawling over my right arm, which was outstretched in involuntary command against all evil beings. Sometimes I felt myself touched, but not by them; invisible hands touched me. Once I felt the clutch as of cold soft fingers at my throat. I was still equally conscious that if I gave way to fear I should be in bodily peril; and I concentrated all my faculties in the single focus of resisting, stubborn will. And I turned my sight from the Shadow—above all, from those strange serpent eyes—eyes that had now become distinctly visible. For there, though in nought else round me, I was aware that there was a WILL, and a will of intense, creative, working evil, which might crush down on my own.

The pale atmosphere in the room began now to redden as if in the air of some near conflagration. The larvae grew lurid as things that live in fire. Again the room vibrated; again were heard the three measured knocks; and again all things were swallowed up in the darkness of the dark Shadow, as if out of that darkness all had come, into that darkness all returned.

As the gloom receded, the Shadow was wholly gone. Slowly as it had been withdrawn, the flame grew again into the candles on the table, again into the fuel in the grate. The whole room came once more calmly, healthfully into sight.

The two doors were still closed, the door communicating with the servant's room still locked. In the corner of the wall into which he had so convulsively niched himself, lay the dog. I called to him—no movement; I approached—the animal was dead; his eyes protruded; his tongue out of his mouth; the froth gathered round his jaws. I took him in my arms; I brought him to the fire, I felt acute grief for the loss of my poor favorite—acute self-reproach; I accused myself of his death; I imagined he had died of fright. But what was my surprise on finding that his neck was actually broken. Had this been done in the dark?—must it not have been by a hand human as mine?—must there not have been a human agency all the while in that room? Good cause to suspect it. I cannot tell. I cannot do more than state the fact fairly; the reader may draw his own inference.

Another surprising circumstance—my watch was restored to the table from which it had been so mysteriously withdrawn; but it had stopped at the very moment it was so withdrawn; nor, despite all the skill of the watchmaker, has it ever gone since—that is, it will go in a strange erractic way for a few hours, and then come to a dead stop—it is worthless.

Nothing more chanced for the rest of the night. Nor, indeed, had I long to wait before the dawn broke. Nor till it was broad daylight did I quit the haunted house. Before I did so, I revisited the little blind room in which my servant and myself had been for a time imprisoned. I had a strong impression—for which I could not account—that from that room had originated the mechanism of the phenomena—if I may use the term —which had been experienced in my chamber. And though I entered it now in the clear day, with the sun peering through the filmy window, I still felt, as I stood on its floor, the creep of the horror which I had first there experienced the night before, and which had been so aggravated by what had passed in my own chamber. I could not, indeed, bear to stay more than half a minute within those walls. I descended the stairs, and again I heard the footfall before me; and when I opened the street door, I thought I could distinguish a very low laugh. I gained my own home, expecting to find my runaway servant there. But he had not presented himself; nor did I hear more of him for three days, when I received a letter from him, dated from Liverpool to this effect:

"HONORED SIR—I humbly entreat your pardon, though I can scarcely hope that you will think I deserve it, unless—which Heaven forbid—you saw what I did. I feel that it will be years before I can recover myself: and as to being fit for service, it is out of the question. I am therefore going to my brother-in-law at Melbourne. The ship sails tomorrow. Perhaps the long voyage may set me up. I do nothing now but start and tremble, and fancy IT is behind me. I humbly beg you, honored sir, to order my clothes, and whatever wages are due to me, to be sent to my mother's, at Walworth. John knows her address."

The letter ended with additional apologies, somewhat incoherent, and explanatory details as to effects that had been under the writer's charge.

This flight may perhaps warrant a suspicion that the man wished to go to Australia, and had been somehow or other fraudulently mixed up with the events of the night. I say nothing in refutation of that conjecture; rather, I suggest it as one that would seem to many persons the most probable solution of improbable occurrences. My belief in my own theory remained unshaken. I returned in the evening to the house, to bring away in a hack cab the things I had left up there, with my poor dog's body. In the task I was not disturbed, nor did any incident worth note befall me, except that still, on ascending and descending the stairs, I heard the same footfall in advance. On leaving the house, I went to Mr. J———'s. He was at home. I returned him the keys, told him that my curiosity was sufficiently gratified, and was about to relate quickly what had passed, when he stopped me, and said, though with much politeness, that he had no longer any interest in a mystery which none had ever solved.

I determined at least to tell him of the two letters in which I had read, as well as of the extraordinary manner in which they had disappeared, and I then inquired if he thought they had been addressed to the woman who had died in the house, and if there were anything in her early history which could possibly confirm the dark suspicions to which the letters gave rise. Mr. J——— seemed startled, and, after musing a few moments, answered, "I am but little acquainted with the woman's earlier history, except, as I before told you, that her family were known to mine. But you revive some vague reminiscences to her prejudice. I will make inquiries, and inform you of their result. Still, even if we could admit the popular superstition that a person who had been either the perpetrator or the victim of dark crimes in life could revisit, as a restless spirit, the scene in which those crimes had been committed, I should observe that the house was infested by strange sights and sounds before the old woman died—you smile—what would you say?"

"I would say this, that I am convinced, if we could get to the bottom of these mysteries, we should find a living human agency."

"What! you believe it is all an imposture? for what object?"

"Not an imposture in the ordinary sense of the word. If suddenly I were to sink into a deep sleep, from which you could not awake me, but in that sleep could answer questions with an accuracy which I could not pretend to when awake—tell you what money you had in your pocket—nay, describe your very thoughts—it is not necessarily an imposture, any more than it is necessarily supernatural. I should be, unconsciously to myself, under a mesmeric influence, conveyed to me from a distance by a human being who had acquired power over me by previous *rapport.*"

"But if a mesmerizer could so affect another living being, can you suppose that a mesmerizer could also affect inanimate objects: move chairs—open and shut doors?"

"Or impress our senses with the belief in such effects—we never having been *en rapport* with the person acting on us? No. What is commonly called mesmerism could not do this; but there may be a power akin to mesmerism, and superior to it—the power that in the old days was called Magic. That such a power may extend to all inanimate objects of matter I do not say; but if so, it would not be against nature—it would be only a rare power in nature which might be given to constitutions with certain peculiarities, and cultivated by practice to an extraordinary degree. That such a power might extend over the dead—that is, over certain thoughts and memories that the dead may still retain—and compel, not that which ought properly to be called the soul, and which is far beyond human reach, but rather a phantom of what has been most earth-stained on earth, to make itself apparent to our senses—is a very ancient though obsolete theory, upon which I will hazard no opinion. But I do not conceive the power would be supernatural. Let me illustrate what I mean from an experiment which Paracelsus describes as not difficult, and which the author of the *Curiosities of Literature* cites as credible: A flower perishes; you burn it. Whatever were the elements of that flower while it lived are gone, dispersed, you know not whither; you can never discover nor re-collect them. But you can, by chemistry, out of the burnt dust of that flower, raise a spectrum of the flower, just as it seemed in life. It may be the same with the human being. The soul has as much escaped you as the essence or elements of the flower. Still you may make a spectrum of it.

"And this phantom, though in the popular superstition it is held to be the soul of the departed, must not be confounded with the true soul; it is but an eidolon of the dead form. Hence, like the best attested stories of ghosts or spirits, the thing that most strikes us is the absence of what we hold to be soul; that is, of superior emancipated intelligence. These apparitions come for little or no object—they seldom speak when they do come; if they speak, they utter no ideas above those of an ordinary person on earth. American spirit-seers have published volumes of communications in prose and verse, which they assert to be given in the names of the most illustrious dead—Shakespeare, Bacon—heaven knows whom. Those communications, taking the best, are certainly not a whit of higher order than would be communications from living persons of fair talent and education; they are wondrously inferior to what Bacon, Shakespeare, and Plato said and wrote when on earth. Nor, what is more noticeable, do they ever contain an idea that was not on the earth before. Wonderful, therefore, as such phenomena may be (granting them to be truthful), I see much that philosophy may question, nothing that it is incumbent on philosophy to deny, viz., nothing supernatural. They are but ideas conveyed somehow or other (we have not yet discovered the means) from one mortal brain to another. Whether, in so doing, tables walk of their own accord, or fiend-like shapes appear in a magic circle, or bodyless hands rise and remove material objects, or a Thing of Darkness, such as presented itself to me, freeze our blood—still am I persuaded that these are but agencies conveyed, as if by electric wires, to my own brain from the brain of another. In some constitutions there is a natural chemistry, and these constitutions may produce chemic wonders—in others a natural fluid, call it electricity, and these may produce electric wonders.

"But the wonders differ from Normal Science in this—they are alike objectless, purposeless, puerile, frivolous. They lead on to no grand results; and therefore the world does not heed, and true sages have not cultivated them. But sure I am, that of all I saw or heard, a man, human as myself, was the remote originator; and I believe unconsciously to himself as to the exact effects produced, for this reason: no two persons, you say, have ever told you that they experienced exactly the same thing. Well, observe, no two persons ever experience exactly the same dream. If this were an ordinary imposture, the machinery would be arranged for results that would but little vary; if it were a supernatural agency permitted by the Almighty, it would surely be for some definite end. These phenomena belong to neither class; my persuasion is, that they originate in some brain now far distant; that that brain had no distinct volition in anything that occurred; that what does occur reflects but its devious, motley, ever-shifting, half-formed thoughts; in short, that it has been the dreams of such a brain put into action and invested with a semi-substance. That this brain is of immense power, that it can set matter into movement, that it is malignant and destructive, I believe; some material force must have killed my dog; the same force might, for aught I know, have sufficed to kill myself, had I been as subjugated by terror as the dog—had my intellect or my spirit given me no countervailing resistance in my will."

"It killed your dog! that is fearful! indeed it is strange that no animal can be induced to stay in that house; not even a cat. Rats and mice are never found in it."

"The instincts of the brute creation detect influences deadly to their existence. Man's reason has a sense less subtle, because it has a resisting power more supreme. But enough; do you comprehend my theory?"

"Yes, though imperfectly—and I accept any crotchet (pardon the word), however odd, rather than embrace at once the notion of ghosts and hobgoblins we imbibed in our nurseries. Still, to my unfortunate house the evil is the same. What on earth can I do with the house?"

"I will tell you what I would do. I am convinced from my own internal feelings that the small unfurnished room at right angles to the door of the bedroom which I occupied, forms a starting point or receptacle for the influences which haunt the house; and I strongly advise you to have the walls opened, the floor removed—nay, the whole room pulled down. I observed that it is detached from the body of the house, built over the small back yard, and could be removed without injury to the rest of the building."

"And you think, if I did that—"

"You would cut off the telegraph wires. Try it. I am so persuaded that I am right, that I will pay half the expenses if you will allow me to direct the operations."

"Nay, I am well able to afford the cost; for the rest, allow me to write to you."

About ten days afterwards I received a letter from Mr. J——, telling me that he had visited the house since I had seen him; that he had found the two letters I had described replaced in the drawer from which I had taken them; that he had read them with misgivings like my own; that he had instituted a cautious inquiry about the woman to whom I rightly conjectured they had been written. It seemed that thirty-six years ago (a year before the date of the letters) she had married, against the wish of her relations, an American of very suspicious character, in fact, he was generally believed to have been a pirate. She herself was the daughter of very respectable tradespeople, and had served in the capacity of nursery governess before her marriage. She had a brother, a widower, who was considered wealthy, and who had one child of about six years old. A month after the marriage, the body of this brother was found in the Thames, near London Bridge; there seemed some marks of violence about his throat, but they were not deemed sufficient to warrant the inquest in any other verdict than that of "found drowned."

The American and his wife took charge of the little boy, the deceased brother having by his will left his sister the guardian of his only child—and in the event of the child's death, the sister inherited. The child died about six months afterwards—it was supposed to have been neglected and ill-treated. The neighbors deposed to have heard it shriek at night. The surgeon who had examined it after death said that it was emaciated as if from want of nourishment, and the body was covered with livid bruises. It seemed that one winter night the child had sought to escape—crept out into the back yard—tried to scale the wall—fallen back exhausted, and been found at morning on the stones in a dying state. But though there was some evidence of cruelty, there was none of murder; and the aunt and her husband had sought to palliate cruelty by alleging the exceeding stubbornness and perversity of the child, who was declared to be half-witted. Be that as it may, at the orphan's death the aunt inherited her brother's fortune. Before the first wedded year was out the American quitted England abruptly, and never returned to it. He obtained a cruising vessel, which was lost in the Atlantic two years afterwards. The widow was left in affluence; but reverses of various kinds had befallen her; a bank broke—an investment failed—she went into a small business and became insolvent—then she entered into the service, sinking lower and lower, from housekeeper down to maid-of-all work—never long retaining a place, though nothing decided against her character was ever alleged. She was considered sober, honest, and peculiarly quiet in her ways; still nothing prospered with her. And so she had dropped into the workhouse, from which Mr. J—— had taken her, to be placed in charge of the very house which she had rented as mistress in the first years of her wedded life.

Mr. J—— added that he had passed an hour alone in the unfurnished room which I had urged him to destroy, and that his impressions of dread while there were so great, though he had neither heard nor seen anything, that he was eager to have the walls bared and the floors removed as I had suggested. He had engaged persons for the work, and would commence any day I would name.

The day was accordingly fixed. I repaired to the haunted house—he went into the blind dreary room, took up the skirting, and then the floors. Under the rafters, covered with rubbish, was found a trap-door, quite large enough to admit a man. It was closely nailed down, with clamps and rivets of iron. On removing these we descended into a room below, the existence of which had never been suspected. In this room there had been a window and a flue, but they had been bricked over, evidently for many years. By the help of candles we examined this place; it still retained some mouldering furniture—three chairs, an oak settle, a table—all of the fashion of about eighty years ago. There was a chest of drawers against the wall, in which we found, half-rotted away, old-fashioned articles of a man's dress, such as might have been worn eighty or a hundred years ago by a gentleman of some rank—costly steel buckles and buttons, like those yet worn in court-dresses, a handsome court sword—in a waistcoat which had once been rich with gold-lace, but which was now blackened and foul with damp, we found five guineas, a few silver coins, and an ivory ticket, probably for some place of entertainment long since passed away. But our main discovery was in a kind of iron safe fixed to the wall, the lock of which it cost us much trouble to get picked.

In this safe were three shelves, and two small drawers. Ranged on the shelves were several bottles of crystal, hermetically stopped. They contained colorless volatile essences, of the nature of which I shall only say that they were not poisons—phosphor and ammonia entered into some of them. There were also some very curious glass tubes, and a small pointed rod of iron, with a large lump of rock-crystal, and another of amber—also a loadstone of great power.

In one of the drawers we found a miniature portrait set in gold, and retaining the freshness of its colors most remarkably, considering the length of time it had probably been there. The portrait was that of a man who might be somewhat advanced in middle life, perhaps forty-seven or forty-eight.

It was a remarkable face—a most impressive face. If you could fancy some mighty serpent transformed into a man, preserving in the human lineaments the old serpent type, you would have a better idea of that countenance than long descriptions can convey: the width and flatness of frontal—the tapering elegance of contour disguising the strength of the deadly jaw—the long, large, terrible eye, glittering and green as the emerald—and withal a certain ruthless calm, as if from the consciousness of an immense power.

Mechanically I turned round the miniature to examine the back of it, and on the back was engraved a pentacle; in the middle of the pentacle a ladder, and the third step of the ladder was formed by the date 1765. Examining still more minutely, I detected a spring; this, on being pressed, opened the back of the miniature as a lid. Withinside the lid were engraved, "Marianna to thee—be faithful in life and in death to———." Here follows a name that I will not mention, but it was not unfamiliar to me. I had heard it spoken by old men in my childhood as the name borne by a dazzling charlatan who had made a great sensation in London for a year or so, and had fled the country on the charge of a double murder within his own house—that of his mistress and his rival. I said nothing of this to Mr. J——, to whom reluctantly I resigned the miniature.

We had found no difficulty in opening the first drawer within the iron safe; we found great difficulty in opening the second: it was not locked, but it resisted all efforts, till we inserted in the chinks the edge of a chisel. When we had thus drawn it forth we found a very singular apparatus in the nicest order. Upon a small thin book, or rather tablet, was placed a saucer of crystal: this saucer was filled with a clear liquid—on that liquid floated a kind of compass, with a needle shifting rapidly round; but instead of the usual points of a compass were seven strange characters, not very unlike those used by astrologers to denote the planets.

A particular, but not strong nor displeasing odor came from this drawer, which was lined with a wood that we afterwards discovered to be hazel. Whatever the cause of this odor, it produced a material effect on the nerves. We all felt it, even the two workmen who were in the room—a creeping tingling sensation from the tips of the fingers to the roots of the hair. Impatient to examine the tablet, I removed the saucer. As I did so the needle of the compass went round and round with exceeding swiftness, and I felt a shock that ran through my whole frame, so that I dropped the saucer on the floor. The liquid was spilt—the saucer was broken—the compass rolled to the end of the room—and at that instant the walls shook to and fro, as if a giant had swayed and rocked them.

The two workmen were so frightened that they ran up the ladder by which we had descended from the trapdoor; but seeing that nothing more happened, they were easily induced to return.

Meanwhile I had opened the tablet: it was bound in plain red leather, with a silver clasp; it contained but one sheet of thick vellum, and on that sheet were inscribed within a double pentacle, words in old monkish Latin, which are literally to be translated thus:

> *On all that it can reach within these walls—sentient or inanimate, living or dead—as moves the needle, so work my will! Accursed be the house, and restless be the dwellers therein.*

We found no more. Mr. J—— burnt the tablet and its anathema. He razed to the foundations the part of the building containing the secret room with the chamber over it. He had then the courage to inhabit the house himself for a month, and a quieter, better-conditioned house could not be found in all London. Subsequently he let it to advantage, and his tenant has made no complaints.

SWEET WILLIAM'S GHOST

There came a ghost to Margret's door,
   With many a grievous groan,
And ay he tirled at the pin,
   But answer made she none.

'Is that my father Philip,
   Or is't my brother John?
Or is't my true-love, Willy,
   From Scotland new come home?'

'T is not thy father Philip,
   Nor yet thy brother John;
But 't is thy true-love, Willy,
   From Scotland new come home.

'O sweet Margret, O dear Margret,
   I pray thee speak to me;
Give me my faith and troth, Margret,
   As I gave it to thee.'

'Thy faith and troth thou's never get,
   Nor yet will I thee lend,
Till that thou come within my bower
   And kiss my cheek and chin.'

'If I shoud come within thy bower,
   I am no earthly man;
And shoud I kiss thy rosy lips,
   Thy days will not be lang.'

'O sweet Margret, O dear Margret,
   I pray thee speak to me;
Give me my faith and troth, Margret,
   As I gave it to thee.'

'Thy faith and troth thou's never get,
   Nor yet will I thee lend,
Till you take me to yon kirk
   And wed me with a ring.'

'My bones are buried in yon kirk-yard,
　　Afar beyond the sea,
And it is but my spirit, Margret,
　　That's now speaking to thee.'

'She stretched out her lilly-white hand,
　　And, for to do her best,
Hae, there's your faith and troth, Willy,
　　God send your soul good rest.'

Now she has kilted her robes of green
　　A piece below her knee,
And a' the live-lang winter night
　　The dead corp followed she.

'Is there any room at your head, Willy?
　　Or any room at your feet?
Or any room at your side, Willy,
　　Wherein that I may creep?'

'There's no room at my head, Margret,
　　There's no room at my feet;
There's no room at my side, Margret,
　　My coffin's made so meet.'

Then up and crew the red, red cock,
　　And up then crew the gray:
'T is time, 't is time, my dear Margret
　　That you were going away.'

No more the ghost to Margret said,
　　But, with a grievous groan,
Evanished in a cloud of mist,
　　And left her all alone.

'O stay, my only true-love, stay,'
　　The constant Margret cry'd;
Wan grew her cheeks, she closed her een,
　　Stretched her soft limbs, and dy'd.

Anonymous

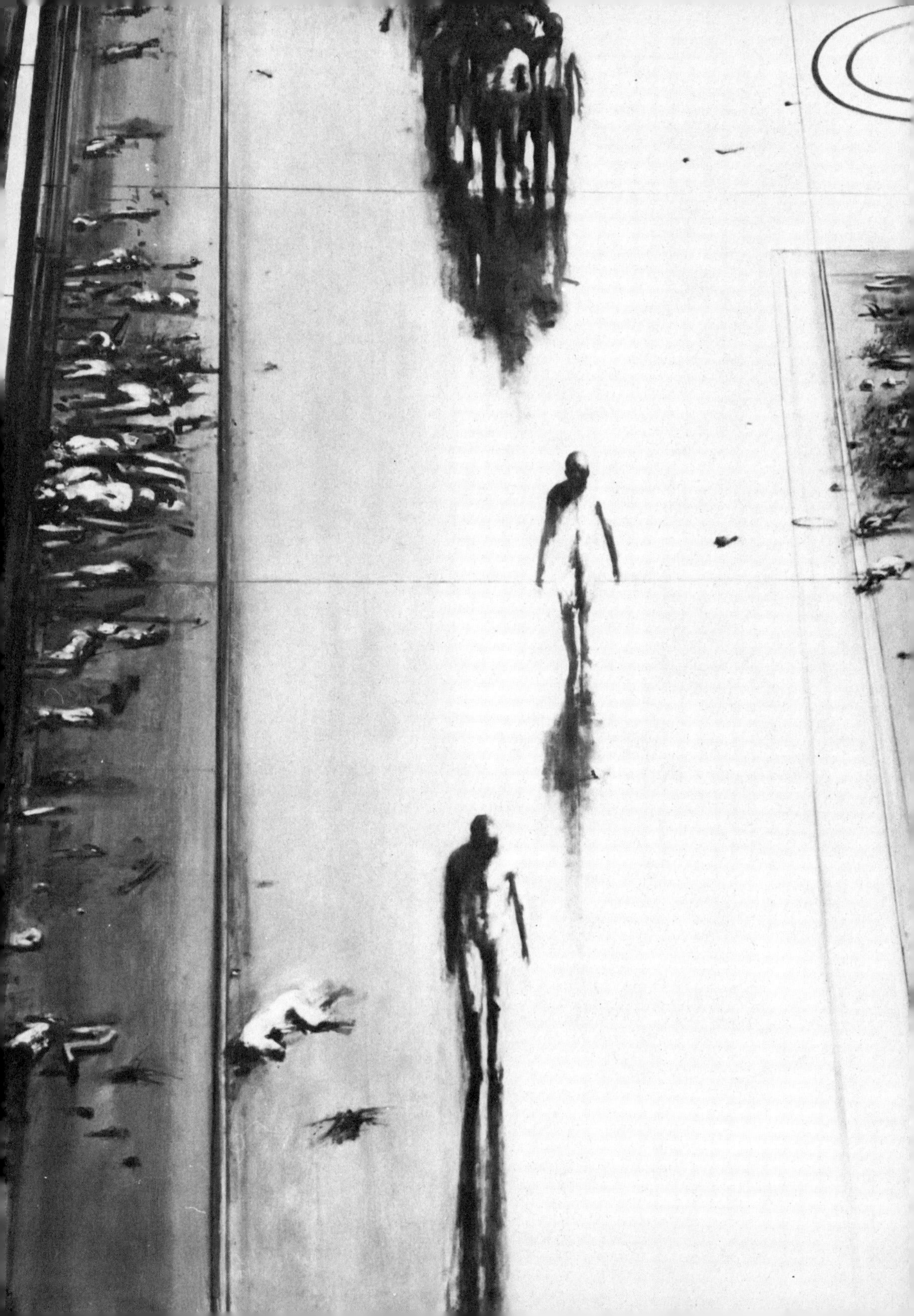

Footsteps Invisible

Robert Arthur

The night was dark, and violent with storm. Rain beat down as if from an angry heaven, and beneath its force all the noises of a metropolis blended oddly, so that to Jorman they sounded like the muted grumble of the city itself.

He himself was comfortable enough, however. The little box-sized newsstand beside the subway entrance was tight against the rain.

The window that he kept open to hear prospective customers, take in change, and pass out papers let in a wet chill, but a tiny oil heater in one corner gave out a glow of warmth that beat it back.

A midget radio shrilled sweetly, and Foxfire, his toy wire-haired terrier, snored at his feet.

Jorman reached up and switched the radio off. There were times when it gave him pleasure. But more often he preferred to listen to life itself, as it poured past his stand like a river.

Tonight, though, even Times Square was deserted to the storm gods. Jorman listened and could not hear a single footstep, though his inner time sense—reenforced by a radio announcement a moment before—told him it was barely half past twelve.

He lit a pipe and puffed contentedly.

After a moment he lifted his head. Footsteps were approaching: slow, measured, familiar footsteps. They paused in front of his stand momentarily, and he smiled.

"Hello, Clancy," he greeted the cop on the beat. "A nice night for ducks."

"If I only had web feet," the big officer grumbled, "'twould suit me fine. You're a funny one, now, staying out so late on a night like this, and not a customer in sight."

"I like it." Jorman grinned. "Like to listen to the storm. Makes my imagination work."

"Mine, too," Clancy grunted. "But the only thing it can imagine is my own apartment, with a hot tub and a hot drink waitin'. Arrgh!"

He shook himself, and with a goodnight trampled onward.

Jorman heard the officer's footsteps diminish. There was silence for a while, save for the rush of the rain and the occasional splashing whir of a cab sloshing past. Then he heard more steps.

This time they came toward him from the side street, and he listened intently to them, head cocked a little to one side.

They were—he searched for the right word—well, odd. *Shuffle-shuffle,* as if made by large feet encased in sneakers, and they slid along the pavement for a few inches with each step. *Shuffle-shuffle—shuffle-shuffle,* they came toward him slowly, hesitantly, as if the walker were pausing every few feet to look about him.

Jorman wondered whether the approaching man could be a cripple. A clubfoot, perhaps, dragging one foot with each step. For a moment he had the absurd thought that the sounds were made by four feet, not two; but he dismissed it with a smile and listened more closely.

The footprints were passing him now, and though the rain made it hard to distinguish clearly, he had the impression that each shuffling step was accompanied by a slight clicking noise.

As he was trying to hear more distinctly, Foxfire woke from his slumbers. Jorman felt the little dog move his feet, then heard the animal growling deep in its chest. He rached down and found Foxfire huddled against his shoe, tail tucked under, hair bristling.

"Quiet, boy!" he whispered. "I'm trying to hear."

Foxfire quieted. Jorman held his muzzle and listened. The footsteps of the stranger had shuffled past him to the corner. There they paused, as if in irresolution. Then they turned south on Seventh Avenue, and after a moment were engulfed in the storm noise.

Jorman released his hold on his dog and rubbed his chin perplexedly, wondering what there could have been about the pedestrian's scent to arouse Foxfire so.

For a moment Jorman sat very still, his pipe clenched in his hand. Then with a rush of relief he heard Clancy's returning tramp. The cop came up and stopped, and Jorman did not wait for him to speak. He leaned out his little window.

"Clancy," he asked, trying to keep the excitement out of his voice, "what does that fellow look like down the block there—the one heading south on Seventh? He ought to be about in the middle of the block."

"Huh?" Clancy said. "I don't see any guy. Somebody snitch a paper?"

"No." Jorman shook his head. "I was just curious. You say there isn't anyone—"

"Not in sight," the cop told him. "Must have turned in some place.

You and me have this town to ourselves tonight. Well, be good. I got to try some more doors."

He sloshed away, the rain pattering audibly off his broad, rubber-coated back, and Jorman settled back into his chair chuckling to himself. It was funny what tricks sounds played on you, especially in the rain.

He relit his pipe and was thinking of shutting up for the night when his last customer of the evening approached. This time he recognized the steps. It was a source of pride to him—and of revenue as well—that he could call most of his regulars by name if they came up when the street wasn't too crowded.

This one, though he didn't come often and had never come before at night, was easy. The step was a firm, decisive one. *Click*—that was the heel coming down—*slap*—that was the sole being planted firmly. *Click-slap*—the other foot. Simple. He could have distinguished it in a crowd.

"Good morning, Sir Andrew," Jorman said pleasantly as the steps came up to his stand. *"Times?"*

"Thanks." It was a typically British voice that answered. "Know me, do you?"

"Oh, yes." Jorman grinned. It was usually a source of mystification to his customers that he knew their names. But names were not too hard to learn, if the owners of them lived or worked nearby. "A bellboy from your hotel was buying a paper last time you stopped. When you'd gone on, he told me who you were."

"That easy, eh?" Sir Andrew Carraden exclaimed. "Don't know as I like it so much, though, being kept track of. Prefer to lose myself these days. Had enough of notoriety in the past."

"Had plenty of it four years ago, I suppose," Jorman suggested. "I followed the newspaper accounts of your tomb-hunting expedition. Interesting work, archaeology. Always wished I could poke around in the past that way, sometime."

"Don't!" The word was sharp. "Take my advice and stay snug and cozy in the present. The past is an uncomfortable place. Sometimes you peer into it and then spend the rest of your life trying to get away from it. And— But I mustn't stop here chatting. Not in this storm. Here's your money. No, here on the counter . . ."

And then, as Jorman fumbled for and found the pennies, Sir Andrew Carraden exclaimed again.

"I say!" he said. "I'm sorry."

"Perfectly all right," Jorman told him. "It pleases me when people don't notice. A lot don't, you know, in spite of the sign."

"Blind newsdealer," Sir Andrew Carraden read the little placard tacked to the stand. "I say—"

"Wounded in the war," Jorman told him. "Sight failed progressively. Went entirely a couple of years ago. So I took up this. But I don't mind. Compensations, you know. Amazing what a lot a man can hear when he listens. But you're going to ask me how I knew you, aren't you? By your footsteps. They're very recognizable. Sort a *click-slap, click-slap.*"

His customer was silent for a moment. Jorman was about to ask whether anything was wrong when the Englishman spoke.

"Look. I"—and his tone took on an almost hungry eagerness—"I've got to talk to somebody, or blow my top. I mean, go barmy. Completely mad. Maybe I am, already. I don't know. You—you might have a few minutes to spare? You might be willing to keep me company for an hour? I—it might not be too dull."

Jorman hesitated in answering. Not because he intended to refuse—the urgency in the man's voice was unmistakable—but there was something of a hunted tone in Sir Andrew Carraden's voice that aroused Jorman's curiosity.

It was absurd—but Jorman's ears were seldom wrong. The Englishman, the archaeologist whose name had been so prominent a few years back, was a hunted man. Perhaps a desperate man. A fugitive—from what?

Jorman did not try to guess. He nodded.

"I have time," he agreed.

He bent down and picked up Foxfire, attached the leash, threw an old ulster over his shoulders, and turned down his bright gasoline lantern. With Foxfire straining at the leash, he swung up his racks and padlocked the stand.

"This way," Sir Andrew Carraden said at his side. "Not half a block. Like to take my arm?"

"Thanks." Jorman touched the other's elbow. The touch told him what he remembered from photographs in the papers he had seen, years back. The Britisher was a big man. Not the kind to fear anything. Yet now he was afraid.

They bowed their heads to the somewhat lessened rain and walked the short distance to the hotel.

They turned into the lobby, their heels loud on marble. Jorman knew the place: the Hotel Russet. Respectable, but a bit run down.

As they passed the desk, a sleepy clerk called out.

"Oh, pardon me. There's a message here for you. From the manager.

Relative to some work we've been doing—"

"Thanks, thanks," Jorman's companion answered impatiently, and Jorman heard paper stuffed into a pocket. "Here's the elevator. Step up just a bit."

They had been seated in easy chairs for some minutes, pipes going, hot drinks in front of them, before Sir Andrew Carraden made any further reference to the thing that was obviously on his mind.

The room they were in was fairly spacious, judging from the reverberations of their voices, and since it seemed to be a sitting room, probably was joined to a bedroom beyond. Foxfire slumbering at Jorman's feet, they had been talking of inconsequentials—when the Englishman interrupted himself abruptly.

"Jorman," he said, "I'm a desperate man. I'm being hunted."

Jorman heard coffee splash as an unsteady hand let the cup rattle against the saucer.

"I guessed so," he confessed. "It was in your voice. The police?"

Sir Andrew Carraden laughed, a harsh, explosive sound.

"Your ears *are* sharp," he said. "The police? I wish it were! No. By a—a personal enemy."

"Then couldn't the police—" Jorman began. The other cut him short.

"No! They can't help me. Nobody in this world can help me. And God have mercy on me, nobody in the next!"

Jorman passed over the emphatic exclamation.

"But surely—"

"Take my word for it, I'm on my own," Sir Andrew Carraden told him, his voice grim. "This is a—a feud, you might say. And I'm the hunted one. I've done a lot of hunting in my day, and now I know the other side of it. It's not pleasant."

Jorman sipped at his drink.

"You—this enemy. He's been after you long?"

"Three years." The Englishman's voice was low, a bit unsteady. In his mind Jorman could see the big man leaning forward, arm braced against knee, face set in grim lines.

"It began one night in London. A rainy night like this. I was running over some clay tablets that were waiting deciphering. Part of the loot from the tomb of Tut-Ankh-Tothet. The one the stories in the papers you referred to were about.

"I'd been working pretty hard. I knocked off for a pipe and stood at the window looking out. Then I heard it."

"Heard it?"

"Heard him." Carraden corrected himself swiftly. "Heard *him* hunting for me. Heard his footsteps—"

"Footsteps?"

"Yes. In the pitch-black night. Heard him tramping back and forth as he tried to locate me. Then he picked up my trail and came up the garden path."

Sir Andrew paused, and Jorman heard the coffee cup being raised again.

"My dog, a great Dane, scented him. It was frightened, poor beast, and with reason. But it tried to attack. He tore the dog to pieces on my own doorstep. I couldn't see the fight, but I could hear. The beast held him up long enough for me to run for it. Out the back door, into the storm.

"There was a stream half a mile away. I made for that, plunged into it, floated two miles down, went ashore, picked up a ride to London. Next morning I left London on a freighter for Australia before he could pick up my trail again."

Jorman heard the archaeologist draw a deep breath.

"It took him six months to get on to me again, up in the Australian gold country. Again I heard him in time. I got away on a horse as he was forcing his way into my cabin, caught a cargo plane for Melbourne, took a fast boat to Shanghai. But I didn't stay there long."

"Why not?" Jorman asked. He fancied that Carraden had shuddered slightly.

"Too much like his own country. Conditions were—favorable for him in the Orient. Unfavorable for me. I had a hunch. I hurried on to Manila and took a plane for the States there. Got a letter from an old Chinese servant that *he* arrived the next night."

Jorman sipped slowly at his coffee, his brow knitted. He did not doubt the man's sincerity, but the story *was* a bit puzzling.

"This fellow, this enemy of yours," he commented slowly, "you said the Orient was too much like his own country. I assume you mean Egypt."

"Yes. He comes from Egypt. I incurred his—well, his enmity there."

"He's a native then? An Egyptian native?"

Carraden hesitated, seeming to choose his words.

"Well, yes," he said firmly. "In a way you might call him a native of Egypt. Though, strictly speaking, he comes from another—another country. One less well known."

"But," Jorman persisted, "I should think that you, a man of wealth, would have all kinds of recourse against a native, no matter where he might be from. After all, the man is bound to be conspicuous, and ought to be easy to pick up. I know you said the police could not help you, but have you tried? And how in the world does the fellow follow you so persistently? From London to Australia to Shanghai—that's a thin trail to run down."

"I know you're puzzled," the other told him. "But take my word for it, the police are no good. This chap—well, he just isn't conspicuous, that's all. He moves mostly by night. But even so he can go anywhere.

"He has—well, methods. And as for following me, he has his own ways of doing that, too. He's persistent. So awfully, awfully persistent. That's the horror of it: that blind, stubborn persistence with which he keeps on my trail."

Jorman was silent. Then he shook his head.

"I admit you've got me curious," he told Carraden. "I can see easily enough there are some things you don't want to tell me. I suppose the reason he's hunting you so doggedly is one of them."

"Right," the Englishman admitted. "It was while the expedition was digging out old Tut-Ankh-Tothet. It was something I did. A law I violated. A law I was aware of, but—well, I went ahead anyway.

"You see, there were some things we found buried with old Tothet the press didn't hear of. Some papyri, some clay tablets. And off the main tomb a smaller one. . . .

"Well, I can't tell you more. I violated an ancient law, then got panicky and tried to escape the consequences. In doing so, I ran afoul of this—this fellow. And brought him down on my neck. If you don't mind—"

There was a desperate note in his host's voice. Jorman nodded.

"Certainly," he agreed. "I'll drop the subject. After all, it's your business. You've never tried to ambush the fellow and have it out with him, I suppose?"

He imagined Carraden shaking his head.

"No use," the other said shortly. "My only safety is in flight. So I've kept running. When I got to 'Frisco, I thought I was safe for a while. But this time he was on my heels almost at once. I heard him coming up the street for me late one foggy night. I got out the back door and ran for it. Got away to the Canadian plains.

"I planted myself out in the middle of nowhere, on a great, rolling grassy plain with no neighbor for miles. Where no one would ever think of me, much less speak to me or utter my name. I was safe there almost a year. But in the end it was—well, almost a mistake."

Carraden put down his cup with a clatter. Jorman imagined it was because the cup had almost slipped from shaking fingers.

"You see, out there on the prairie, there were no footsteps. This time he came at night, as usual, and he was almost on me before I was aware of it. And my horse was lame. I got away. But it was a near thing. Nearer than I like to remember...

"So I came to New York. I've been here since, in the very heart of the city. It's the best place of all to hide. Among people. So many millions crossing and recrossing my path muddy up my trail, confuse the scent—"

"Confuse the scent?" Jorman exclaimed.

Carraden coughed. "Said more than I meant to, that time," he admitted. "Yes, it's true. He scents me out. In part, at least.

"It's hard to explain. Call it the intangible evidences of my passage."

"I see." The man's voice pleaded so for belief that Jorman nodded, though he was far from seeing.

"I've been here almost a year now," the Englishman told him. "Almost twelve months with no sign of him. I've been cautious; man, how cautious I've been! Lying in my burrow like a terrified rabbit.

"Most of that time I've been right here, close to Times Square, where a million people a day cut my trail. I've huddled in my two rooms here—there's a bedroom beyond—going out only by day. He is usually most active at night. In the day people confuse him. It's the lonely reaches of the late night hours he likes best. And it's during them I huddle here, listening wakefully....

"Except on stormy nights like this. Storms make his job more difficult. The rain washes away my scent, the confusion of the winds and the raging of the elements dissipates my more intangible trail. That's why I ventured out tonight.

"Some day, even here, he'll find me," Sir Andrew Carraden said continuing, his voice tight with strain. "I'm prepared. I'll hear him coming—I hope—and as he forces this door, I'll get out through the other one, the one in the bedroom, and get away. I early learned the folly of holing up in a burrow with only one exit. Now I always have at least one emergency doorway.

"Believe me, man, it's a ghastly existence. The lying awake in the quiet hours of the night, listening, listening for him; the clutch at the heart, the sitting bolt upright, the constant and continuing terror—"

Carraden did not finish his sentence. He was silent for several minutes, fighting, Jorman imagined, for self-control. Then the springs of his easy chair squeaked as he leaned forward.

"Look," the Englishman said then, in such desperate earnestness that his voice trembled a bit. "You must wonder whether I just brought you up here to tell you this tale. I didn't. I had a purpose. I told you the story to see how you reacted. And I'm satisfied. Anyway, you didn't openly disbelieve me; and if you think I'm crazy, maybe you'll humor me anyway. I have a proposition to make."

Jorman sat up a bit straighter.

"Yes?" he asked, his face expressing uncertainty. "What—"

"What kind of proposition?" Carraden finished the sentence for him. "This. That you can help me out by listening for him."

Jorman jerked his head up involuntarily, so that if he had not been blind he would have been staring into the other's face.

"Listen for your enemy?"

"Yes," the Englishman told him, voice hoarse. "Listen for his approach. Like a sentinel. An outpost. Look, man, you're down there in your little stand every evening from six on, I've noticed. You stay until late at night. You're posted there not fifty yards from this hotel.

"When he comes, he'll go by you. He's bound to have cast about a bit, to unravel the trail—double back and forth like a hunting dog, you know, until he gets it straightened out.

"He may go by three or four times before he's sure. You have a keen ear. If he goes by while you're on the job, you're bound to hear him."

Carraden's voice quickened, became desperately persuasive.

"And if you do, you can let me know. I'll instruct the doorman to come over if you signal. Or you can leave your stand and come up here; you can make it easily enough, only fifty paces. But somehow you must warn me. Say you will, man!"

Jorman hesitated in his answer. Sir Andrew mistook his silence.

"If you're frightened," he said, "there's no need to be. He won't attack you. Only me."

"That part's all right," Jorman told him honestly. "What you've told me isn't altogether clear, and—I'll be frank—I'm not absolutely sure whether you're sane or not. But I wouldn't mind listening for you. Only, don't you see, I wouldn't have any way of recognizing your enemy's step."

Carraden gave a little whistling sigh that he checked at once.

"Good man!" The exclamation was quiet, but his voice showed relief. "Just so you'll do it. That last bit is easy enough. I've heard him several times. I can imitate his step for you, I think. There's only one thing worrying me.

"He—not everyone can hear him. But I'm counting on your blindness to give your ears the extra sensitivity— No matter. We have to have a go at it. Give me a moment."

Jorman sat in silence and waited. The rain, beating against the panes of two windows, was distinctly lessening. Somewhere distant a fire siren wailed, a banshee sound.

Carraden was making a few tentative scrapings, with his hands or his feet, on the floor.

"Got it!" he announced. "I've put a bedroom slipper on each hand. It's a noise like this."

With the soft-soled slippers, he made a noise like the shuffle of a bare foot—a double sound, *shuffle-shuffle,* followed by a pause, then repeated.

"If you're extra keen," he announced, "you can hear a faint click or scratch at each step. But—"

Then Jorman heard him sit up straight, knew Carraden was staring at his face.

"What is it, man?" the Englishman cried in alarm. "What's wrong?"

Jorman sat very tense, his fingers gripping the arms of his chair.

"Sir Andrew," he whispered, his lips stiff, "Sir Andrew! I've already heard those footsteps. An hour ago in the rain he went by my stand."

In the long silence that followed, Jorman could guess how the blood was draining from the other man's ruddy face, how the knuckles of his hands clenched.

"Tonight?" Carraden asked then, his voice harsh and so low that Jorman could hardly hear him. "Tonight, man?"

"Just a few minutes before you came by," Jorman blurted. "I heard footsteps—*his* steps—shuffling by. The dog woke up and whimpered. They approached me slowly, pausing, then going on."

The Englishman breathed, "Go on, man! What then?"

"They turned. He went down Seventh Avenue, going south."

Sir Andrew Carraden leaped to his feet, paced across the room, wheeled, came back.

"He's tracked me down at last!" he said in a tight voice, from which a note of hysteria was not far absent. "I've got to go. Tonight. Now. You say he turned south?"

Jorman nodded.

"But that means nothing." Carraden spoke swiftly, as if thinking out loud. "He'll find he's lost the track. He'll turn back. And since he passed, I've made a fresh trail. The rain may not have washed it quite away. He may have picked it up. He may be coming up those stairs now. Where's my bag? My passport? My money? All in my bureau. Excuse me. Sit tight."

Jorman heard a door flung open, heard the man rush into the adjoining bedroom, heard a tight bureau drawer squeal.

Then Carraden's footsteps again. A moment after, a bolt on a door pulled back. Then the door itself rattled. A pause, and it rattled again, urgently. Once again, this time violently. Jorman could hear Carraden's loud breathing in the silence that followed.

"The door won't open!" There was an edge of fear in the Englishman's voice as he called out. "There's a key or something in the lock. From the outside."

He came back into the sitting room with a rush, paused beside Jorman.

"That message!" The words came through Carraden's teeth. "The one the bloody clerk handed me. I wonder if—"

Paper ripped, rattled. Sir Andrew Carraden began to curse.

"The fool!" he almost sobbed. "Oh, the bloody, bloody fool. 'Dear sir' "—Carraden's voice was shaking now—" 'redecoration of the corridor on the north side of your suite necessitated our opening your door this afternoon to facilitate the painting of it. In closing and locking it, a key inadvertently jammed in the lock, and we could not at once extricate it. Our locksmith will repair your lock promptly in the morning. Trusting you will not be inconvenienced—'

"God deliver us from fools!" Sir Andrew gasped. "Luckily there's still time to get out this way. Come on, man, don't sit there. I'll show you down. But we must hurry, hurry."

Jorman heard the other man's teeth chattering faintly together in the excess of emotion that was shaking him, felt the musclar quivering of near-panic in the big man as he put out his hand and took Sir Andrew's arm to help himself rise. And then, as he was about to lift himself, his fingers clamped tight about the Englishman's wrist.

"Carraden!" he whispered. "Carraden! *Listen!*"

The other asked no question. Jorman felt the quivering muscles beneath his fingers tense. And a silence that was like a hand squeezing them breathless seemed to envelop the room. There was not even the faint, distant sound of traffic to break it.

Then they both heard it. In the hallway, coming toward the door. The faint padding sound of shuffling footsteps . . .

It was Foxfire, whimpering piteously at their feet, that broke the spell momentarily holding them.

"He"—Carraden's word was a gasp—"he's out there!"

He left Jorman's side. Jorman heard him shoving with desperate strength at something heavy. Castors squeaked. Some piece of furniture tipped over and fell with a crash against the inside of the door.

"There!" Carraden groaned. "The desk. And the door's bolted. That'll hold him a moment. Sit tight, man. Hold the pup. He'll ignore you. It's me he wants. I've got to get that other door open before he can come through."

His footsteps raced away into the bedroom. Jorman sat where he was, Foxfire under his arm, so tense that his muscles ached from sheer fright.

In the bedroom there was a crash, as of a man plunging against a closed door that stubbornly would not give. But above the noise from the bedroom, Jorman could hear the barricaded door—the door beyond which *he* was—start to give.

Nails screamed as they came forth from wood. Hinges groaned. And the whole mass—door, lintels, desk—moved inward an inch or so. A pause, and then the terrible, inexorable pressure from the other side came again. With a vast rending the door gave way and crashed inward over the barricading furniture.

And in the echoes of the crash he heard the almost soundless *shuffle-shuffle* of feet crossing the room toward the bedroom.

In the bedroom Sir Andrew Carraden's efforts to force the jammed door ceased suddenly. Then the Englishman screamed, an animal cry of pure terror from which all intelligence was gone. The window in the bedroom crashed up with a violence that shattered the glass.

After that there was silence for a moment, until Jorman's acute hearing caught, from the street outside and five floors down, the sound of an object striking the pavement.

Sir Andrew Carraden had jumped . . .

Somehow Jorman found the strength to stumble to his feet. He dashed straight forward toward the door, and fell over the wreckage of it. Hurt, but not feeling it, he scrambled up again and stumbled into the hall and down the corridor.

Somehow his questing hands found a door that was sheathed in metal, and he thrust it open. Beyond were bannisters. Stairs. By the sense of feel he rushed down recklessly.

How many minutes it took to reach the lobby, to feel his way blindly past the startled desk clerk out to the street, he did not know. Or whether he had gotten down before *he* had.

Once outside on the wet pavement, cool night air on his cheek, he paused, his breath coming in sobbing gasps. And as he stood there, footsteps, shuffling footsteps, passed close by him from behind and turned westward.

Then Jorman heard an astounding thing. He heard Sir Andrew Carraden's footsteps also, a dozen yards distant, hurrying away from him.

Sir Andrew Carraden had leaped five floors. And still could walk....

No, run. For the tempo of the man's steps was increasing. He was trotting now. Now running. And behind the running footsteps of Carraden were *his* steps, moving more swiftly, too, something scratching loudly on the concrete each time he brought a foot down.

"Sir Andrew!" Jorman called loudly, senselessly. "Sir An—"

Then he stumbled and almost fell, trying to follow. Behind him the desk clerk came hurrying up. He exclaimed something in shocked tones, but Jorman did not even hear him. He was bending down, his hand exploring the object over which he had stumbled.

"Listen!" Jorman gasped with a dry mouth to the desk clerk, jittering above him. "Tell me quick! I've got to know. What did the man look like who followed me out of the hotel just now?"

"F-followed you?" the clerk stuttered. "Nobody f-followed you. Nobody but you has gone in or out in the last h-half hour. Listen, why did he do it? Why did he jump?"

Jorman did not answer him.

"Dear God," he was whispering, and in a way it was a prayer. "Oh, dear God!"

His hand was touching the dead body of Andrew Carraden, lying broken and bloody on the pavement.

But his ears still heard those footsteps of pursued and pursuer, far down the block, racing away until not even he could make them out any longer.

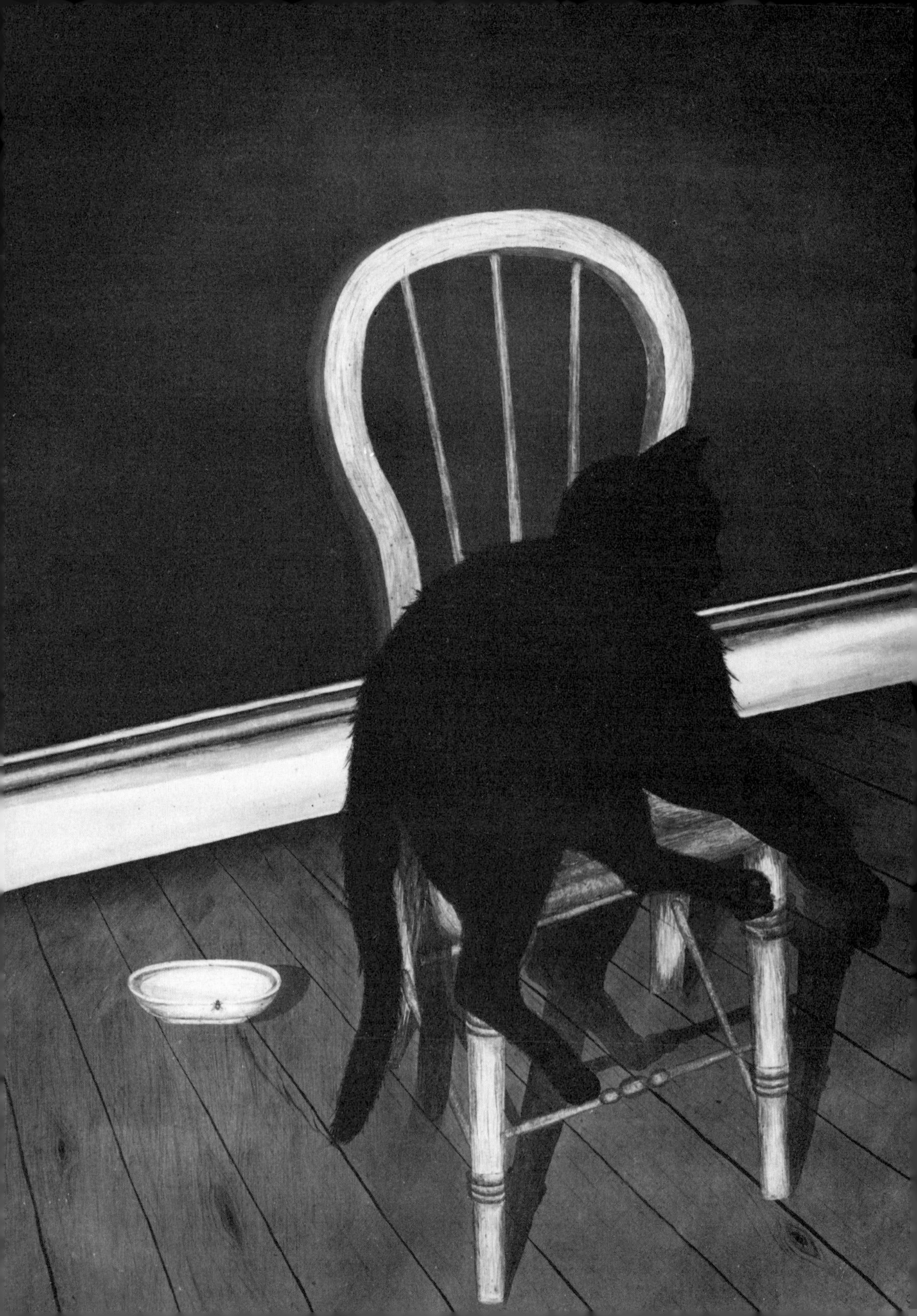

The Black Cat

Edgar Allan Poe

For the most wild yet most homely narrative which I am about to pen, I neither expect nor solicit belief. Mad indeed would I be to expect it, in a case where my very senses reject their own evidence. Yet, mad am I not—and very surely do I not dream. But to-morrow I die, and today I would unburden my soul. My immediate purpose is to place before the world, plainly, succinctly, and without comment, a series of mere household events. In their consequences, these events have terrified—have tortured—have destroyed me. Yet I will not attempt to expound them. To me, they have presented little but horror—to many they will seem less terrible than *baroques*. Hereafter, perhaps, some intellect may be found which will reduce my phantasm to the commonplace—some intellect more calm, more logical, and far less excitable than my own, which will perceive, in the circumstances I detail with awe, nothing more than an ordinary succession of very natural causes and effects.

From my infancy I was noted for the docility and humanity of my disposition. My tenderness of heart was even so conspicuous as to make me the jest of my companions. I was especially fond of animals, and was indulged by my parents with a great variety of pets. With these I spent most of my time, and never was so happy as when feeding and caressing them. This peculiarity of character grew with my growth, and, in my manhood, I derived from it one of my principal sources of pleasure. To those who have cherished an affection for a faithful and sagacious dog, I need hardly be at the trouble of explaining the nature or the intensity of the gratification thus derivable. There is something in the unselfish and self-sacrificing love of a brute, which goes directly to the heart of him who has had frequent occasion to test the paltry friendship and gossamer fidelity of mere *Man*.

I married early, and was happy to find in my wife a disposition not uncongenial with my own. Observing my partiality for domestic pets, she lost no opportunity of procuring those of the most agreeable kind. We had birds, goldfish, a fine dog, rabbits, a small monkey, and a *cat*.

This latter was a remarkably large and beautiful animal, entirely black, and sagacious to an astonishing degree. In speaking of his intelligence, my wife, who at heart was not a little tinctured with superstition, made frequent allusion to the ancient popular notion, which regarded all black cats as witches in disguise. Not that she was ever *serious* upon this point —and I mention the matter at all for no better reason than that it happens, just now, to be remembered.

Pluto—this was the cat's name—was my favorite pet and playmate. I alone fed him, and he attended me wherever I went about the house. It was even with difficulty that I could prevent him from following me through the streets.

Our friendship lasted, in this manner, for several years, during which my general temperament and character—through the instrumentality of the Fiend Intemperance—had (I blush to confess it) experienced a radical alteration for the worse. I grew, day by day, more moody, more irritable, more regardless of the feelings of others. I suffered myself to use intemperate language to my wife. At length, I even offered her personal violence. My pets, of course, were made to feel the change in my disposition. I not only neglected, but ill-used them. For Pluto, however, I still retained sufficient regard to restrain me from maltreating him, as I made no scruple of maltreating the rabbits, the monkey, or even the dog, when, by accident, or through affection, they came in my way. But my disease grew upon me—for what disease is like Alcohol!—and at length even Pluto, who was now becoming old, and consequently somewhat peevish—even Pluto began to experience the effects of my ill temper.

One night, returning home, much intoxicated, from one of my haunts about town, I fancied that the cat avoided my presence. I seized him; when, in his fright at my violence, he inflicted a slight wound upon my hand with his teeth. The fury of a demon instantly possessed me. I knew myself no longer. My original soul seemed, at once, to make its flight from my body; and a more than fiendish malevolence, gin-nurtured, thrilled every fibre of my frame. I took from my waistcoat-pocket a penknife, opened it, grasped the poor beast by the throat, and deliberately cut one of its eyes from the socket! I blush, I burn, I shudder, while I pen the damnable atrocity.

When reason returned with the morning—when I had slept off the fumes of the night's debauch—I experienced a sentiment half of horror, half of remorse, for the crime of which I had been guilty; but it was, at best, a feeble and equivocal feeling, and the soul remained untouched. I again plunged into excess, and soon drowned in wine all memory of the deed.

In the meantime the cat slowly recovered. The socket of the lost eye presented, it is true, a frightful appearance, but he no longer appeared to suffer any pain. He went about the house as usual, but, as might be expected, fled in extreme terror at my approach. I had so much of my old heart left, as to be at first grieved by this evident dislike on the part of a creature which had once so loved me. But this feeling soon gave place to irritation. And then came, as if to my final and irrevocable overthrow, the spirit of PERVERSENESS. Of this spirit philosophy takes no account. Yet I am not more sure that my soul lives, than I am that perverseness is one of the primitive impulses of the human heart—one of the indivisible primary faculties, or sentiments, which give direction to the character of Man. Who has not, a hundred times, found himself committing a vile or a stupid action, for no other reason than because he knows he should *not?* Have we not a perpetual inclination, in the teeth of our best judgment, to violate that which is *Law,* merely because we understand it to be such? This spirit of perverseness, I say, came to my final overthrow. It was this unfathomable longing of the soul *to vex itself*—to offer violence to its own nature—to do wrong for the wrong's sake only—that urged me to continue and finally to consummate the injury I had inflicted upon the unoffending brute. One morning, in cold blood, I slipped a noose about its neck and hung it to the limb of a tree;—hung it with the tears streaming from my eyes, and with the bitterest remorse at my heart;—hung it *because* I knew that it had loved me, and *because* I felt it had given me no reason of offense;—hung it *because* I knew that in so doing I was committing a sin—a deadly sin that would so jeopardize my immortal soul as to place it—if such a thing were possible—even beyond the reach of the infinite mercy of the Most Merciful and Most Terrible God.

On the night of the day on which this most cruel deed was done, I was aroused from sleep by the cry of fire. The curtains of my bed were in flames. The whole house was blazing. It was with great difficulty that my wife, a servant, and myself, made our escape from the conflagration. The destruction was complete. My entire worldly wealth was swallowed up, and I resigned myself thenceforward to despair.

I am above the weakness of seeking to establish a sequence of cause and effect, between the disaster and the atrocity. But I am detailing a chain of facts—and wish not to leave even a possible link imperfect. On the day succeeding the fire, I visited the ruins. The walls, with one exception, had fallen in. This exception was found in a compartment wall, not very thick, which stood about the middle of the house, and against which had rested the head of my bed. The plastering had here, in great measure, resisted the action of the fire—a fact which I attributed to its having been recently spread. About this wall a dense crowd were collected, and many persons seemed to be examining a particular portion of it with very minute and eager attention. The words "strange!" "singular!" and other similar expressions, excited my curiosity. I approached and saw, as if graven in *bas-relief* upon the white surface, the figure of a gigantic *cat*. The impression was given with an accuracy truly marvellous. There was a rope about the animal's neck.

When I first beheld this apparition—for I could scarcely regard it as less—my wonder and my terror were extreme. But at length reflection came to my aid. The cat, I remembered, had been hung in a garden adjacent to the house. Upon the alarm of fire, this garden had been immediately filled by the crowd—by some one of whom the animal must have been cut from the tree and thrown, through an open window, into my chamber. This had probably been done with the view of arousing me from sleep. The falling of other walls had compressed the victim of my cruelty into the substance of the freshly-spread plaster; the lime of which, with the flames, and the *ammonia* from the carcass, had then accomplished the portraiture as I saw it.

Although I thus readily accounted to my reason, if not altogether to my conscience, for the startling fact just detailed, it did not the less fail to make a deep impression upon my fancy. For months I could not rid myself of the phantasm of the cat; and, during this period, there came back into my spirit a half-sentiment that seemed, but was not, remorse. I went so far as to regret the loss of the animal, and to look about me, among the vile haunts which I now habitually frequented, for another pet of the same species, and of somewhat similar appearance, with which to supply its place.

One night as I sat, half stupefied, in a den of more than infamy, my attention was suddenly drawn to some black object, reposing upon the head of one of the immense hogsheads of gin, or of rum, which constituted the chief furniture of the apartment. I had been looking steadily at the top of this hogshead for some minutes, and what now caused me surprise was the fact that I had not sooner perceived the object thereupon. I approached it, and touched it with my hand. It was a black cat—a very large one—fully as large as Pluto, and closely resembling him in every respect but one. Pluto had not a white hair upon any portion of his body; but this cat had a large, although indefinite splotch of white, covering nearly the whole region of the breast.

Upon my touching him, he immediately arose, purred loudly, rubbed against my hand, and appeared delighted with my notice. This, then, was the very creature of which I was in search. I at once offered to purchase it of the landlord; but this person made no claim to it—knew nothing of it—had never seen it before.

I continued my caresses, and when I prepared to go home, the animal evinced a disposition to accompany me. I permitted it to do so; occasionally stooping and patting it as I proceeded. When it reached the house it domesticated itself at once, and became immediately a great favorite with my wife.

For my own part, I soon found a dislike to it arising within me. This was just the reverse of what I had anticipated; but—I know not how or why it was—its evident fondness for myself rather disgusted and annoyed me. By slow degrees these feelings of disgust and annoyance rose into the bitterness of hatred. I avoided the creature; a certain sense of shame, and the remembrance of my former deed of cruelty, preventing me from physically abusing it. I did not, for some weeks, strike, or otherwise violently ill use it; but gradually—very gradually—I came to look upon it with unutterable loathing, and to flee silently from its odious presence, as from the breath of a pestilence.

What added, no doubt, to my hatred of the beast, was the discovery, on the morning after I brought it home, that, like Pluto, it also had been deprived of one of its eyes. This circumstance, however, only endeared it to my wife, who, as I have already said, possessed, in a high degree, that humanity of feeling which had once been my distinguishing trait, and the source of many of my simplest and purest pleasures.

With my aversion to this cat, however, its partiality for myself seemed to increase. It followed my footsteps with a pertinacity which it would be difficult to make the reader comprehend. Whenever I sat, it would crouch beneath my chair, or spring upon my knees, covering me with its loathsome caresses. If I arose to walk it would get between my feet and thus nearly throw me down, or, fastening its long and sharp claws in my dress, clamber, in this manner, to my breast. As such times, although I longed to destroy it with a blow, I was yet withheld from so doing, partly by a memory of my former crime, but chiefly—let me confess it at once—by absolute *dread* of the beast.

This dread was not exactly a dread of physical evil—and yet I should be at a loss how otherwise to define it. I am almost ashamed to own—yes, even in this felon's cell, I am almost ashamed to own—that the terror and horror with which the animal inspired me, had been heightened by one of the merest chimeras it would be possible to conceive. My wife had called my attention, more than once, to the character of the mark of white hair, of which I have spoken, and which constituted the sole visible difference between the strange beast and the one I had destroyed. The reader will remember that this mark, although large, had been originally very indefinite; but, by slow degrees—degrees nearly imperceptible, and which for a long time my reason struggled to reject as fanciful—it had, at length, assumed a rigorous distinctness of outline. It was now the representation of an object that I shudder to name—and for this, above all, I loathed, and dreaded, and would have rid myself of the monster *had I dared*—it was now, I say, the image of a hideous—of a ghastly thing—of the GALLOWS!—oh, mournful and terrible engine of Horror and of Crime—of Agony and of Death!

And now was I indeed wretched beyond the wretchedness of mere Humanity. And *a brute beast*—whose fellow I had contemptuously destroyed—*a brute beast* to work out for *me*—for me, a man fashioned in the image of the High God—so much of insufferable woe! Alas! neither by day nor by night knew I the blessing of rest any more! During the former the creature left me no moment alone, and in the latter I started hourly from dreams of unutterable fear to find the hot breath of *the thing* upon my face, and its vast weight—an incarnate nightmare that I had no power to shake off—incumbent eternally upon my *heart!*

Beneath the pressure of torments such as these the feeble remnant of the good within me succumbed. Evil thoughts became my sole intimates—the darkest and most evil of thoughts. The moodiness of my usual temper increased to hatred of all things and of all mankind; while from the sudden, frequent, and ungovernable outbursts of a fury to which I now blindly abandoned myself, my uncomplaining wife, alas, was the most usual and the most patient of sufferers.

One day she accompanied me, upon some household errand, into the cellar of the old building which our poverty compelled us to inhabit. The cat followed me down the steep stairs, and nearly throwing me headlong, exasperated me to madness. Uplifting an axe, and forgetting in my wrath the childish dread which had hitherto stayed my hand, I aimed a blow at the animal, which, of course, would have proved instantly fatal had it descended as I wished. But this blow was arrested by the hand of my wife. Goaded by the interference into a rage more than demoniacal, I withdrew my arm from her grasp and buried the axe in her brain. She fell dead upon the spot without a groan.

This hideous murder accomplished, I set myself forthwith, and with entire deliberation, to the task of concealing the body. I knew that I could not remove it from the house, either by day or by night, without the risk of being observed by the neighbors. Many projects entered my mind. At one period I thought of cutting the corpse into minute fragments, and destroying them by fire. At another, I resolved to dig a grave for it in the floor of the cellar. Again, I deliberated about casting it in the well in the yard—about packing it in a box, as if merchandise, with the usual arrangements, and so getting a porter to take it from the house. Finally I hit upon what I considered a far better expedient than either of these. I determined to wall it up in the cellar, as the monks of the Middle Ages are recorded to have walled up their victims.

For a purpose such as this the cellar was well adapted. Its walls were loosely constructed, and had lately been plastered throughout with a rough plaster, which the dampness of the atmosphere had prevented from hardening. Moreover, in one of the walls was a projection, caused by a false chimney, or fireplace, that had been filled up and made to resemble the rest of the cellar. I made no doubt that I could readily displace the bricks at this point, insert the corpse, and wall the whole up as before, so that no eye could detect any thing suspicious.

And in this calculation I was not deceived. By means of a crowbar I easily dislodged the bricks, and, having carefully deposited the body against the inner wall, I propped it in that position, while with little trouble I relaid the whole structure as it originally stood. Having procured mortar, sand, and hair, with every possible precaution, I prepared a plaster which could not be distinguished from the old, and with this I very carefully went over the new brickwork. When I had finished, I felt satisfied that all was right. The wall did not present the slightest appearance of having been disturbed. The rubbish on the floor was picked up with the minutest care. I looked around triumphantly, and said to myself: "Here at least, then, my labor has not been in vain."

My next step was to look for the beast which had been the cause of so much wretchedness; for I had, at length, firmly resolved to put it to death. Had I been able to meet with it at the moment, there could have been no doubt of its fate; but it appeared that the crafty animal had been alarmed at the violence of my previous anger, and forbore to present itself in my present mood. It is impossible to describe or to imagine the deep, the blissful sense of relief which the absence of the detested creature occasioned in my bosom. It did not make its appearance during the night; and thus for one night, at least, since its introduction into the house, I soundly and tranquilly slept; aye, *slept* even with the burden of murder upon my soul.

The second and the third day passed, and still my tormentor came not.

The Black Cat

Once again I breathed as a freeman. The monster, in terror, had fled the premises forever! I should behold it no more! My happiness was supreme! The guilt of my dark deed disturbed me but little. Some few inquiries had been made, but these had been readily answered. Even a search had been instituted—but of course nothing was to be discovered. I looked upon my future felicity as secured.

Upon the fourth day of the assassination, a party of the police came, very unexpectedly, into the house, and proceeded again to make rigorous investigation of the premises. Secure, however, in the inscrutability of my place of concealment, I felt no embarrassment whatever. The officers bade me accompany them in their search. They left no nook or corner unexplored. At length, for the third or fourth time, they descended into the cellar. I quivered not in a muscle. My heart beat calmly as that of one who slumbers in innocence. I walked the cellar from end to end. I folded my arms upon my bosom, and roamed easily to and fro. The police were thoroughly satisfied and prepared to depart. The glee at my heart was too strong to be restrained. I burned to say if but one word, by way of triumph, and to render doubly sure their assurance of my guiltlessness.

"Gentlemen," I said at last, as the party ascended the steps, "I delight to have allayed your suspicions. I wish you all health and a little more courtesy. By the bye, gentlemen, this—this is a very well-constructed house," (in the rabid desire to say something easily, I scarcely knew what I uttered at all),—"I may say an *excellently* well-constructed house. These walls—are you going, gentlemen?—these walls are solidly put together"; and here, through the mere frenzy of bravado, I rapped heavily with a cane which I held in my hand, upon that very portion of the brickwork behind which stood the corpse of the wife of my bosom.

But may God shield and deliver me from the fangs of the Arch-Fiend! No sooner had the reverberation of my blows sunk into silence, than I was answered by a voice from within the tomb!—by a cry, at first muffled and broken, like the sobbing of a child, and then quickly swelling into one long, loud, and continuous scream, utterly anomalous and inhuman—a howl—a wailing shriek, half of horror and half of triumph, such as might have arisen only out of hell, conjointly from the throats of the damned in their agony and of the demons that exult in the damnation.

Of my own thoughts it is folly to speak. Swooning, I staggered to the opposite wall. For one instant the party on the stairs remained motionless, through extremity of terror and awe. In the next a dozen stout arms were toiling at the wall. It fell bodily. The corpse, already greatly decayed and clotted with gore, stood erect before the eyes of the spectators. Upon its

Edgar Allan Poe

head, with red extended mouth and solitary eye of fire, sat the hideous beast whose craft had seduced me into murder, and whose informing voice had consigned me to the hangman. I had walled the monster up within the tomb.

READINGS, FORECASTS, PERSONAL GUIDANCE

It is not   I swear it by every fiery omen to be seen these nights
    in every quarter of the heavens, I affirm it by all the monstrous portents
    of the earth and of the sea
It is not that my belief in the true and mystic science is shaken,
    nor that I have lost faith in the magic of the cards,
    or in the augury of dreams, or in the great and good divinity of the stars.
No, I know still whose science fits the promise to the inquirer's need,
    invariably, for a change: Mine. My science foretells the wished-for journey,
    the business adjustment, the handsome stranger.
    (Each of these is considered a decided change.)
And I know whose skill weighs matrimony, risks a flyer in steel or wheat
    against the vagaries of the moon.
(Planet of dreams, of mothers and of children, goddess of sailors
    and of all adventurers, forgive the liberty. But a man must eat.) My skill,
Mine, and the cunning and the patience. (Two dollars for the horoscope in brief
    and five for a twelve months' forecast in detail.)

No, it is this: The wonders that I have seen with my own eyes.

It is this: That still these people know, as I do not, that what has never been
    on earth before may still well come to pass,
That always, always there are new and brighter things beneath the sun,
That surely, in bargain basements or in walk-up flats, it must be so
    that still from time to time they hear wild angel voices speak.

It is this: That I have known them for what they are,
Seen thievery written plainly in their planets, found greed and murder
    and worse in their birth dates and their numbers,
    guilt etched in every line of every palm;
But still a light burns through the eyes they turn to me, a need more moving
    than the damned and dirty dollars (which I must take)
    that form the pattern of their larger hopes and deeper fears.

And it comes to this: That always I feel another hand, not mine,
    has drawn and turned the card to find some incredible ace.
Always another word I did not write appears in the spirit parchment
    prepared by me,
Always another face I do not know shows in the dream, the crystal globe,
    or the flame.

And finally, this: Corrupt, in a world bankrupt and corrupt,
    what have I got to do with these miracles?
If they want miracles, let them consult someone else.
Would they, in extremity, ask them of a physician? Or expect them,
    in desperation, of an attorney? Or of a priest? Or of a poet?

Nevertheless, a man must eat.
Mrs. Raeburn is expected at five. She will communicate
    with a number of friends and relatives long deceased.

Kenneth Fearing

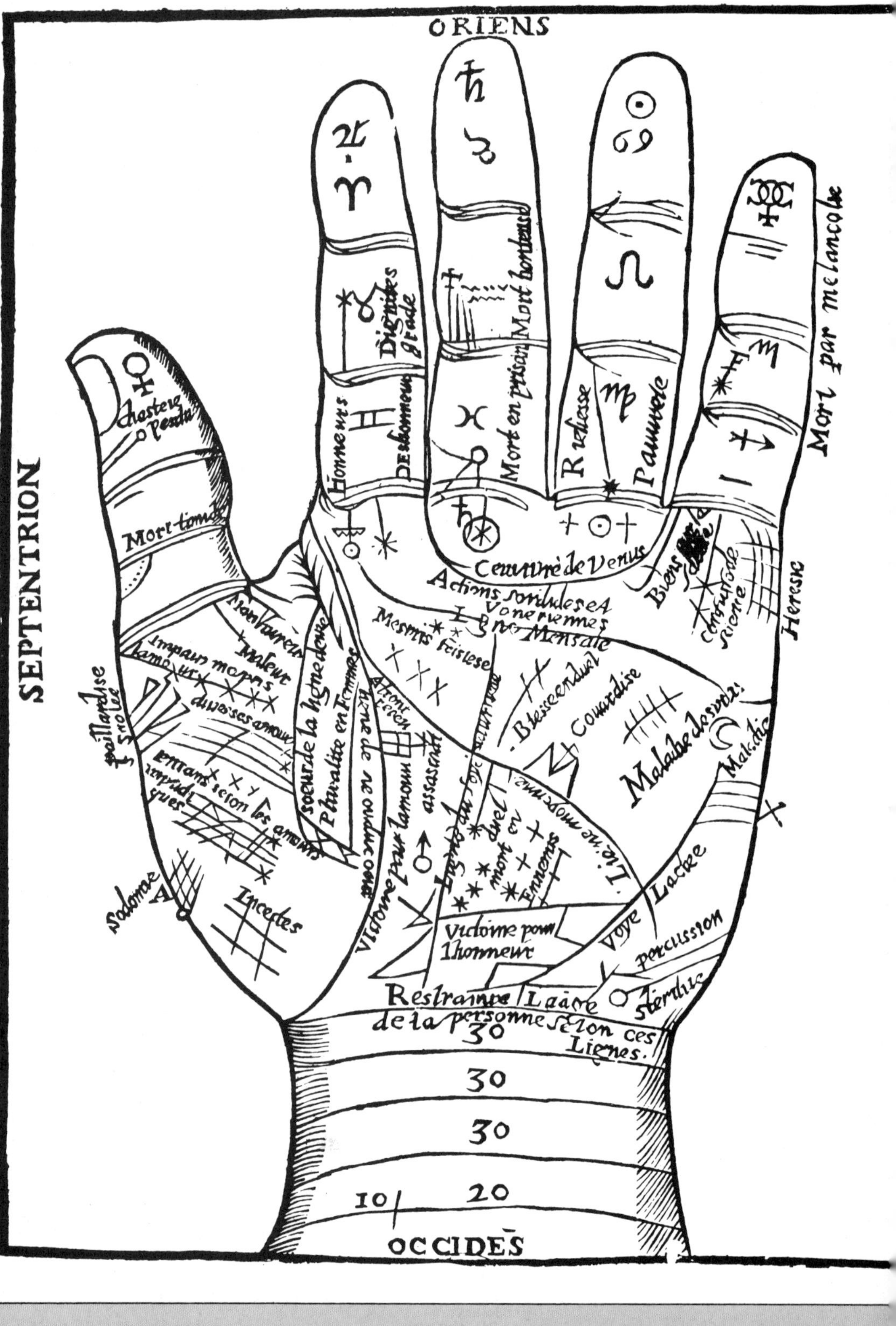

EN of WANDS. | WHEEL of FORTUNE. | FOUR of SWORDS.

E of PENTACLES | THE HANGED MAN. | TEN of CUPS.

The Furnished Room

O. Henry

Restless, shifting, fugacious as time itself is a certain vast bulk of the population of the red brick district of the lower West Side. Homeless, they have a hundred homes. They flit from furnished room to furnished room, transients forever—transients in abode, transients in heart and mind. They sing "Home, Sweet Home" in ragtime; they carry their *lares et penates* in a bandbox; their vine is entwined about a picture hat; a rubber plant is their fig tree.

Hence the houses of this district, having had a thousand dwellers, should have a thousand tales to tell, mostly dull ones, no doubt; but it would be strange if there could not be found a ghost or two in the wake of all these vagrant guests.

One evening after dark a young man prowled among these crumbling red mansions, ringing their bells. At the twelfth he rested his lean hand-baggage upon the step and wiped the dust from his hatband and forehead. The bell sounded faint and far away in some remote, hollow depths.

To the door of this, the twelfth house whose bell he had rung, came a housekeeper who made him think of an unwholesome, surfeited worm that had eaten its nut to a hollow shell and now sought to fill the vacancy with edible lodgers.

He asked if there was a room to let.

"Come in," said the housekeeper. Her voice came from her throat; her throat seemed lined with fur. "I have the third-floor back, vacant since a week back. Should you wish to look at it?"

The young man followed her up the stairs. A faint light from no particular source mitigated the shadows of the halls. They trod noiselessly upon a stair carpet that its own loom would have forsworn. It seemed to have become vegetable; to have degenerated in that rank, sunless air to lush lichen or spreading moss that grew in patches to the staircase and was viscid under the foot like organic matter. At each turn of the stairs were vacant niches in the wall. Perhaps plants had once been set within them. If so they had died in that foul and tainted air. It may be that statues of the saints had stood there, but it was not difficult to conceive that imps and devils had dragged them forth in the darkness and down to the unholy depths of some furnished pit below.

"This is the room," said the housekeeper, from her furry throat. "It's a nice room. It ain't often vacant. I had some most elegant people in it last summer—no trouble at all, and paid in advance to the minute. The water's at the end of the hall. Sprowls and Mooney kept it three months. They done a vaudeville sketch. Miss B'retta Sprowls—you may have heard of her—Oh, that was just the stage names—right there over the dresser is where the marriage certificate hung, framed. The gas is here, and you see there is plenty of closet room. It's a room everybody likes. It never stays idle long."

"Do you have many theatrical people rooming here?" asked the young man.

"They comes and goes. A good proportion of my lodgers is connected with the theatres. Yes, sir, this is the theatrical district. Actor people never stays long anywhere. I get my share. Yes, they comes and they goes."

He engaged the room, paying for a week in advance. He was tired, he said, and would take possession at once. He counted out the money. The room had been made ready, she said, even to the towels and water. As the housekeeper moved away he put, for the thousandth time, the question that he carried at the end of his tongue.

"A young girl—Miss Vashner—Miss Eloise Vashner—do you remember such a one among your lodgers? She would be singing on the stage, most likely. A fair girl, of medium height and slender, with reddish, gold hair and dark mole near her left eyebrow."

"No, I don't remember the name. Them stage people has names they change as often as their rooms. They comes and they goes. No, I don't call that one to mind."

No. Always no. Five months of ceaseless interrogation and the inevitable negative. So much time spent by day in questioning managers, agents, schools and choruses; by night among the audience of theatres from all-star casts down to music halls so low that he dreaded to find what he most hoped for. He who had loved her best had tried to find her. He was sure that since her disappearance from home this great, water-girt city held her somewhere, but it was like a monstrous quicksand, shifting its particles constantly, with no foundation, its upper granules of today buried tomorrow in ooze and slime.

The furnished room received its latest guest with a first glow of pseudo-hospitality, a hectic, haggard, perfunctory welcome like the specious

The Furnished Room

smile of a demirep. The sophistical comfort came in reflected gleams from the decayed furniture, the ragged brocade upholstery of a couch and two chairs, a foot-wide cheap pier glass between the two windows, from one or two gilt picture frames and a brass bedstead in a corner.

The guest reclined, inert, upon a chair, while the room, confused in speech as though it were an apartment in Babel, tried to discourse to him of its divers tenantry.

A polychromatic rug like some brilliant-flowered, rectangular, tropical islet lay surrounded by a billowy sea of soiled matting. Upon the gay-papered wall were those pictures that pursue the homeless one from house to house—the Huguenot Lovers, The First Quarrel, The Wedding Breakfast, Psyche at the Fountain. The mantel's chastely severe outline was ingloriously veiled behind some pert drapery drawn rakishly askew like the sashes of the Amazonian ballet. Upon it was some desolate flotsam cast aside by the room's marooned when a lucky sail had borne them to a fresh port—a trifling vase or two, pictures of actresses, a medicine bottle, some stray cards out of a deck.

One by one, as the characters of a cryptograph become explicit, the little signs left by the furnished room's procession of guests developed a significance. The threadbare space in the rug in front of the dresser told that lovely woman had marched in the throng. The tiny fingerprints on the wall spoke of little prisoners trying to feel their way to sun and air. A splattered stain, raying like the shadow of a bursting bomb, witnessed where a hurled glass or bottle had splintered with its contents against the wall. Across the pier glass had been scrawled with a diamond in staggering letters the name "Marie." It seemed that the succession of dwellers in the furnished room had turned in fury—perhaps tempted beyond forbearance by its garish coldness—and wreaked upon it their passions. The furniture was chipped and bruised; the couch, distorted by bursting springs, seemed a horrible monster that had been slain during the stress of some grotesque convulsion. Some more potent upheaval had cloven a great slice from the marble mantel. Each plank in the floor owned its particular cant and shriek as from a separate and individual agony. It seemed incredible that all this malice and injury had been wrought upon the room by those who had called it for a time their home; and yet it may have been the cheated home instinct surviving blindly, the resentful rage at false household gods that had kindled their wrath. A hut that is our own we can sweep and adorn and cherish.

The young tenant in the chair allowed these thoughts to file, soft-shod, through his mind, while there drifted into the room furnished sounds and furnished scents. He heard in one room a tittering and incontinent, slack laughter; in others the monologue of a scold, the rattling of dice, a lullaby, and one crying dully; above him a banjo tinkled with spirit. Doors banged somewhere; the elevated trains roared intermittently; a cat yowled miserably upon a back fence. And he breathed the breath of the house—a dank savor rather than a smell—a cold, musty effluvium as from underground vaults mingled with the reeking exhalations of linoleum and mildewed and rotten woodwork.

Then suddenly, as he rested there, the room was filled with the strong, sweet odor of mignonette. It came as upon a single buffet of wind with such sureness and fragrance and emphasis that it almost seemed a living visitant. And the man cried aloud: "What, dear?" as if he had been called, and sprang up and faced about. The rich odor clung to him and wrapped him around. He reached out his arms for it, all his senses for the time confused and commingled. How could one be peremptorily called by an odor? Surely it must have been a sound. But, was it not the sound that had touched, that had caressed him?

"She has been in this room," he cried, and he sprang to wrest from it a token, for he knew he would recognize the smallest thing that had belonged to her or that she had touched. This enveloping scent of mignonette, the odor that she had loved and made her own—whence came it?

The room had been but carelessly set in order. Scattered upon the flimsy dresser scarf were half a dozen hairpins—those discreet, indistinguishable friends of womankind, feminine of gender, infinite of mood and uncommunicative of tense. These he ignored, conscious of their triumphant lack of identity. Ransacking the drawers of the dresser he came upon a discarded, tiny, ragged handkerchief. He pressed it to his face. It was racy and insolent with heliotrope; he hurled it to the floor. In another drawer he found odd buttons, a theatre programme, a pawnbroker's card, two lost marshmallows, a book on the divination of dreams. In the last was a woman's black satin hair bow, which halted him, poised between ice and fire. But the black satin hair bow also is femininity's demure, impersonal common ornament and tells no tales.

And then he traversed the room like a hound on the scent, skimming the walls, considering the corners of the bulging matting on his hands and knees, rummaging mantel and tables, the curtains and hangings, the drunken cabinet in the corner, for a visible sign, unable to perceive that she was there beside, around, against, within, above him, clinging to him, wooing him, calling him so poignantly through the finer senses that even his grosser ones became cognizant of the call. Once again he

The Furnished Room

answered loudly: "Yes, dear!" and turned, wild-eyed, to gaze on vacancy, for he could not yet discern form and color and love and outstretched arms in the odor of mignonette. Oh, God! whence that odor, and since when have odors had a voice to call? Thus he groped.

He burrowed in crevices and corners, and found corks and cigarettes. These he passed in passive contempt. But once he found in a fold of the matting a half-smoked cigar, and this he ground beneath his heel with a green and trenchant oath. He sifted the room from end to end. He found dreary and ignoble records of many a peripatetic tenant; but of her whom he sought, and who may have lodged there, and whose spirit seemed to hover there, he found no trace.

And then he thought of the housekeeper.

He ran from the haunted room downstairs and to a door that showed a crack of light. She came out to his knock. He smothered his excitement as best he could.

"Will you tell me, madam," he besought her, "who occupied the room I have before I came?"

"Yes, sir. I can tell you again. 'Twas Sprowls and Mooney, as I said. Miss B'retta Sprowls it was in the theatres, but Missis Mooney she was. My house is well known for respectability. The marriage certificate hung, framed, on a nail over—"

"What kind of a lady was Miss Sprowls—in looks, I mean?"

"Why, black-haired, sir, short, and stout, with a comical face. They left a week ago Tuesday."

"And before they occupied it?"

"Why, there was a single gentleman connected with the draying business. He left owing me a week. Before him was Missis Crowder and her two children, that stayed four months; and back of them was old Mr. Doyle, whose sons paid for him. He kept the room six months. That goes back a year, sir, and further I do not remember."

He thanked her and crept back to his room. The room was dead. The essence that had vivified it was gone. The perfume of mignonette had departed. In its place was the old, stale odor of mouldy house furniture, of atmosphere in storage.

The ebbing of his hope drained his faith. He sat staring at the yellow, singing gaslight. Soon he walked to the bed and began to tear the sheets into strips. With the blade of his knife he drove them tightly into every crevice around windows and doors. When all was snug and taut he turned out the light, turned the gas full on again and laid himself gratefully upon the bed.

It was Mrs. McCool's night to go with the can for beer. So she fetched it and sat with Mrs. Purdy in one of those subterranean retreats where housekeepers foregather and the worm dieth seldom.

"I rented out my third-floor-back this evening," said Mrs. Purdy, across a fine circle of foam. "A young man took it. He went up to bed two hours ago."

"Now, did ye, Mrs. Purdy, ma'am?" said Mrs. McCool, with intense admiration. "You do be a wonder for rentin' rooms of that kind. And did ye tell him, then?" she concluded in a husky whisper laden with mystery.

"Rooms," said Mrs. Purdy, in her furriest tones, "are furnished for to rent. I did not tell him, Mrs. McCool."

"'Tis right ye are, ma'am; 'tis by renting rooms we kape alive. Ye have the rale sense for business, ma'am. There be many people will rayjict the rentin' of a room if they be tould a suicide has been after dyin' in the bed of it."

"As you say, we has our living to be making," remarked Mrs. Purdy.

"Yis, ma'am; 'tis true. 'Tis just one wake ago this day I helped ye lay out the third-floor-back. A pretty slip of a colleen she was to be killin' herself wid the gas—a swate little face she had, Mrs. Purdy, ma'am."

"She'd a-been called handsome, as you say," said Mrs. Purdy, assenting but critical, "but for that mole she had a-growin' by her left eyebrow. Do fill up your glass again, Mrs. McCool."

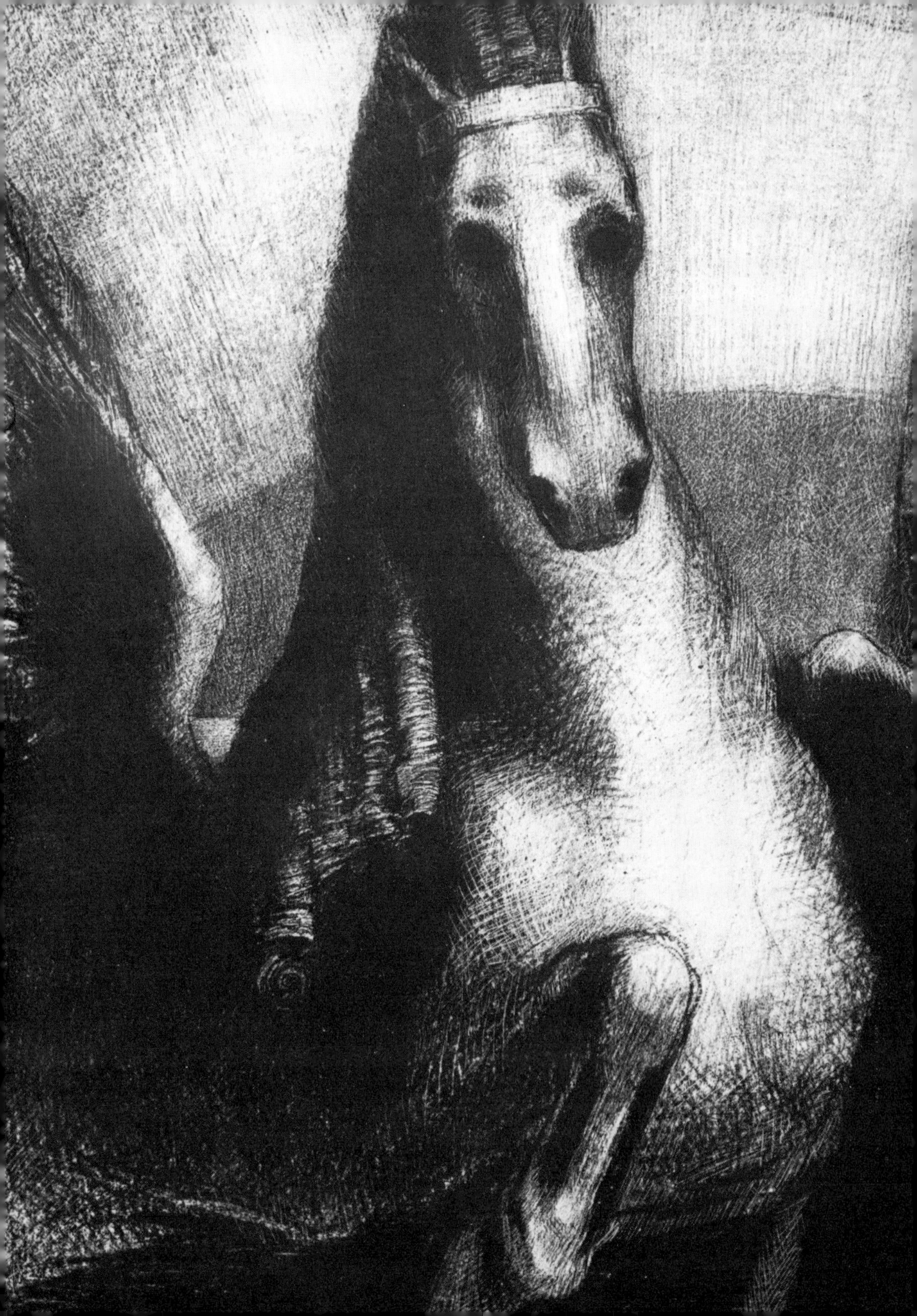

The Tradition

Algernon Blackwood

The noises outside the little flat at first were very disconcerting after living in the country. They made sleep difficult. At the cottage in Sussex where the family had lived, night brought deep, comfortable silence, unless the wind was high, when the pine trees round the duck pond made a sound like surf, or, if the gale was from the southwest, the orchard roared a bit unpleasantly.

But in London it was very different; sleep was easier in the daytime than at night. For, after nightfall, the rumble of the traffic became spasmodic instead of continuous; the motor-horns startled like warnings of alarm; after comparative silence the furious rushing of a taxicab touched the nerves. From dinner till eleven o'clock the streets subsided gradually; then came the army from theatres, parties, and late dinners, hurrying home to bed. The motor-horns during this hour were lively and incessant, like bugles of a regiment moving into battle. The parents rarely retired until this attack was over. If quick about it, sleep was possible then before the flying of the night-birds—an uncertain squadron—screamed half the street awake again. But, these finally disposed of, a delightful hush settled down upon the neighborhood, profounder far than any peace of the countryside. The deep rumble of the produce wagons, coming in to the big London markets from the farms—generally about three a.m.—held no disturbing quality.

But sometimes in the stillness of very early morning, when streets were empty and pavements all deserted, there was a sound of another kind that was startling and unwelcome. For it was ominous. It came with a clattering violence that made nerves quiver and forced the heart to pause and listen. A strange resonance was in it, a volume of sound, moreover, that was hardly justified by its cause. For it was hoofs. A horse swept hurrying up the deserted street, and was close upon the building in a moment. It was audible suddenly, no gradual approach from a distance, but as though it turned a corner from soft ground that muffled the hoofs, on to the echoing, hard paving that emphasized the dreadful clatter. Nor did it die away again when once the house was reached. It ceased as abruptly as it came. The hoofs did not go away.

It was the mother who heard them first, and drew her husband's attention to their disagreeable quality.

"It is the mail-vans, dear," he answered. "They go at four a.m. to catch the early trains into the country."

She looked up sharply, as though something in his tone surprised her.

"But there's no sound of wheels," she said. And then, as he did not reply, she added gravely, "You have heard it too, John. I can tell."

"I have," he said. "I have heard it—twice."

And they looked at one another searchingly, each trying to read the other's mind. She did not question him; he did not propose writing to complain in a newspaper; both understood something that neither of them quite believed.

"I heard it first," she then said softly, "the night before Jack got the fever. And, as I listened, I heard him crying. But when I went in to see he was asleep. The noise stopped just outside the building." There was a shadow in her eyes as she said this, and a hush crept between her words. "I did not hear it *go*." She said this almost beneath her breath.

He looked a moment at the ground; then, coming towards her, he took her in his arms and kissed her. And she clung very tightly to him.

"Sometimes," he said in a quiet voice, "a mounted policeman passes down the street, I think."

"It is a horse," she answered. But whether it was a question or mere corroboration he did not ask, for at that moment the doctor arrived, and the question of little Jack's health became the paramount matter of immediate interest. The great man's verdict was uncommonly disquieting.

All that night they sat up in the sick room. It was strangely still, as though by one accord the traffic avoided the house where a little boy hung between life and death. The motor-horns even had a muffled sound, and heavy drays and wagons used the side streets; there were fewer taxicabs about, or else they flew by noiselessly. Yet no straw was down, the expense prohibited that. And towards morning, very early, the mother decided to watch alone. She had been a trained nurse before her marriage, accustomed when she was younger to long vigils. "You go down, dear, and get a little sleep," she urged in a whisper. "He's quiet now. At five o'clock I'll come for you to take my place."

"You'll fetch me at once," he whispered, "if—" then hesitated—as though breath failed him. A moment he stood there staring from her face to the bed. "If you hear anything," he finished. She nodded, and he went downstairs to his study, not to his bedroom. He left the door ajar. He sat in darkness, listening. Mother, he knew, was listening, too, beside the bed. His heart was very full, for he did not believe the boy could live till morning. The picture of the room was all the time before his eyes—the shaded lamp, the table with the medicines, the little wasted figure beneath the blankets, and mother close beside it, listening. He sat alert, ready to fly upstairs at the smallest cry.

But no sound broke the stillness; the entire neighborhood was silent; all London slept. He heard the clock strike three in the dining room at the end of the corridor. It was still enough for that. There was not even the heavy rumble of a single produce wagon, though usually they passed about this time on their way to Smithfield and Covent Garden markets. He waited, far too anxious to close his eyes. . . . At four o'clock he would go up and relieve her vigil. Four, he knew, was the time when life sinks to its lowest ebb. . . . Then, in the middle of his reflections, thought stopped dead, and it seemed his heart stopped too.

Far away, but coming nearer with extraordinary rapidity, a sharp, clear sound broke out of the surrounding stillness—a horse's hoofs. At first it was so distant that it might have been almost on the high roads of the country, but the amazing speed with which it came closer, and the sudden increase of the beating sound was such, that by the time he turned his head it seemed to have entered the street outside. It was within a hundred yards of the building. The next second it was before the very door. And something in him blenched. He knew a moment's complete paralysis. The abrupt cessation of the heavy clatter was strangest of all. It came like lightning, it struck, it paused. It did not go away again. Yet the sound of it was still beating in his ears as he dashed upstairs three steps at a time. It seemed in the house as well, on the stairs behind him, in the little passage-way, *inside the very bedroom.* It was an appalling sound. Yet he entered a room that was quiet, orderly, and calm. It was silent. Beside the bed his wife sat, holding Jack's hand, stroking it. She was soothing him; her face was very peaceful. No sound but her gentle whisper was audible.

He controlled himself by a tremendous effort, but his face betrayed his consternation and distress. "Hush," she said beneath her breath, "he's sleeping much more calmly now. The crisis, bless God, is over, I do believe. I dared not leave him."

He saw in a moment that she was right, and an untellable relief passed over him. He sat down beside her, very cold, yet perspiring with heat.

"You heard—?" he asked after a pause.

"Nothing," she replied quickly, "except his pitiful, wild words when the delirium was on him. It's passed. It lasted but a moment, or I'd have called you."

He stared closely into her tired eyes. "And his words?" he asked in a whisper. Whereupon she told him quietly that the little chap had sat up with wide-opened eyes and talked excitedly about a "great, great horse" he heard, but that was not "coming for him." He laughed and said he would not go with it because he "was not ready yet." "Some scrap of talk he had overheard from us," she added, "when we discussed the traffic once...."

"But *you* heard nothing?" he repeated almost impatiently.

No, she had heard nothing. After all, then, he *had* dozed a moment in his chair....

Four weeks later Jack, entirely convalescent, was playing a restricted game of hide-and-seek with his sister in the flat. It was really a forbidden joy, owing to noise and risk of breakages, but he had unusual privileges after his grave illness. It was dusk. The lamps in the street were being lit. "Quietly, remember; your mother's resting in her room," were the father's orders. She had just returned from a week by the sea, recuperating from the strain of nursing for so many nights. The traffic rolled and boomed along the streets below.

"Jack! Do come on and hide. It's your turn. I hid last."

But the boy was standing spellbound by the window, staring hard at something on the pavement. Sybil called and tugged in vain. Tears threatened. Jack would not budge. He declared he saw something.

"Oh, you're always seeing something. I wish you'd go and hide. It's only because you can't think of a good place, really."

"Look!" he cried in a voice of wonder. And as he said it his father rose quickly from his chair before the fire.

"Look," the child repeated with delight and excitement. "It's a great, great horse. And it's perfectly white all over." His sister joined him at the window. "Where? Where? I can't see it. Oh, *do* show me!"

Their father was standing close behind them now. "I heard it," he was whispering, but so low the children did not notice him. His face was very pale.

"Straight in front of our door, stupid! Can't you see it? Oh, I do wish it had come for me. It's *such* a beauty!" And he clapped his hands with pleasure and excitement. "Quick, quick! I can hear it. It's going away again!"

But, while the children stood half squabbling by the window their father leaned over a sofa in the adjoining room above a figure whose heart in sleep had quietly stopped its beating. The great, great horse had come. But this time he had not only heard its wonderful arrival. He had also heard it go. It seemed he heard the awful hoofs beat down the sky, far far away, and very swiftly, dying into silence, finally up among the stars.

The Demon Lover

Elizabeth Bowen

Towards the end of her day in London Mrs. Drover went round to her shut-up house to look for several things she wanted to take away. Some belonged to herself, some to her family, who were by now used to their country life. It was late August; it had been a steamy, showery day: at the moment the trees down the pavement glittered in an escape of humid yellow afternoon sun. Against the next batch of clouds, already piling up ink-dark, broken chimneys and parapets stood out. In her once familiar street, as in any unused channel, an unfamiliar queerness had silted up; a cat wove itself in and out of railings, but no human eye watched Mrs. Drover's return. Shifting some parcels under her arm, she slowly forced round her latchkey in an unwilling lock, then gave the door, which had warped, a push with her knee. Dead air came out to meet her as she went in.

The staircase window having been boarded up, no light came down into the hall. But one door, she could just see, stood ajar, so she went quickly through into the room and unshuttered the big window in there. Now the prosaic woman, looking about her, was more perplexed than she knew by everything that she saw, by traces of her long former habit of life—the yellow smoke-stain up the white marble mantelpiece, the ring left by a vase on the top of the escritoire; the bruise in the wallpaper where, on the door being thrown open widely, the china handle had always hit the wall. The piano, having gone away to be stored, had left what looked like claw-marks on its part of the parquet. Though not much dust had seeped in, each object wore a film of another kind; and, the only ventilation being the chimney, the whole drawing room smelled of the cold hearth. Mrs. Drover put down her parcels on the escritoire and left the room to proceed upstairs; the things she wanted were in the bedroom chest.

She had been anxious to see how the house was—the part-time caretaker she shared with some neighbors was away this week on his holiday, known to be not yet back. At the best of times he did not look in often, and she was never sure that she trusted him. There were some cracks in the structure, left by the last bombing, on which she was anxious to keep an eye. Not that one could do anything—

A shaft of refracted daylight now lay across the hall. She stopped dead and stared at the hall table—on this lay a letter addressed to her.

She thought first—then the caretaker *must* be back. All the same, who, seeing the house shuttered, would have dropped a letter in at the box? It was not a circular, it was not a bill. And the post office redirected, to the address in the country, everything for her that came through the post. The caretaker (even if he *were* back) did not know she was due in London today—her call here had been planned to be a surprise—so his negligence in the matter of this letter, leaving it to wait in the dusk and dust, annoyed her. Annoyed, she picked up the letter, which bore no stamp. But it cannot be important, or they would know. . . . She took the letter rapidly upstairs with her, without a stop to look at the writing till she reached what had been her bedroom, where she let in light. The room looked over the garden and other gardens: the sun had gone in; as the clouds sharpened and lowered, the trees and rank lawns seemed already to smoke with dark. Her reluctance to look again at the letter came from the fact that she felt intruded upon—and by someone contemptuous of her ways. However, in the tenseness preceding the fall of rain she read it: it was a few lines.

Dear Kathleen,
You will not have forgotten that today is our anniversary, and the day we said. The years have gone by at once slowly and fast. In view of the fact that nothing has changed, I shall rely upon you to keep your promise. I was sorry to see you leave London, but was satisfied that you would be back in time. You may expect me, therefore, at the hour arranged.
                                            Until then . . .
                                                    K.

Mrs. Drover looked for the date: it was today's. She dropped the letter on to the bedsprings, then picked it up to see the writing again—her lips, beneath the remains of lipstick, beginning to go white. She felt so much the change in her own face that she went to the mirror, polished a clear patch in it and looked at once urgently and stealthily in. She was confronted by a woman of forty-four, with eyes staring out under a hat brim that had been rather carelessly pulled down. She had not put on any more powder since she left the shop where she ate her solitary tea. The pearls her husband had given her on their marriage hung loose round her now rather thinner throat, slipping into the V of the pink wool jumper her sister knitted last autumn as they sat round the fire. Mrs. Drover's most normal expression was one of controlled worry, but of assent. Since the birth of the third of her little boys, attended by a quite serious illness, she had had an intermittent muscular flicker to the left of her mouth, but in spite of this she could always sustain a manner that was at once energetic and calm.

Turning from her own face as precipitately as she had gone to meet it, she went to the chest where the things were, unlocked it, threw up the lid and knelt to search. But as the rain began to come crashing down she could not keep from looking over her shoulder at the stripped bed on which the letter lay. Behind the blanket of rain the clock of the church that still stood struck six—with rapidly heightening apprehension she counted each of the slow strokes. "The hour arranged. . . . My God," she said, "*what* hour? How should I . . . ? After twenty-five years . . ."

The young girl talking to the soldier in the garden had not ever completely seen his face. It was dark; they were saying goodbye under a tree. Now and then—for it felt, from not seeing him at this intense moment, as though she had never seen him at all—she verified his presence for these few moments longer by putting out a hand, which he each time pressed, without very much kindness, and painfully, on to one of the breast buttons of his uniform. That cut of the button on the palm of her hand was, principally, what she was to carry away. This was so near the end of a leave from France that she could only wish him already gone. It was August 1916. Being not kissed, being drawn away from and looked at intimidated Kathleen till she imagined spectral glitters in the place of his eyes. Turning away and looking back up the lawn she saw, through branches of trees, the drawing room window alight: she caught a breath for the moment when she could go running back there into the safe arms of her mother and sister, and cry: "What shall I do, what shall I do? He has gone."

Hearing her catch her breath, her fiancé said, without feeling: "Cold?"
"You're going away such a long way."
"Not so far as you think."
"I don't understand?"
"You don't have to," he said. "You will. You know what we said."
"But that was—suppose you—I mean, suppose."
"I shall be with you," he said, "sooner or later. You won't forget that. You need do nothing but wait."

Only a little more than a minute later she was free to run up the silent lawn. Looking in through the window at her mother and sister, who did not for the moment perceive her, she already felt that unnatural promise drive down between her and the rest of all human kind. No other way of having given herself could have made her feel so apart, lost and forsworn. She could not have plighted a more sinister troth.

Kathleen behaved well when, some months later, her fiancé was reported missing, presumed killed. Her family not only supported her but were able to praise her courage without stint because they could not regret, as a husband for her, the man they knew almost nothing about. They hoped she would, in a year or two, console herself—and had it been only a question of consolation things might have gone much straighter ahead. But her trouble, behind just a little grief, was a complete dislocation from everything. She did not reject other lovers, for these failed to appear: for years she failed to attract men—and with the approach of her thirties she became natural enough to share her family's anxiousness on this score. She began to put herself out, to wonder; and at thirty-two she was very greatly relieved to find herself being courted by William Drover. She married him, and the two of them settled down in this quiet, arboreal part of Kensington: in this house the years piled up, her children were born and they all lived till they were driven out by the bombs of the next war. Her movements as Mrs. Drover were circumscribed, and she dismissed any idea that they were still watched.

As things were—dead or living the letter-writer sent her only a threat. Unable, for some minutes, to go on kneeling with her back exposed to the empty room, Mrs. Drover rose from the chest to sit on an upright chair whose back was firmly against the wall. The desuetude of her former bedroom, her married London home's whole air of being a cracked cup from which memory, with its reassuring power, had either evaporated or leaked away, made a crisis—and at just this crisis the letter-writer had, knowledgeably, struck. The hollowness of the house this evening cancelled years on years of voices, habits and steps. Through the shut windows she only heard rain fall on the roofs around. To rally herself, she said she was in a mood—and, for two or three seconds shutting her eyes, told herself that she had imagined the letter. But she opened them—there it lay on the bed.

On the supernatural side of the letter's entrance she was not permitting her mind to dwell. Who, in London, knew she meant to call at the house today? Evidently, however, this had been known. The caretaker, *had* he come back, had had no cause to expect her: he would have taken the letter in his pocket, to forward it, at his own time, through the post. There was no other sign that the caretaker had been in—but, if not? Letters dropped in at doors of deserted houses do not fly or walk to tables in halls. They do not sit on the dust of empty tables with the air of certainty that they will be found. There is needed some human hand—but nobody but the caretaker had a key. Under circumstances she did not care to consider, a house can be entered without a key. It was possible that she was not alone now. She might be being waited for, downstairs. Waited for—until when? Until "the hour arranged." At least that was not six o'clock: six had struck.

She rose from the chair and went over and locked the door.

The thing was, to get out. To fly? No, not that: she had to catch her train. As a woman whose utter dependability was the keystone of her family life she was not willing to return to the country, to her husband, her little boys and her sister, without the objects she had come up to fetch. Resuming work at the chest she set about making up a number of parcels in a rapid, fumbling-decisive way. These, with her shopping parcels, would be too much to carry; these meant a taxi—at the thought of the taxi her heart went up and her normal breathing resumed. I will ring up the taxi now; the taxi cannot come too soon: I shall hear the taxi out there running its engine, till I walk calmly down to it through the hall. "I'll ring up— But no: the telephone is cut off. . . . She tugged at a knot she had tied wrong.

The idea of flight . . . He was never kind to me, not really. I don't remember him kind at all. Mother said he never considered me. He was set on me, that was what it was—not love. Not love, not meaning a person well. What did he do, to make me promise like that? I can't remember. —But she found that she could.

She remembered with such dreadful acuteness that the twenty-five years since then dissolved like smoke and she instinctively looked for the weal left by the button on the palm of her hand. She remembered not only all that he said and did but the complete suspension of *her* existence during that August week. I was not myself—they all told me so at the time. She remembered—but with one white burning blank as where acid has dropped on a photograph: *under no conditions* could she remember his face.

So, wherever he may be waiting, I shall not know him. You have no time to run from a face you do not expect.

The thing was to get to the taxi before any clock struck what could be the hour. She would slip down the street and round the side of the square to where the square gave on the main road. She would return in the taxi, safe, to her own door, and bring the solid driver into the house with her to pick up the parcels from room to room. The idea of the taxi driver made her decisive, bold: she unlocked her door, went to the top of the staircase and listened down.

She heard nothing—but while she was hearing nothing the *passé* air of the staircase was disturbed by a draught that travelled up to her face. It emanated from the basement: down there a door or window was being opened by someone who chose this moment to leave the house.

The rain had stopped; the pavements steamily shone as Mrs. Drover let herself out by inches from her own front door into the empty street. The unoccupied houses opposite continued to meet her look with their damaged stare. Making towards the thoroughfare and the taxi, she tried not to keep looking behind. Indeed, the silence was so intense—one of those creeks of London silence exaggerated this summer by the damage of war—that no tread could have gained on hers unheard. Where her street debouched on the square where people went on living she grew conscious of and checked her unnatural pace. Across the open end of the square two buses impassively passed each other; women, a perambulator, cyclists, a man wheeling a barrow signalized, once again, the ordinary flow of life. At the square's most populous corner should be—and was—the short taxi rank. This evening, only one taxi—but this, although it presented its blank rump, appeared already to be alertly waiting for her. Indeed, without looking round the driver started his engine as she panted up from behind and put her hand on the door. As she did so, the clock struck seven. The taxi faced the main road: to make the trip back to her house it would have to turn—she had settled back on the seat and the taxi *had* turned before she, surprised by its knowing movement, recollected that she had not "said where." She leaned forward to scratch at the glass panel that divided the driver's head from her own.

The driver braked to what was almost a stop, turned round and slid the glass panel back: the jolt of this flung Mrs. Drover forward till her face was almost into the glass. Through the aperture driver and passenger, not six inches between them, remained for an eternity eye to eye. Mrs. Drover's mouth hung open for some seconds before she could issue her first scream. After that she continued to scream freely and to beat with her gloved hands on the glass all round as the taxi, accelerating without mercy, made off with her into the hinterland of deserted streets.

In Ghostly Japan

Lafcadio Hearn

And it was the hour of sunset that they came to the foot of the mountain. There was in that place no sign of life, —neither token of water, nor trace of plant, nor shadow of flying bird, —nothing but desolation rising to desolation. And the summit was lost in heaven.

Then the Bodhisattva said to his young companion: —"What you have asked to see will be shown to you. But the place of the Vision is far; and the way is rude. Follow after me, and do not fear: strength will be given you."

Twilight gloomed about them as they climbed. There was no beaten path, nor any mark of former human visitation; and the way was over an endless heaping of tumbled fragments that rolled or turned beneath the foot. Sometimes a mass dislodged would clatter down with hollow echoings; —sometimes the substance trodden would burst like an empty shell. . . . Stars pointed and thrilled; —and the darkness deepened.

"Do not fear, my son," said the Bodhisattva, guiding: "danger there is none, though the way be grim."

Under the stars they climbed, —fast, fast, —mounting by help of power superhuman. High zones of mist they passed; and they saw below them, ever widening as they climbed, a soundless flood of cloud, like the tide of a milky sea.

Hour after hour they climbed; —and forms invisible yielded to their tread with dull soft crashings; —and faint cold fires lighted and died at every breaking.

And once the pilgrim-youth laid hand on a something smooth that was not stone, —and lifted it, —and dimly saw the cheekless gibe of death.

"Linger not thus, my son!" urged the voice of the teacher; —"the summit that we must gain is very far away!"

On through the dark they climbed, —and felt continually beneath them the soft strange breakings —and saw the icy fires worm and die, —till the rim of the night turned grey, and the stars began to fail, and the east began to bloom.

Yet still they climbed, —fast, fast, —mounting by help of power superhuman. About them now was frigidness of death, —and silence tremendous. . . . A gold flame kindled in the east.

Then first to the pilgrim's gaze the steeps revealed their nakedness; — and a trembling seized him, —and a ghastly fear. For there was not any ground, —neither beneath him nor about him nor above him, —but a heaping only, monstrous and measureless, of skulls and fragments of skulls and dust of bone, —with a shimmer of shed teeth strown through the drift of it, like the shimmer of scrags of shell in the wrack of a tide.

"Do not fear my son!" cried the voice of the Bodhisattva; —"only the strong of heart can win to the place of the Vision!"

Behind them the world had vanished. Nothing remained but the clouds beneath, and the sky above, and the heaping of skulls between, —upslanting out of sight.

Then the sun climbed with the climbers; and there was no warmth in the light of him, but coldness sharp as a sword. And the horror of stupendous height, and the nightmare of stupendous depth, and the terror of silence, ever grew and grew, and weighed upon the pilgrim, and held his feet, —so that suddenly all power departed from him, and he moaned like a sleeper in dreams.

"Hasten, hasten, my son!" cried the Bodhisattva: "the day is brief, and the summit is very far away."

But the pilgrim shrieked, —

"I fear! I fear unspeakably! —and the power has departed from me!"

"The power will return, my son," made answer the Bodhisattva. . . . "Look now below you and above you and about you, and tell me what you see."

"I cannot," cried the pilgrim, trembling and clinging; —"I dare not look beneath! Before me and about me there is nothing but skulls of men."

"And yet, my son," said the Bodhisattva, laughing softly, —"and yet you do not know of what this mountain is made."

The other, shuddering, repeated: —

"I fear! —unutterably I fear! . . . there is nothing but skulls of men!"

"A mountain of skulls it is," responded the Bodhisattva. "But know, my son, that all of them ARE YOUR OWN! Each has at some time been the nest of your dreams and delusions and desires. Not even one of them is the skull of any other being. All, —all without exception, —have been yours, in the billions of your former lives."

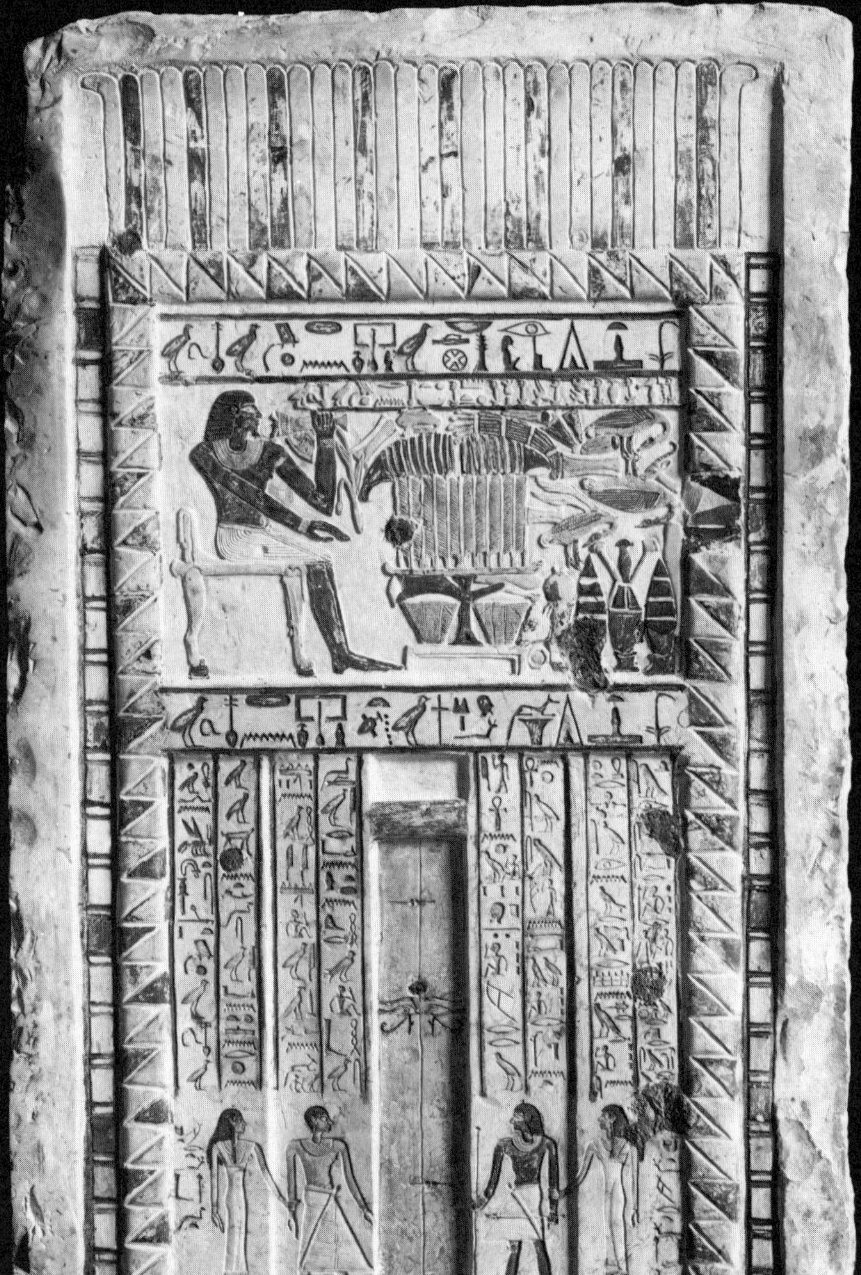

THE OTHER WORLD

from The Book of the Dead

Here are cakes for thy body,
Cool water for thy throat,
Sweet breezes for thy nostrils,
And thou art satisfied.

No longer dost thou stumble
Upon thy chosen path,
From thy mind all evil
And darkness fall away.

Here by the river,
Drink and bathe thy limbs,
Or cast thy net, and surely
It shall be filled with fish.

The holy cow of Hapi
Shall give thee of her milk,
The ale of gods triumphant
Shall be thy daily draught.

White linen is thy tunic,
Thy sandals shine with gold;
Victorious thy weapons,
That death come not again.

Now upon the whirlwind
Thou followest thy Prince,
Now thou hast refreshment
Under the leafy tree.

Take wings to climb the zenith,
Or sleep in Fields of Peace;
By day the Sun shall keep thee,
By night the rising Star.

Translated by Robert Hillyer

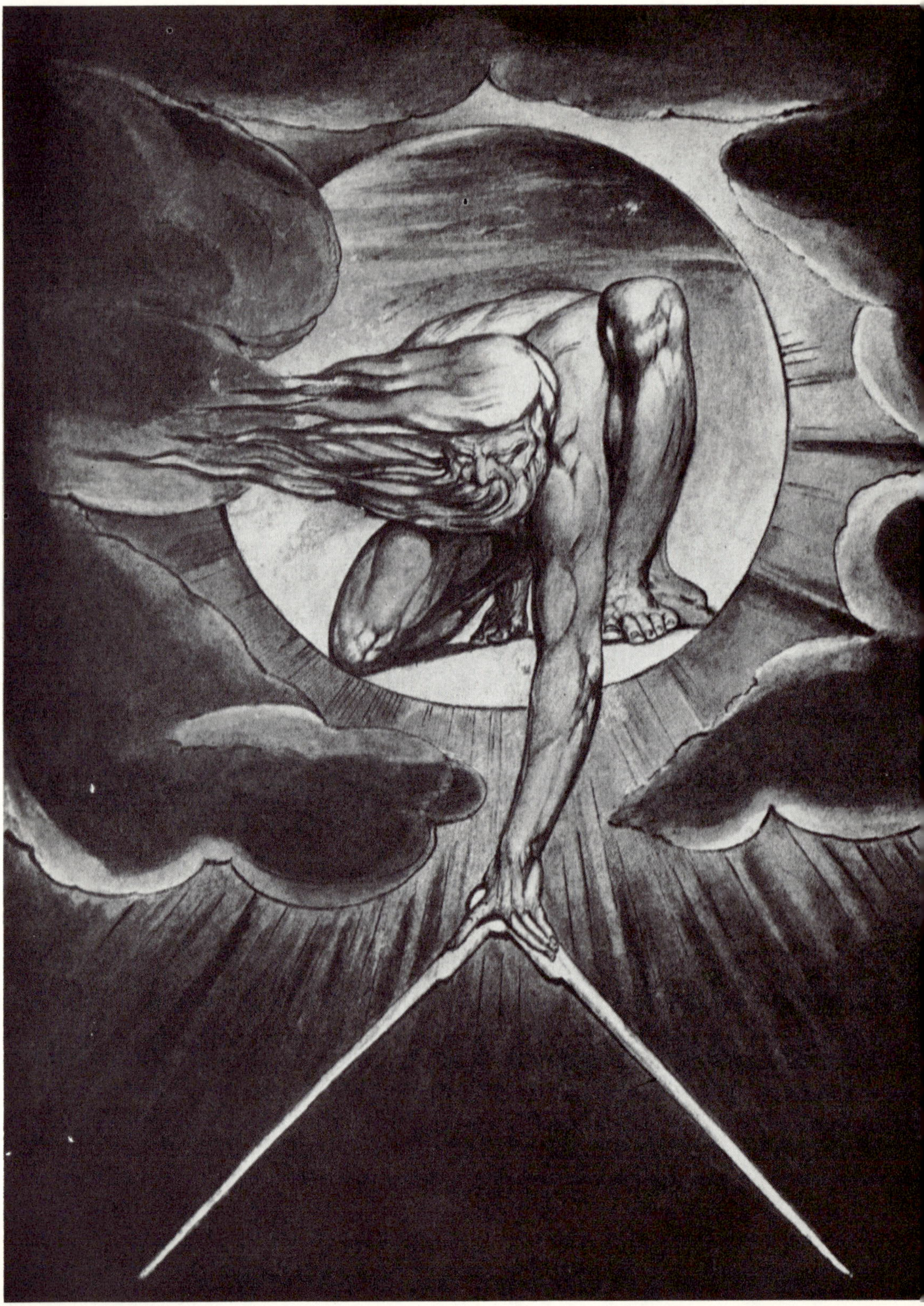

THE NINE ANGELIC CIRCLES

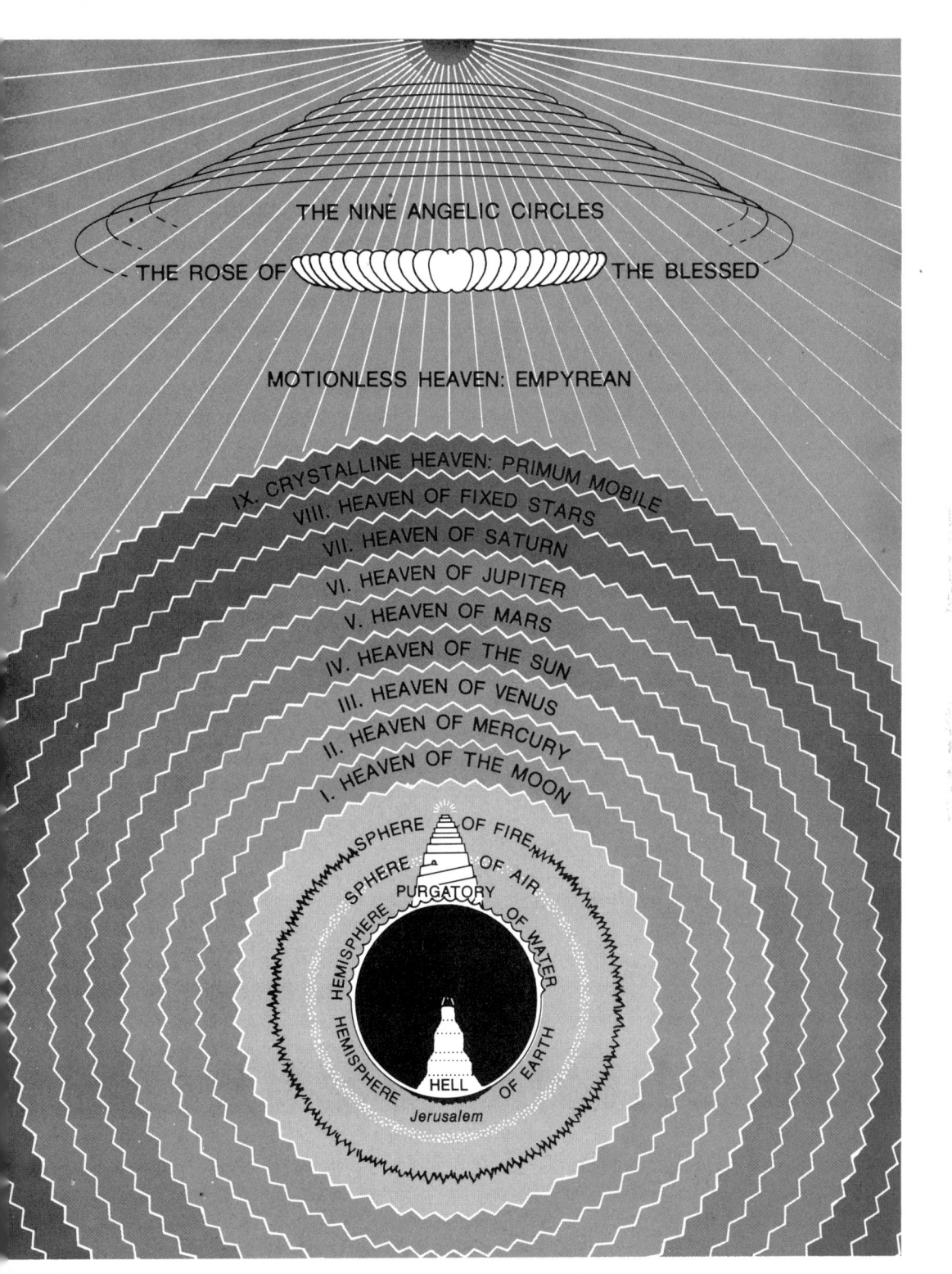

THE ROSE OF THE BLESSED

MOTIONLESS HEAVEN: EMPYREAN

IX. CRYSTALLINE HEAVEN: PRIMUM MOBILE
VIII. HEAVEN OF FIXED STARS
VII. HEAVEN OF SATURN
VI. HEAVEN OF JUPITER
V. HEAVEN OF MARS
IV. HEAVEN OF THE SUN
III. HEAVEN OF VENUS
II. HEAVEN OF MERCURY
I. HEAVEN OF THE MOON

SPHERE OF FIRE
SPHERE OF AIR
HEMISPHERE OF WATER
PURGATORY
HEMISPHERE OF EARTH
HELL
Jerusalem

The Universe

TERRESTRIAL PARADISE

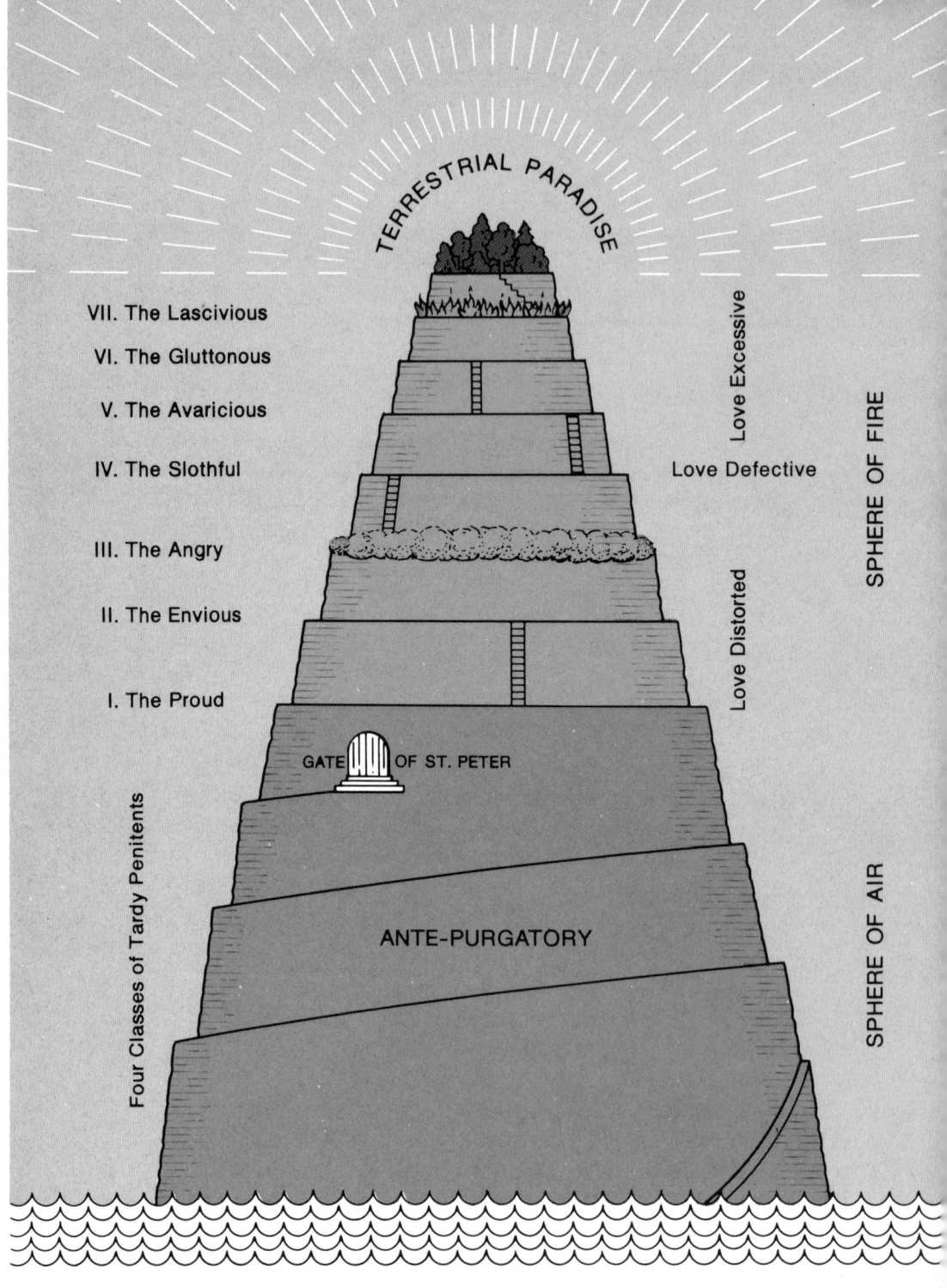

VII. The Lascivious
VI. The Gluttonous
V. The Avaricious
IV. The Slothful
III. The Angry
II. The Envious
I. The Proud

Love Excessive
Love Defective
Love Distorted

SPHERE OF FIRE

GATE OF ST. PETER

Four Classes of Tardy Penitents

ANTE-PURGATORY

SPHERE OF AIR

Purgatory

Dark Wood | JERUSALEM

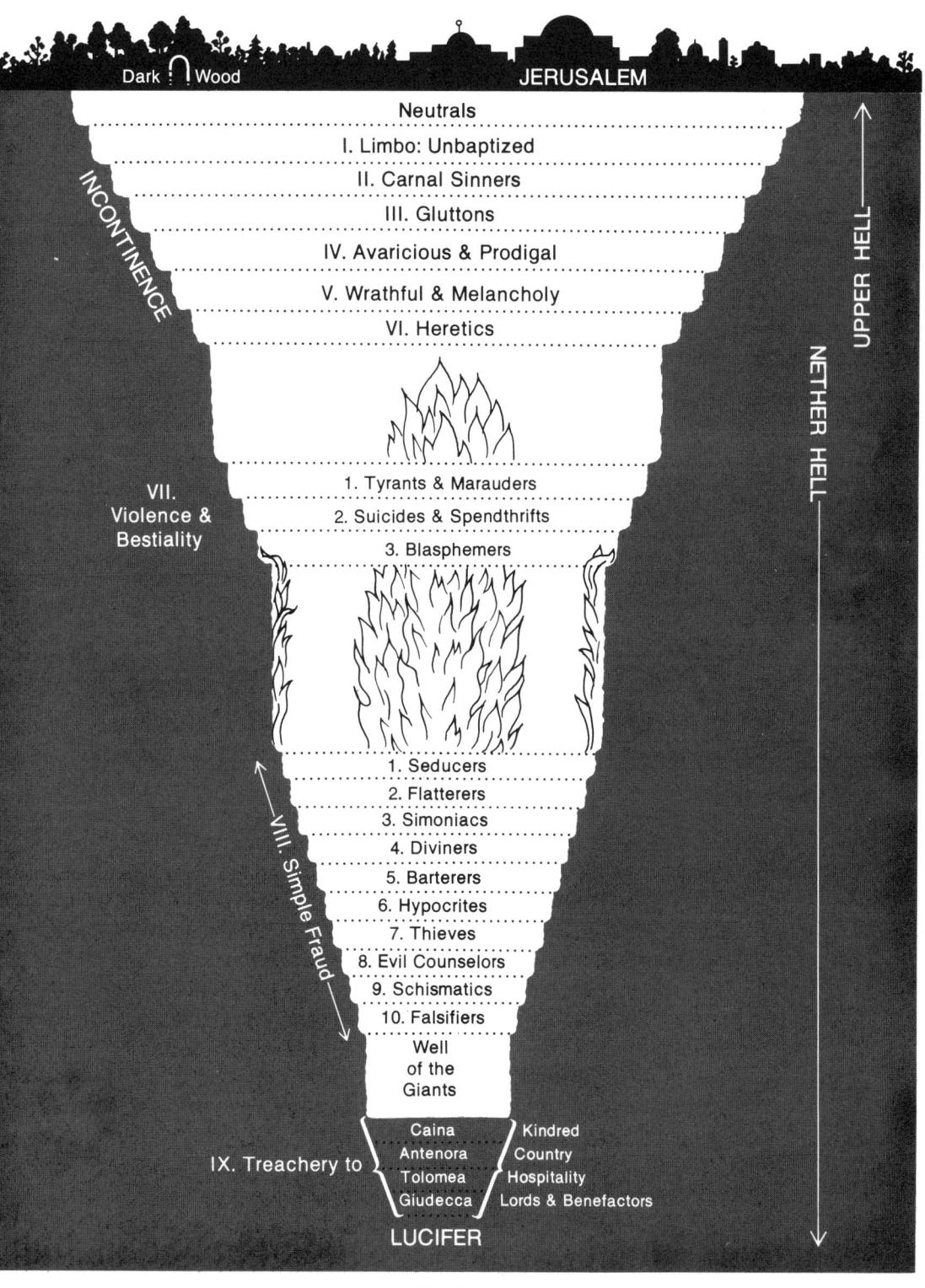

Neutrals

I. Limbo: Unbaptized

II. Carnal Sinners

III. Gluttons

IV. Avaricious & Prodigal

V. Wrathful & Melancholy

VI. Heretics

INCONTINENCE

UPPER HELL

NETHER HELL

VII. Violence & Bestiality
1. Tyrants & Marauders
2. Suicides & Spendthrifts
3. Blasphemers

VIII. Simple Fraud
1. Seducers
2. Flatterers
3. Simoniacs
4. Diviners
5. Barterers
6. Hypocrites
7. Thieves
8. Evil Counselors
9. Schismatics
10. Falsifiers

Well of the Giants

IX. Treachery to
- Caina — Kindred
- Antenora — Country
- Tolomea — Hospitality
- Giudecca — Lords & Benefactors

LUCIFER

Hell

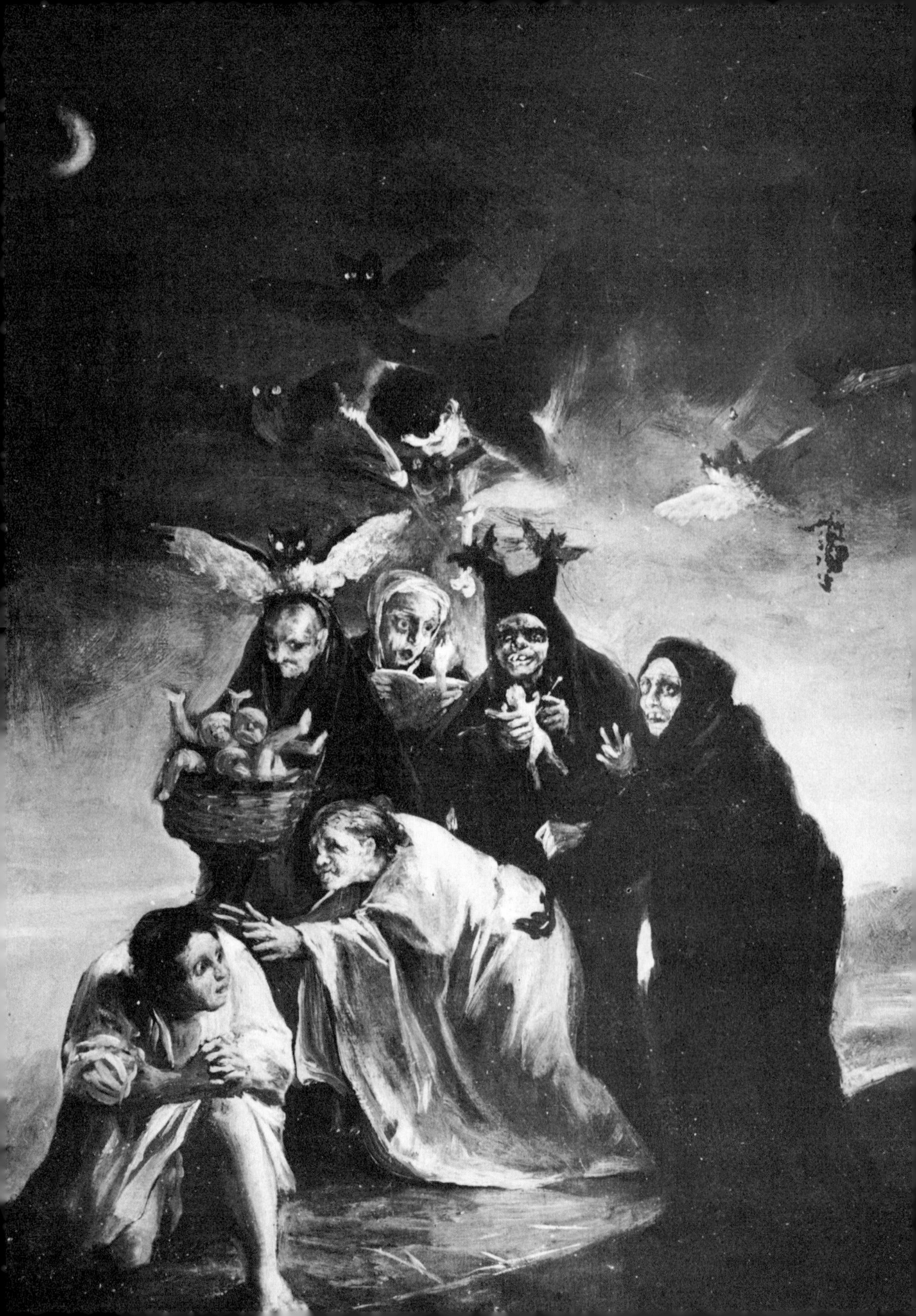

The Witch Mania

Charles Mackay

Countrymen. Hang her! beat her! kill her!

Justice. How now? Forbear this violence!

Mother Sawyer. A crew of villains—a knot of bloody hangmen! set to torment me! I know not why.

Justice. Alas, neighbour Banks! are you a ringleader in mischief? Fie! to abuse an aged woman!

Banks. Woman! a she hell-cat, a witch! To prove her one, we no sooner set fire on the thatch of her house, but in she came running, as if the devil had sent her in a barrel of gunpowder.

Ford's Witch of Edmonton

The belief that disembodied spirits may be permitted to revisit this world has its foundation upon that sublime hope of immortality which is at once the chief solace and greatest triumph of our reason. Even if revelation did not teach us, we feel that we have that within us which shall never die; and all our experience of this life but makes us cling the more fondly to that one repaying hope. But in the early days of "little knowledge" this grand belief became the source of a whole train of superstitions, which, in their turn, became the fount from whence flowed a deluge of blood and horror. Europe, for a period of two centuries and a half, brooded upon the idea, not only that parted spirits walked the earth to meddle in the affairs of men, but that men had power to summon evil spirits to their aid to work woe upon their fellows. An epidemic terror seized upon the nations; no man thought himself secure, either in his person or possessions, from the machinations of the devil and his agents. Every calamity that befell him he attributed to a witch. If a storm arose and blew down his barn, it was witchcraft; if his cattle died of a murrain —if disease fastened upon his limbs, or death entered suddenly and snatched a beloved face from his hearth—they were not visitations of Providence, but the works of some neighboring hag, whose wretchedness or insanity caused the ignorant to raise their finger and point at her as a

The Witch Mania

witch. The word was upon everybody's tongue. France, Italy, Germany, England, Scotland, and the far north successively ran mad upon this subject, and for a long series of years furnished their tribunals with so many trials for witchcraft, that other crimes were seldom or never spoken of. Thousands upon thousands of unhappy persons fell victims to this cruel and absurd delusion. In many cities of Germany, as will be shown more fully in its due place hereafter, the average number of executions for this pretended crime was six hundred annually, or two every day, if we leave out the Sundays, when it is to be supposed that even this madness refrained from its work.

A misunderstanding of the famous text of the Mosaic law, "Thou shalt not suffer a witch to live," no doubt led many conscientious men astray, whose superstition, warm enough before, wanted but a little corroboration to blaze out with desolating fury. In all ages of the world men have tried to hold converse with superior beings, and to pierce by their means the secrets of futurity. In the time of Moses, it is evident that there were impostors who trafficked upon the credulity of mankind, and insulted the supreme majesty of the true God by pretending to the power of divination. Hence the law which Moses, by divine command, promulgated against these criminals; but it did not follow, as the superstitious monomaniacs of the middle ages imagined, that the Bible established the existence of the power of divination by its edicts against those who pretended to it. From the best authorities, it appears that the Hebrew word, which has been rendered *venefica* and *witch*, means a poisoner and divineress, a dabbler in spells, or fortune-teller. The modern witch was a very different character, and joined to her pretended power of foretelling future events that of working evil upon the life, limbs, and possessions of mankind. This power was only to be acquired by an express compact, signed in blood, with the devil himself, by which the wizard or witch renounced baptism, and sold his or her immortal soul to the evil one, without any saving clause of redemption.

There are so many wondrous appearances in nature for which science and philosophy cannot even now account, that it is not surprising that, when natural laws were still less understood, men should have attributed to supernatural agency every appearance which they could not otherwise explain. The merest tyro now understands various phenomena which the wisest of old could not fathom. The schoolboy knows why, upon high mountains, there should on certain occasions appear three or four suns in the firmament at once, and why the figure of a traveller upon one eminence should be reproduced, inverted and of a gigantic stature, upon another. We all know the strange pranks which imagination can play in certain diseases; that the hypochondriac can see visions and spectres; and that there have been cases in which men were perfectly persuaded that they were teapots. Science has lifted up the veil, and rolled away all the fantastic horrors in which our forefathers shrouded these and similar cases. The man who now imagines himself a wolf is sent to the hospital instead of to the stake, as in the days of the witch mania; and earth, air, and sea are unpeopled of the grotesque spirits that were once believed to haunt them.

Before entering further into the history of Witchcraft, it may be as well if we consider the absurd impersonation of the evil principle formed by the monks in their legends. We must make acquaintance with the *primum mobile,* and understand what sort of a personage it was who gave the witches, in exchange for their souls, the power to torment their fellow creatures. The popular notion of the devil was, that he was a large, ill-formed, hairy sprite, with horns, a long tail, cloven feet, and dragon's wings. In this shape he was constantly brought on the stage by the monks in their early "miracles" and "mysteries." In these representations he was an important personage, and answered the purpose of the clown in the modern pantomime. The great fun for the people was to see him well belabored by the saints with clubs or cudgels, and to hear him howl with pain as he limped off, maimed by the blow of some vigorous anchorite. St. Dunstan generally served him the glorious trick for which he is renowned, catching hold of his nose with a pair of red-hot pincers, till

> Rocks and distant dells resounded with his cries.

Some of the saints spat in his face, to his very great annoyance; and others chopped pieces off his tail, which, however, always grew on again. This was paying him in his own coin, and amused the populace mightily, for they all remembered the scurvy tricks he had played them and their forefathers. It was believed that he endeavored to trip people up by laying his long invisible tail in their way, and giving it a sudden whisk when their legs were over it;—that he used to get drunk, and swear like a trooper, and be so mischievous in his cups as to raise tempests and earthquakes, to destroy the fruits of the earth, and the barns and homesteads of true believers;—that he used to run invisible spits into people by way of amusing himself in the long winter evenings, and to proceed to taverns and regale himself with the best, offering in payment pieces of gold which, on the dawn of the following morning, invariably turned into slates. Sometimes, disguised as a large drake, he used to lurk among the bulrushes, and frighten the weary traveller out of his wits by his awful quack. The reader will remember the lines of Burns in his address to the "De'il," which so well express the popular notion on this point:

> Ae dreary, windy, winter night,
> The stars shot down wi' sklentin light,
> Wi' you mysel' I got a fright
>   Ayont the lough;
> Ye, like a rash-bush, stood in sight,
>   Wi' waving sough.
> The cudgel in my nieve did shake,
> Each bristled hair stood like a stake,
> When wi' an eldritch stour, 'quaick! quaick!'
>   Among the springs
> Awa' ye squattered, like a drake,
>   On whistling wings.

In all the stories circulated and believed about him, he was represented as an ugly, petty, mischievous spirit, who rejoiced in playing off all manner of fantastic tricks upon poor humanity. Milton seems to have been the first who succeeded in giving any but a ludicrous description of him. The sublime pride, which is the quintessence of evil, was unconceived before his time. All the other limners made him merely grotesque, but Milton made him awful. In this the monks showed themselves but miserable romancers; for their object undoubtedly was to represent the fiend as terrible as possible. But there was nothing grand about their Satan; on the contrary, he was a low, mean devil, whom it was easy to circumvent, and fine fun to play tricks with. But, as is well and eloquently remarked by a modern writer, the subject has also its serious side. An Indian deity, with its wild distorted shape and grotesque attitude, appears merely ridiculous when separated from its accessories and viewed by daylight in a museum; but restore it to the darkness of its own hideous temple, bring back to our recollection the victims that have bled upon its altar or been crushed beneath its car, and our sense of the ridiculous subsides into aversion and horror. So, while the superstitious dreams of former times are regarded as mere speculative insanities, we may be for a moment amused with the wild incoherencies of the patients; but when we reflect that out of these hideous misconceptions of the principle of evil arose the belief in witchcraft—that this was no dead faith, but one operating on the whole being of society, urging on the wisest and the mildest to deeds of murder, or cruelties scarcely less than murder—that the learned and the beautiful, young and old, male and female, were devoted by its influence to the stake and the scaffold—every feeling disappears, except that of astonishment that such things could be, and humiliation at the thought that the delusion was as lasting as it was universal.

Besides this chief personage, there was an infinite number of inferior demons, who played conspicuous parts in the creed of witchcraft. The pages of Bekker, Leloyer, Bodin, Delrio, and De Lancre, abound with descriptions of the qualities of these imps, and the functions which were assigned them. From these authors,—three of whom were commissioners for the trial of witches, and who wrote from the confessions made by the supposed criminals and the evidence delivered against them,—and from the more recent work of M. Jules Garinet, the following summary of the creed has been, with great pains, extracted. The student who is desirous of knowing more is referred to the works in question; he will find enough in every leaf to make his blood curdle with shame and horror: but the purity of these pages shall not be soiled by any thing so ineffably humiliating and disgusting as a complete exposition of them; what is here culled will be a sufficient sample of the popular belief, and the reader would but lose time who should seek in the writings of the demonologists for more ample details. He will gain nothing by lifting the veil which covers their unutterable obscenities, unless, like Sterne, he wishes to gather fresh evidence of "what a beast man is." In that case, he will find plenty there to convince him that the beast would be libelled by the comparison.

It was thought that the earth swarmed with millions of demons of both sexes, many of whom, like the human race, traced their lineage up to Adam, who after the fall was led astray by devils, assuming the forms of beautiful women to deceive him. These demons "increased and multiplied" among themselves with the most extraordinary rapidity. Their bodies were of the thin air, and they could pass through the hardest substances with the greatest ease. They had no fixed residence or abiding-place, but were tossed to and fro in the immensity of space. When thrown together in great multitudes, they excited whirlwinds in the air and tempests in the waters, and took delight in destroying the beauty of nature and the monuments of the industry of man. Although they increased among themselves like ordinary creatures, their numbers were daily augmented by the souls of wicked men, of children still-born, of women who died in childbed, and of persons killed in duels. The whole air was supposed to be full of them, and many unfortunate men and women drew them by thousands into their mouths and nostrils at every inspiration; and the demons, lodging in their bowels or other parts of their bodies, tormented them with pains and diseases of every kind, and sent them frightful dreams. St. Gregory of Nice relates a story of a nun who forgot to say her *benedicite* and make the sign of the cross before she sat down to supper, and who in consequence swallowed a demon concealed among the leaves of a lettuce. Most persons said the number of these demons was so great that they could not be counted, but Wierus asserted that they amounted to no more than seven millions four hundred and five thousand nine hundred and twenty-six; and that they were divided into seventy-two companies or battalions, to each of which there was a prince or captain. They could assume any shape they pleased. When they were male, they were called incubi; and when female, succubi. They sometimes made themselves hideous; and at other times they assumed shapes of such transcendent loveliness, that mortal eyes never saw beauty to compete with theirs.

Although the devil and his legions could appear to mankind at any time, it was generally understood that he preferred the night between Friday and Saturday. If Satan himself appeared in human shape, he was never perfectly and in all respects like a man. He was either too black or too white, too large or too small, or some of his limbs were out of proportion to the rest of his body. Most commonly his feet were deformed, and he was obliged to curl up and conceal his tail in some part of his habiliments; for, take what shape he would, he could not get rid of that encumbrance. He sometimes changed himself into a tree or a river; and upon one occasion he transformed himself into a barrister. In the reign of Philippe le Bel, he appeared to a monk in the shape of a dark man riding a tall black horse, then as a friar, afterwards as an ass, and finally as a coach wheel. Instances are not rare in which both he and his inferior demons have taken the form of handsome young men, and, successfully concealing their tails, have married beautiful young women, who have had children by them. Such children were easily recognizable by their continual shrieking, by their requiring five nurses to suckle them, and by their never growing fat.

All these demons were at the command of any individual who would give up his immortal soul to the prince of evil for the privilege of enjoying their services for a stated period. The wizard or witch could send them to execute the most difficult missions: whatever the witch commanded was performed, except it was a good action, in which case the order was disobeyed, and evil worked upon herself instead.

At intervals, according to the pleasure of Satan, there was a general meeting of the demons and all the witches. This meeting was called the Sabbath, from its taking place on the Saturday or immediately after midnight on Fridays. These sabbaths were sometimes held for one district, sometimes for another, and once at least every year it was held on the Brocken, or among other high mountains, as a general sabbath of the fiends for the whole of Christendom.

The devil generally chose a place where four roads met as the scene of this assembly, or if that was not convenient, the neighborhood of a lake. Upon this spot nothing would ever afterwards grow, as the hot feet of the demons and witches burnt the principle of fecundity from the earth, and rendered it barren forever. When orders had been once issued for the meeting of the sabbath, all the wizards and witches who failed to attend it were lashed by demons with a rod made of serpents or scorpions, as a punishment for their inattention or want of punctuality.

In France and England the witches were supposed to ride uniformly upon broomsticks; but in Italy and Spain, the devil himself, in the shape of a goat, used to transport them on his back, which lengthened or shortened according to the number of witches he was desirous of accommodating. No witch, when proceeding to the sabbath, could get out by a door or window, were she to try ever so much. Their general mode of ingress was by the keyhole, and of egress by the chimney, up which they flew, broom and all, with the greatest ease. To prevent the absence of the witches from being noticed by their neighbors, some inferior demon was commanded to assume their shapes and lie in their beds, feigning illness, until the sabbath was over.

When all the wizards and witches had arrived at the place of rendezvous, the infernal ceremonies of the sabbath began. Satan, having assumed his favorite shape of a large he-goat, with a face in front and another in his haunches, took his seat upon a throne; and all present, in succession, paid their respects to him, and kissed him in his face behind. This done, he appointed a master of ceremonies, in company with whom he made a personal examination of all the wizards and witches, to see whether they had the secret mark about them by which they were stamped as the devil's own. This mark was always insensible to pain. Those who had not yet been marked, received the mark from the master of the ceremonies, the devil at the same time bestowing nicknames upon them. This done, they all began to sing and dance in the most furious manner, until some one arrived who was anxious to be admitted into their society. They were then silent for a while, until the newcomer had denied his salvation, kissed the devil, spat upon the Bible, and sworn obedience to him in all things. They then began dancing again with all their might, and singing these words,

> Alegremos, Alegremos!
> Que gente va tenemos!

In the course of an hour or two they generally became wearied of this violent exercise, and then they all sat down and recounted the evil deeds they had done since their last meeting. Those who had not been malicious and mischievous enough towards their fellow-creatures, received personal chastisement from Satan himself, who flogged them with thorns or scorpions till they were covered with blood, and unable to sit or stand.

When this ceremony was concluded, they were all amused by a dance of toads. Thousands of these creatures sprang out of the earth, and standing on their hind legs, danced, while the devil played the bagpipes or the trumpet. These toads were all endowed with the faculty of speech, and entreated the witches to reward them with the flesh of unbaptized babes for their exertions to give them pleasure. The witches promised compliance. The devil bade them remember to keep their word; and then stamping his foot, caused all the toads to sink into the earth in an instant. The place being thus cleared, preparation was made for the banquet, where all manner of disgusting things were served up and greedily devoured by the demons and witches; although the latter were sometimes regaled with choice meats and expensive wines from golden plates and crystal goblets; but they were never thus favored unless they had done an extraordinary number of evil deeds since the last period of meeting.

After the feast, they began dancing again; but such as had no relish for any more exercise in that way, amused themselves by mocking the holy sacrament of baptism. For this purpose, the toads were again called up, and sprinkled with filthy water; the devil making the sign of the cross, and all the witches calling out, *"In nomine Patricâ Aragucaco Petrica, agora! agora! Valentia, jouando goure gaits goustia!"* which meant, "In the name of Patrick, Petrick of Aragon, now, now, all our ills are over!"

When the devil wished to be particularly amused, he made the witches strip off their clothes and dance before him, each with a cat tied round her neck, and another dangling from her body in form of a tail. When the cock crew, they all disappeared, and the sabbath was ended.

This is a summary of the belief which prevailed for many centuries nearly all over Europe, and which is far from eradicated even at this day.

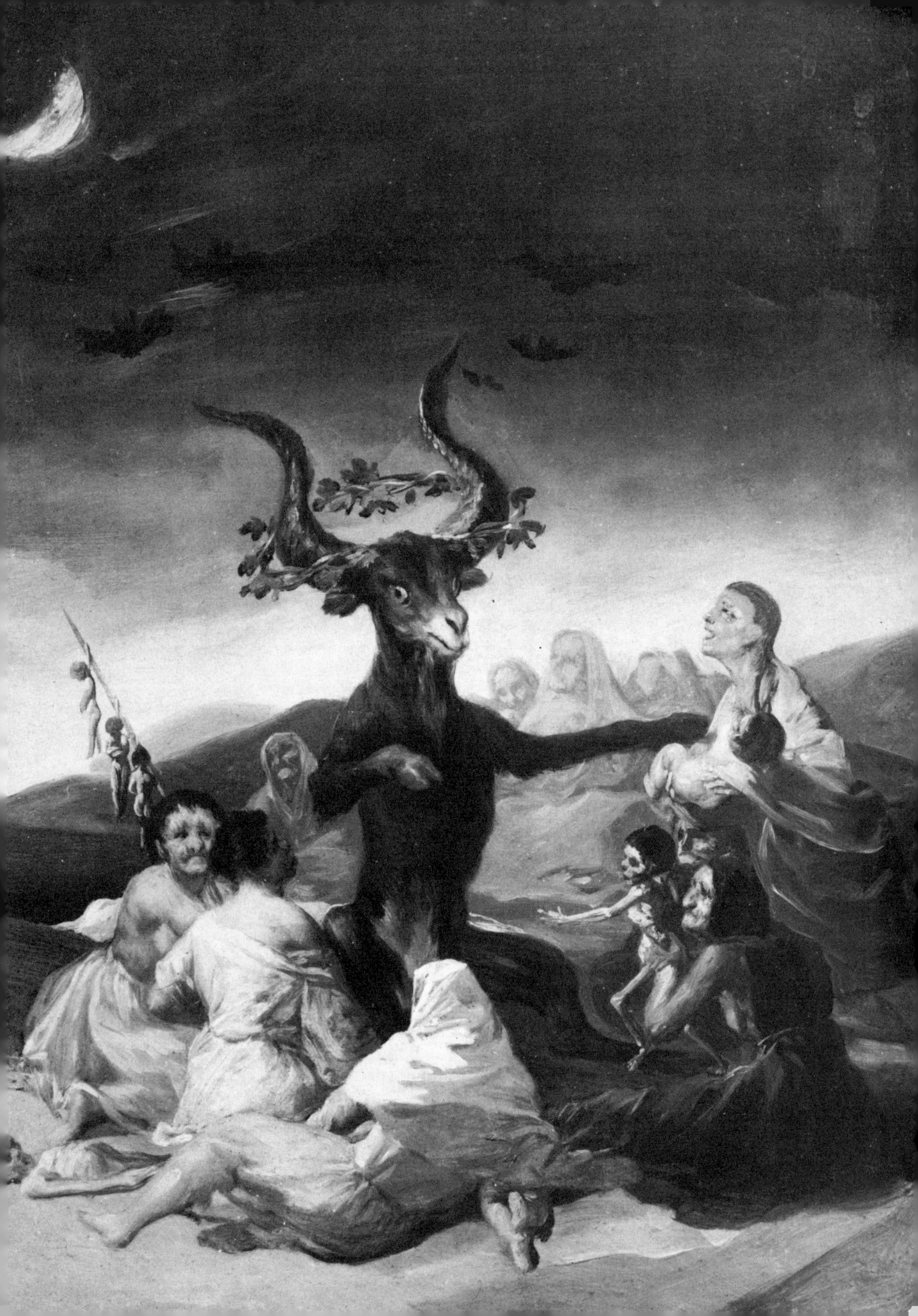

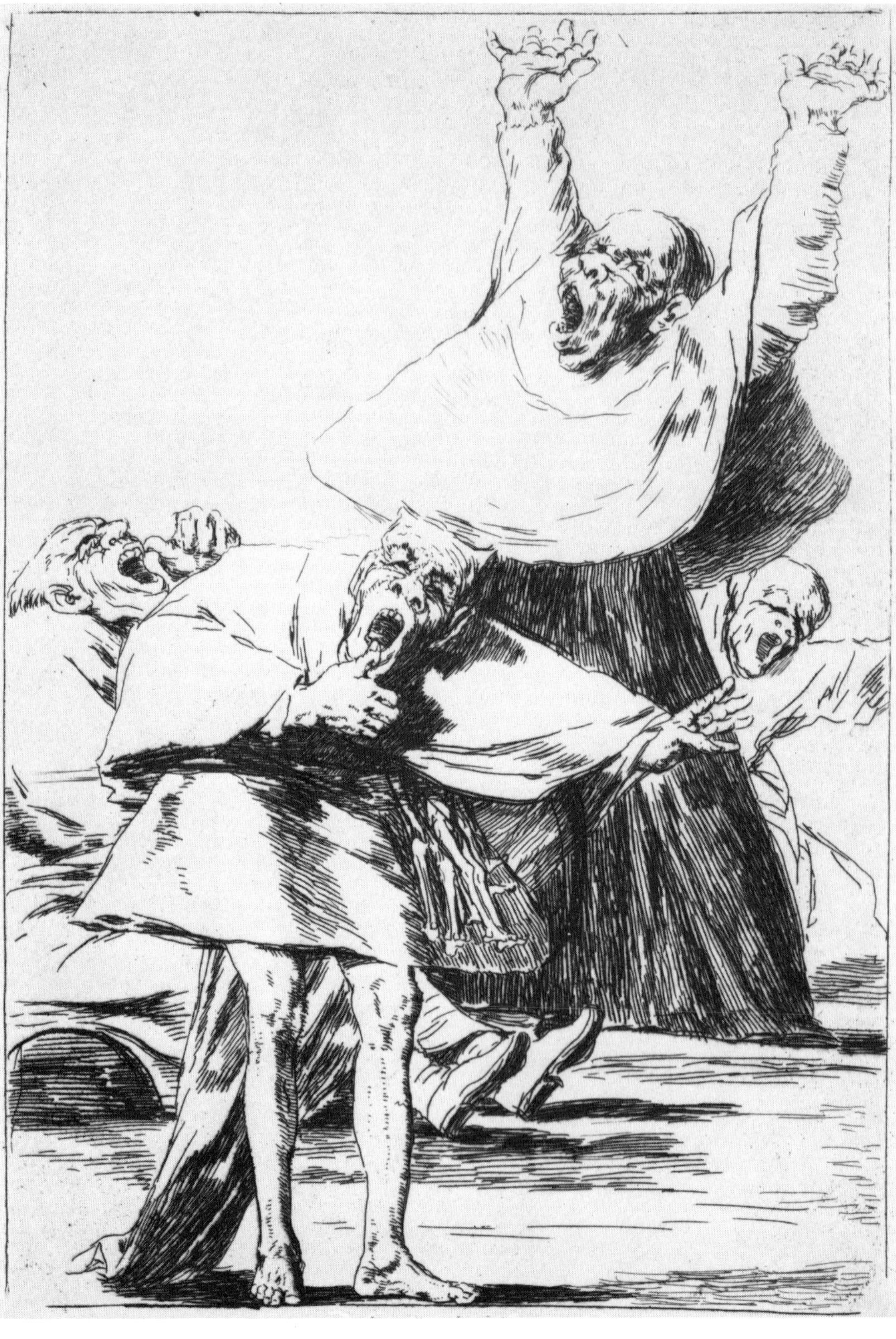

Witches' Spell from Macbeth
William Shakespeare

Act IV, Scene 1   A cavern. In the middle, a boiling cauldron

Thunder. Enter the three WITCHES

1st Witch.   Thrice the brinded cat hath mew'd.

2nd Witch.   Thrice, and once the hedge-pig whin'd.

3rd Witch.   Harpier cries; 'tis time, 'tis time.

1st Witch.   Round about the cauldron go;
In the poison'd entrails throw.
Toad, that under cold stone
Days and nights has thirty-one
Swelter'd venom sleeping got,
Boil thou first i' the charmed pot.

All.   Double, double toil and trouble;
Fire burn and cauldron bubble.

2nd Witch.   Fillet of a fenny snake,
In the cauldron boil and bake;
Eye of newt and toe of frog,
Wool of bat and tongue of dog,
Adder's fork and blind-worm's sting,
Lizard's leg and howlet's wing,
For a charm of powerful trouble,
Like a hell-broth boil and bubble.

All.   Double, double toil and trouble;
Fire burn and cauldron bubble.

3rd Witch.   Scale of dragon, tooth of wolf,
Witches' mummy, maw and gulf
Of the ravin'd salt-sea shark;
Root of hemlock digg'd i' the dark,
Liver of blaspheming Jew,
Gall of goat, and slips of yew
Sliver'd in the moon's eclipse,
Nose of Turk and Tartar's lips,
Finger of birth-strangled babe
Ditch-deliver'd by a drab,
Make the gruel thick and slab:
Add thereto a tiger's chaudron,
For th' ingredients of our cauldron.

All.   Double, double toil and trouble;
Fire burn and cauldron bubble.

2nd Witch.   Cool it with a baboon's blood,
Then the charm is firm and good.

Enter HECATE. *Speaks to the other three* WITCHES

Hecate.   O, well done! I commend your pains;
And every one shall share i' th' gains:
And now about the cauldron sing,
Like elves and fairies in a ring,
Enchanting all that you put in.

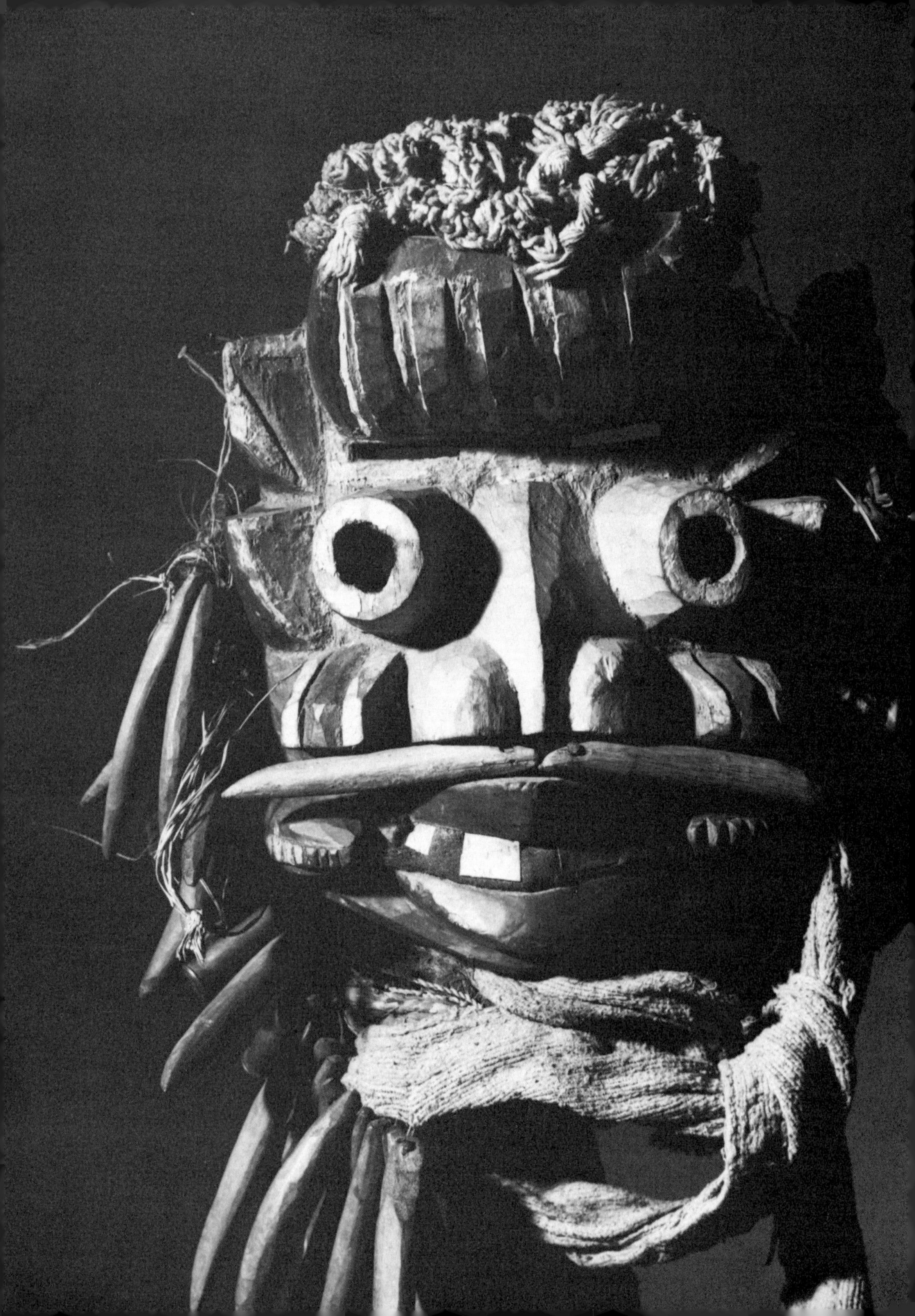

Pollock and the Porroh Man

H.G. Wells

It was in a swampy village on the lagoon river behind the Turner Peninsula that Pollock's first encounter with the Porroh man occurred. The women of that country are famous for their good looks—they are Gallinas with a dash of European blood that dates from the days of Vasco da Gama and the English slave traders, and the Porroh man, too, was possibly inspired by a faint Caucasian taint in his composition. (It's a curious thing to think that some of us may have distant cousins eating men on Sherboro Island or raiding with the Sofas.) At any rate, the Porroh man stabbed the woman to the heart as though he had been a mere low-class Italian, and very narrowly missed Pollock. But Pollock, using his revolver to parry the lightning stab which was aimed at the deltoid muscle, sent the iron dagger flying, and, firing, hit the man in the hand.

He fired again and missed, knocking a sudden window out of the wall of the hut. The Porroh man stooped in the doorway, glancing under his arm at Pollock. Pollock caught a glimpse of the inverted face in the sunlight, and then the Englishman was alone, sick and trembling with the excitement of the affair, in the twilight of the place. It had all happened in less time than it takes to read about it.

The woman was quite dead, and having ascertained this, Pollock went to the entrance of the hut and looked out. Things outside were dazzling bright. Half-a-dozen of the porters of the expedition were standing up in a group near the green huts they occupied, and staring towards him, wondering what the shots might signify. Behind the little group of men was the broad stretch of black fetid mud by the river, a green carpet of rafts of papyrus and water grass, and then the leaden water. The mangroves beyond the stream loomed indistinctly through the blue haze. There were no signs of excitement in the squat village, whose fence was just visible above the cane grass.

Pollock came out of the hut cautiously and walked towards the river, looking over his shoulder at intervals. But the Porroh man had vanished. Pollock clutched his revolver nervously in his hand.

One of his men came to meet him, and as he came, pointed to the bushes behind the hut in which the Porroh man had disappeared. Pollock had an irritating persuasion of having made an absolute fool of himself; he felt bitter, savage, at the turn things had taken. At the same time, he would have to tell Waterhouse—the moral, exemplary, cautious Waterhouse—who would inevitably take the matter seriously. Pollock cursed bitterly at his luck, at Waterhouse, and especially at the West Coast of Africa. He felt consummately sick of the expedition. And in the back of his mind all the time was a speculative doubt where precisely within the visible horizon the Porroh man might be.

It is perhaps rather shocking, but he was not at all upset by the murder that had just happened. He had seen so much brutality during the last three months, so many dead women, burnt huts, drying skeletons, up the Kittam River in the wake of the Sofa cavalry, that his senses were blunted. What disturbed him was the persuasion that this business was only beginning.

He swore savagely at the black, who ventured to ask a question, and went on into the tent under the orange trees where Waterhouse was lying, feeling exasperatingly like a boy going into the headmaster's study.

Waterhouse was still sleeping off the effects of his last dose of chlorodyne, and Pollock sat down on a packing case beside him, and, lighting his pipe, waited for him to awake. About him were scattered the pots and weapons Waterhouse had collected from the Mendi people, and which he had been repacking for the canoe voyage to Sulyma.

Presently Waterhouse woke up, and after judicial stretching, decided he was all right again. Pollock got him some tea. Over the tea the incidents of the afternoon were described by Pollock, after some preliminary beating about the bush. Waterhouse took the matter even more seriously than Pollock had anticipated. He did not simply disapprove, he scolded, he insulted.

"You're one of those infernal fools who think a black man isn't a human being," he said. "I can't be ill a day without you must get into some dirty scrape or other. This is the third time in a month that you have come crossways-on with a native, and this time you're in for it with a vengeance. Porroh, too! They're down upon you enough as it is, about that idol you wrote your silly name on. And they're the most vindictive devils on earth! You make a man ashamed of civilization. To think you come of a decent family! If ever I cumber myself up with a vicious, stupid young lout like you again—"

"Steady on, now," snarled Pollock, in the tone that always exasperated Waterhouse; "steady on."

At that Waterhouse became speechless. He jumped to his feet.

"Look here, Pollock," he said, after a struggle to control his breath. "You must go home. I won't have you any longer. I'm ill enough as it is through you—"

"Keep your hair on," said Pollock, staring in front of him. "I'm ready enough to go."

Waterhouse became calmer again. He sat down on the camp stool. "Very well," he said. "I don't want a row, Pollock, you know, but it's confoundly annoying to have one's plans put out by this kind of thing. I'll come to Sulyma with you, and see you safe aboard—"

"You needn't," said Pollock. "I can go alone. From here."

"Not far," said Waterhouse. "You don't understand this Porroh business."

"How should *I* know she belonged to a Porroh man?" said Pollock bitterly.

"Well, she did," said Waterhouse; "and you can't undo the thing. Go alone, indeed! I wonder what they'd do to you. You don't seem to understand that this Porroh hokey-pokey rules this country, is its law, religion, constitution, medicine, magic. . . . They appoint the chiefs. The Inquisition, at its best, couldn't hold a candle to these chaps. He will probably set Awajale, the chief here, on to us. It's lucky our porters are Mendis. We shall have to shift this little settlement of ours. . . . Confound you, Pollock! And, of course, you must go and miss him."

He thought, and his thoughts seemed disagreeable. Presently he stood up and took his rifle. "I'd keep close for a bit, if I were you," he said, over his shoulder, as he went out. "I'm going out to see what I can find out about it."

Pollock remained sitting in the tent, meditating. "I was meant for a civilized life," he said to himself, regretfully, as he filled his pipe. "The sooner I get back to London or Paris the better for me."

His eyes fell on the sealed case in which Waterhouse had put the featherless poisoned arrows they had bought in the Mendi country. "I wish I had hit the beggar somewhere vital," said Pollock viciously.

Waterhouse came back after a long interval. He was not communicative, though Pollock asked him questions enough. The Porroh man, it seems, was a prominent member of that mystical society. The village was interested, but not threatening. No doubt the witch doctor had gone into the bush. He was a great witch doctor. "Of course, he's up to something," said Waterhouse, and became silent.

"But what can he do?" asked Pollock, unheeded.

"I must get you out of this. There's something brewing, or things would not be so quiet," said Waterhouse, after a gap of silence..Pollock wanted to know what the brew might be. "Dancing in a circle of skulls," said Waterhouse; "brewing a stink in a copper pot." Pollock wanted particulars. Waterhouse was vague, Pollock pressing. At last Waterhouse lost his temper. "How the devil should *I* know?" he said to Pollock's twentieth inquiry what the Porroh man would do. "He tried to kill you offhand in the hut. *Now,* I fancy he will try something more elaborate. But you'll see fast enough. I don't want to help unnerve you. It's probably all nonsense."

That night, as they were sitting at their fire, Pollock again tried to draw Waterhouse out on the subject of Porroh methods. "Better get to sleep," said Waterhouse, when Pollock's bent became apparent; "we start early tomorrow. You may want all your nerve about you."

"But what line will he take?"

"Can't say. They're versatile people. They know a lot of rum dodges. You'd better get that copper devil, Shakespeare, to talk."

There was a flash and a heavy bang out of the darkness behind the huts, and a clay bullet came whistling close to Pollock's head. This, at least, was crude enough. The blacks and half-breeds sitting and yarning round their own fire jumped up, and someone fired into the dark.

"Better go into one of the huts," said Waterhouse quietly, still sitting unmoved.

Pollock stood up by the fire and drew his revolver. Fighting, at least, he was not afraid of. But a man in the dark is in the best of armor. Realizing the wisdom of Waterhouse's advice, Pollock went into the tent and lay down there.

What little sleep he had was disturbed by dreams, variegated dreams, but chiefly of the Porroh man's face, upside down, as he went out of the hut, and looked up under his arm. It was odd that this transitory impression should have stuck so firmly in Pollock's memory. Moreover, he was troubled by queer pains in his limbs.

In the white haze of the early morning, as they were loading the canoes, a barbed arrow suddenly appeared quivering in the ground close to Pollock's foot. The boys made a perfunctory effort to clear out the thicket, but it led to no capture.

After these two occurrences, there was a disposition on the part of the expedition to leave Pollock to himself, and Pollock became, for the first time in his life, anxious to mingle with blacks. Waterhouse took one canoe, and Pollock, in spite of a friendly desire to chat with Waterhouse, had to take the other. He was left all alone in the front part of the canoe, and he had the greatest trouble to make the men—who did not love him—keep to the middle of the river, a clear hundred yards or more from either shore. However, he made Shakespeare, the Freetown half-breed, come up to his own end of the canoe and tell him about Porroh, which Shakespeare, failing in his attempts to leave Pollock alone, presently did with considerable freedom and gusto.

The day passed. The canoe glided swiftly along the ribbon of lagoon water, between the drift of water-figs, fallen trees, papyrus, and palm-wine palms, and with the dark mangrove swamp to the left, through which one could hear now and then the roar of the Atlantic surf. Shakespeare told in his soft, blurred English of how the Porroh could cast spells; how men withered up under their malice; how they could send dreams and devils; how they tormented and killed the sons of Ijibu; how they kidnapped a white trader from Sulyma who had maltreated one of the sect, and how his body looked when it was found. And Pollock after each narrative cursed under his breath at the want of missionary enterprise that allowed such things to be, and at the inert British Government that ruled over this dark heathendom of Sierra Leone. In the evening they came to the Kasi Lake, and sent a score of crocodiles lumbering off the island on which the expedition camped for the night.

The next day they reached Sulyma, and smelt the sea breeze, but Pollock had to put up there for five days before he could get on to Freetown. Waterhouse, considering him to be comparatively safe here, and within the pale of Freetown influence, left him and went back with the expedition to Gbemma, and Pollock became very friendly with Perea, the only resident white trader at Sulyma—so friendly, indeed, that he went about with him everywhere. Perea was a little Portuguese Jew, who had lived in England, and he appreciated the Englishman's friendliness as a great compliment.

For two days nothing happened out of the ordinary; for the most part Pollock and Perea played Nap—the only game they had in common—and Pollock got into debt. Then, on the second evening, Pollock had a disagreeable intimation of the arrival of the Porroh man in Sulyma by getting a flesh wound in the shoulder from a lump of filed iron. It was a long shot, and the missile had nearly spent its force when it hit him. Still it conveyed its message plainly enough. Pollock sat up in his hammock, revolver in hand, all night, and next morning confided, to some extent, in the Anglo-Portuguese.

Perea took the matter seriously. He knew the local customs pretty thoroughly. "It is a personal question, you must know. It is revenge. And of course he is hurried by your leaving de country. None of de natives or half-breeds will interfere wid him very much—unless you make it wort deir while. If you come upon him suddenly, you might shoot him. But den he might shoot you.

"Den dere's dis—infernal magic," said Perea. "Of course, I don't believe in it—superstition—but still it's not nice to tink dat wherever you are, dere is a black man, who spends a moonlight night now and den a-dancing about a fire to send you bad dreams. . . . Had any bad dreams?"

"Rather," said Pollock. "I keep on seeing the beggar's head upside down grinning at me and showing all his teeth as he did in the hut, and coming close up to me, and then going ever so far off, and coming back. It's nothing to be afraid of, but somehow it simply paralyzes me with terror in my sleep. Queer things—dreams. I know it's a dream all the time, and I can't wake up from it."

"It's probably only fancy," said Perea. "Den my niggers say Porroh men can send snakes. Seen any snakes lately?"

"Only one. I killed him this morning, on the floor near my hammock. Almost trod on him as I got up."

"*Ah!*" said Perea, and then, reassuringly, "Of course it is a—coincidence. Still I would keep my eyes open. Den dere's pains in de bones."

"I thought they were due to miasma," said Pollock.

"Probably dey are. When did dey begin?"

Then Pollock remembered that he first noticed them the night after the fight in the hut. "It's my opinion he don't want to kill you," said Perea—"at least not yet. I've heard deir idea is to scare and worry a man wid deir spells, and narrow misses, and rheumatic pains, and bad dreams, and all dat, until he's sick of life. Of course, it's all talk, you know. You mustn't worry about it. . . . But I wonder what he'll be up to next."

"*I* shall have to be up to something first," said Pollock, staring gloomily at the greasy cards that Perea was putting on the table. "It don't suit my dignity to be followed about, and shot at, and blighted in this way. I wonder if Porroh hokey-pokey upsets your luck at cards."

He looked at Perea suspiciously.

"Very likely it does," said Perea warmly, shuffling. "Dey are wonderful people."

That afternoon Pollock killed two snakes in his hammock, and there was also an extraordinary increase in the number of red ants that swarmed over the place; and these annoyances put him in a fit temper to talk over business with a certain Mendi rough he had interviewed before. The Mendi rough showed Pollock a little iron dagger, and demonstrated where one struck in the neck, in a way that made Pollock shiver, and in return for certain considerations Pollock promised him a double-barrelled gun with an ornamental lock.

In the evening, as Pollock and Perea were playing cards, the Mendi rough came in through the doorway, carrying something in a blood-soaked piece of native cloth.

"Not here!" said Pollock very hurriedly. "Not here!"

But he was not quick enough to prevent the man, who was anxious to get to Pollock's side of the bargain, from opening the cloth and throwing the head of the Porroh man upon the table. It bounded from there on to the floor, leaving a red trail on the cards, and rolled into a corner, where it came to rest upside down, but glaring at Pollock.

Perea jumped up as the thing fell among the cards, and began in his excitement to gabble in Portuguese. The Mendi was bowing, with the red cloth in his hand. "De gun!" he cried. Pollock stared back at the head in the corner. It bore exactly the expression it had in his dreams. Something seemed to snap in his own brain as he looked at it.

Then Perea found his English again.

"You got him killed?" he said. "You did not kill him yourself?"

"Why should I?" said Pollock.

"But he will not be able to take it off now!"

"Take *what* off?" said Pollock.

"And all dese cards are spoiled!"

"*What* do you mean by taking off?" said Pollock.

"You must send me a new pack from Freetown. You can buy dem dere."

"But—'take it off'?"

"It is only superstition. I forgot. De niggers say dat if de witches—he was a witch— But it is rubbish. . . . You must make de Porroh man take it off, or kill him yourself. . . . It is very silly."

Pollock swore under his breath, still staring hard at the head in the corner.

"I can't stand that glare," he said. Then suddenly he rushed at the thing and kicked it. It rolled some yards or so, and came to rest in the same position as before, upside down, and looking at him.

"He is ugly," said the Anglo-Portuguese. "Very ugly. Dey do it on deir faces with little knives."

Pollock would have kicked the head again, but the Mendi man touched him on the arm. "De gun?" he said, looking nervously at the head.

"Two—if you will take that beastly thing away," said Pollock.

The Mendi shook his head, and intimated that he only wanted one gun now due to him, and for which he would be obliged. Pollock found neither cajolery nor bullying any good with him. Perea had a gun to sell (at a profit of three hundred per cent), and with that the man presently departed. Then Pollock's eyes, against his will, were recalled to the thing on the floor.

"It is funny dat his head keeps upside down," said Perea, with an uneasy laugh. "His brains must be heavy, like de weight in de little images one sees dat keep always upright wid lead in dem. You will take him wiv you when you go presently. You might take him now. De cards are all spoilt. Dere is a man sell dem in Freetown. De room is in a filthy mess as it is. You should have killed him yourself."

Pollock pulled himself together, and went and picked up the head. He would hang it up by the lamp hook in the middle of the ceiling of his room, and dig a grave for it at once. He was under the impression that he hung it up by the hair, but that must have been wrong, for when he returned for it, it was hanging by the neck upside down.

He buried it before sunset on the north side of the shed he occupied, so that he should not have to pass the grave after dark when he was returning from Perea's. He killed two snakes before he went to sleep. In the darkest part of the night he awoke with a start, and heard a pattering sound and something scraping on the floor. He sat up noiselessly and felt under his pillow for his revolver. A mumbling growl followed, and Pollock fired at the sound. There was a yelp, and something dark passed for a moment across the hazy blue of the doorway. "A dog!" said Pollock, lying down again.

In the early dawn he awoke again with a peculiar sense of unrest. The vague pain in his bones had returned. For some time he lay watching the red ants that were swarming over the ceiling, and then, as the light grew brighter, he looked over the edge of his hammock and saw something dark on the floor. He gave such a violent start that the hammock overset and flung him out.

He found himself lying, perhaps, a yard away from the head of the Porroh man. It had been disinterred by the dog, and the nose was grievously battered. Ants and flies swarmed over it. By an odd coincidence, it was still upside down, and with the same diabolical expression in the inverted eyes.

Pollock sat paralyzed, and stared at the horror for some time. Then he got up and walked round it—giving it a wide berth—and out of the shed. The clear light of the sunrise, the living stir of vegetation before the breath of the dying land breeze, and the empty grave with the marks of the dog's paws, lightened the weight upon his mind a little.

He told Perea of the business as though it was a jest—a jest to be told with white lips. "You should not have frightened de dog," said Perea, with poorly simulated hilarity.

The next two days, until the steamer came, were spent by Pollock in making a more effectual disposition of his possession. Overcoming his aversion to handling the thing, he went down to the river mouth and threw it into the seawater, but by some miracle it escaped the crocodiles, and was cast up by the tide on the mud a little way up the river, to be found by an intelligent Arab half-breed, and offered for sale to Pollock, and Perea as a curiosity, just on the edge of night. The native hung about in the brief twilight, making lower and lower offers, and at last, getting scared in some way by the evident dread these wise white men had for the thing, went off, and passing Pollock's shed, threw his burden in there for Pollock to discover in the morning.

At this Pollock got into a kind of frenzy. He would burn the thing. He went out straightway into the dawn, and had constructed a big pyre of brushwood before the heat of the day. He was interrupted by the hooter of the little paddle streamer from Monrovia to Bathurst, which was coming through the gap in the bar. "Thank Heaven!" said Pollock, with infinite piety, when the meaning of the sound dawned upon him. With trembling hands he lit his pile of wood hastily, threw the head upon it, and went away to pack his portmanteau and make his adieux to Perea.

That afternoon, with a sense of infinite relief, Pollock watched the flat swampy foreshore of Sulyma grow small in the distance. The gap in the long line of white surge became narrower and narrower. It seemed to be closing in and cutting him off from his trouble. The feeling of dread and worry began to slip from him bit by bit. At Sulyma belief in Porroh malignity and Porroh magic had been in the air, his sense of Porroh had been vast, pervading, threatening, dreadful. Now manifestly the domain of Porroh was only a little place, a little black band between the sea and the blue cloudy Mendi uplands.

"Good-bye, Porroh!" said Pollock. "Good-bye—certainly not *au revoir*."

The captain of the steamer came and leaned over the rail beside him, and wished him good-evening, and spat at the froth of the wake in token of friendly ease.

"I picked up a rummy curio on the beach this go," said the captain. "It's a thing I never saw done this side of Indy before."

"What might that be?" said Pollock.

"Pickled 'ed," said the captain.

"*What!*" said Pollock.

"'Ed—smoked. 'Ed of one of these Porroh chaps, all ornamented with knife-cuts. Why! What's up? Nothing? I shouldn't have took you for a nervous chap. Green in the face. By gosh! you're a bad sailor. All right, eh? Lord, how funny you went! . . . Well, this 'ed I was telling you of is a bit rum in a way. I've got it, along with some snakes, in a jar of spirit in my cabin what I keeps for such curios, and I'm hanged if it don't float upsy down. Hullo!"

Pollock had given an incoherent cry, and had his hands in his hair. He ran towards the paddle-boxes with a half-formed idea of jumping into the sea, and then he realized his position and turned back towards the captain.

"Here!" said the captain. "Jack Philips, just keep him off me! Stand off! No nearer, mister! What's the matter with you? Are you mad?"

Pollock put his hand to his head. It was no good explaining. "I believe I am pretty nearly mad at times," he said. "It's a pain I have here. Comes suddenly. You'll excuse me, I hope."

He was white and in a perspiration. He saw suddenly very clearly all the danger he ran of having his sanity doubted. He forced himself to restore the captain's confidence, by answering his sympathetic inquiries, noting his suggestions, even trying a spoonful of neat brandy in his cheek, and, that matter settled, asking a number of questions about the captain's private trade in curiosities. The captain described the head in detail. All the while Pollock was struggling to keep under a preposterous persuasion that the ship was as transparent as glass, and that he could distinctly see the inverted face looking at him from the cabin beneath his feet.

Pollock had a worse time almost on the steamer than he had at Sulyma. All day he had to control himself in spite of his intense perception of the imminent presence of that horrible head that was overshadowing his mind. At night his old nightmare returned, until, with a violent effort, he would force himself awake, rigid with the horror of it, and with the ghost of a hoarse scream in his throat.

He left the actual head behind at Bathurst, where he changed ship for Teneriffe, but not his dreams nor the dull ache in his bones. At Teneriffe Pollock transferred to a Cape liner, but the head followed him. He gambled, he tried chess, he even read books, but he knew the danger of drink. Yet whenever a round black shadow, a round black object came into his range, there he looked for the head, and—saw it. He knew clearly enough that his imagination was growing traitor to him, and yet at times it seemed the ship he sailed in, his fellow passengers, the sailors, the wide sea, were all part of a filmy phantasmagoria that hung, scarcely veiling it, between him and a horrible real world. Then the Porroh man, thrusting his diabolical face through that curtain, was the one real and undeniable thing. At that he would get up and touch things, taste something, gnaw something, burn his hand with a match, or run a needle into himself.

So, struggling grimly and silently with his excited imagination, Pollock reached England. He landed at Southampton, and went on straight from Waterloo to his banker's in Cornhill in a cab. There he transacted some business with the manager in a private room, and all the while the head hung like an ornament under the black marble mantel and dripped upon the fender. He could hear the drops fall, and see the red on the fender.

"A pretty fern," said the manager, following his eyes. "But it makes the fender rusty."

"Very," said Pollock; "a *very* pretty fern. And that reminds me. Can you recommend me a physician for mind troubles? I've got a little—what is it?—hallucination."

The head laughed savagely, wildly. Pollock was surprised the manager did not notice it. But the manager only stared at his face.

With the address of a doctor, Pollock presently emerged in Cornhill. There was no cab in sight, and so he went on down to the western end of the street, and essayed the crossing opposite the Mansion House. The crossing is hardly easy even for the expert Londoner; cabs, vans, carriages, mailcarts, omnibuses go by in one incessant stream; to anyone fresh from the malarious solitudes of Sierra Leone it is a boiling, maddening confusion. But when an inverted head suddenly comes bouncing, like an India-rubber ball, between your legs, leaving distinct smears of blood every time it touches the ground, you can scarcely hope to avoid an accident. Pollock lifted his feet convulsively to avoid it, and then kicked at the thing furiously. Then something hit him violently in the back, and a hot pain ran up his arm.

He had been hit by the pole of an omnibus, and three of the fingers of his left hand smashed by the hoof of one of the horses—the very fingers, as it happened, that he shot from the Porroh man. They pulled him out from between the horses' legs, and found the address of the physician in his crushed hand.

For a couple of days Pollock's sensations were full of the sweet, pungent smell of chloroform, and painful operations that caused him no pain, of lying still and being given food and drink. Then he had a slight fever, and was very thirsty, and his old nightmare came back. It was only when it returned that he noticed it had left him for a day.

"If my skull had been smashed instead of my fingers, it might have gone altogether," said Pollock, staring thoughtfully at the dark cushion that had taken on for the time the shape of the head.

Pollock at the first opportunity told the physician of his mind trouble. He knew clearly that he must go mad unless something should intervene to save him. He explained that he had witnessed a decapitation in Dahomey, and was haunted by one of the heads. Naturally, he did not care to state the actual facts. The physician looked grave.

Presently he spoke hesitatingly. "As a child, did you get very much religious training?"

"Very little," said Pollock.

A shade passed over the physician's face. "I don't know if you have heard of the miraculous cures—it may be, of course, they are not miraculous—at Lourdes."

"Faith healing will hardly suit me, I am afraid," said Pollock, with his eye on the dark cushion.

The head distorted its scarred features in an abominable grimace. The physician went upon a new track. "It's all imagination," he said, speaking with sudden briskness. "A fair case for faith healing, anyhow. Your nervous system has run down, you're in that twilight state of health when the bogles come easiest. The strong impression was too much for you. I must make you up a little mixture that will strengthen your nervous system—especially your brain. And you must take exercise."

"I'm no good for faith healing," said Pollock.

"And therefore we must restore tone. Go in search of stimulating air—Scotland, Norway, the Alps—"

"Jericho, if you like," said Pollock—"where Naaman went."

However, so soon as his fingers would let him, Pollock made a gallant attempt to follow the doctor's suggestion. It was now November. He tried football, but to Pollock the game consisted in kicking a furious inverted head about a field. He was no good at the game. He kicked blindly, with a kind of horror, and when they put him back into goal, and the ball came swooping down upon him, he suddenly yelled and got out of the way. The discreditable stories that had driven him from England to wander in the tropics shut him off from any but men's society, and now his increasingly strange behavior made even his man friends avoid him. The thing was no longer a thing of the eye merely; it gibbered at him, spoke to him. A horrible fear came upon him that presently, when he took hold of the apparition, it would no longer become some mere article of furniture, but would *feel* like a real dissevered head. Alone, he would curse at the thing, defy it, entreat it; once or twice, in spite of his grim self control, he addressed it in the presence of others. He felt the growing suspicion in the eyes of the people that watched him—his landlady, the servant, his man.

One day early in December his cousin Arnold—his next of kin—came to see him and draw him out, and watch his sunken yellow face with narrow eager eyes. And it seemed to Pollock that the hat his cousin carried in his hand was no hat at all, but a Gorgon head that glared at him upside down, and fought with its eyes against his reason. However, he was still resolute to see the matter out. He got a bicycle, and riding over the frosty road from Wandsworth to Kingston, found the thing rolling along at his side, and leaving a dark trail behind it. He set his teeth and rode faster. Then suddenly, as he came down the hill towards Richmond Park, the apparition rolled in front of him and under his wheel, so quickly that he had no time for thought, and, turning quickly to avoid it, was flung violently against a heap of stones and broke his left wrist.

The end came on Christmas morning. All night he had been in a fever, the bandages encircling his wrist like a band of fire, his dreams more vivid and terrible than ever. In the cold, colorless, uncertain light that came before the sunrise, he sat up in his bed, and saw the head upon the bracket in the place of the bronze jar that had stood there overnight.

"I know that is a bronze jar," he said, with a chill doubt at his heart. Presently the doubt was irresistible. He got out of bed slowly, shivering, and advanced to the jar with his hand raised. Surely he would see now his imagination had deceived him, recognize the distinctive sheen of bronze. At last, after an age of hesitation, his fingers came down on the patterned cheek of the head. He withdrew them spasmodically. The last stage was reached. His sense of touch had betrayed him.

Trembling, stumbling against the bed, kicking against his shoes with his bare feet, a dark confusion eddying round him, he groped his way to the dressing table, took his razor from the drawer, and sat down on the bed with this in his hand. In the looking glass he saw his own face, colorless, haggard, full of the ultimate bitterness of despair.

He beheld in swift succession the incidents in the brief tale of his experience. His wretched home, his still more wretched schooldays, the years of vicious life he had led since then, one act of selfish dishonor leading to another; it was all clear and pitiless now, all its squalid folly, in the cold light of the dawn. He came to the hut, to the fight with the Porroh man, to the retreat down the river to Sulyma, to the Mendi assassin and his red parcel, to his frantic endeavors to destroy the head, to the growth of his hallucination. It was a hallucination! He *knew* it was. A hallucination merely. For a moment he snatched at hope. He looked away from the glass, and on the bracket, the inverted head grinned and grimaced at him. . . . With the stiff fingers of his bandaged hand he felt at his neck for the throb of his arteries. The morning was very cold, the steel blade felt like ice.

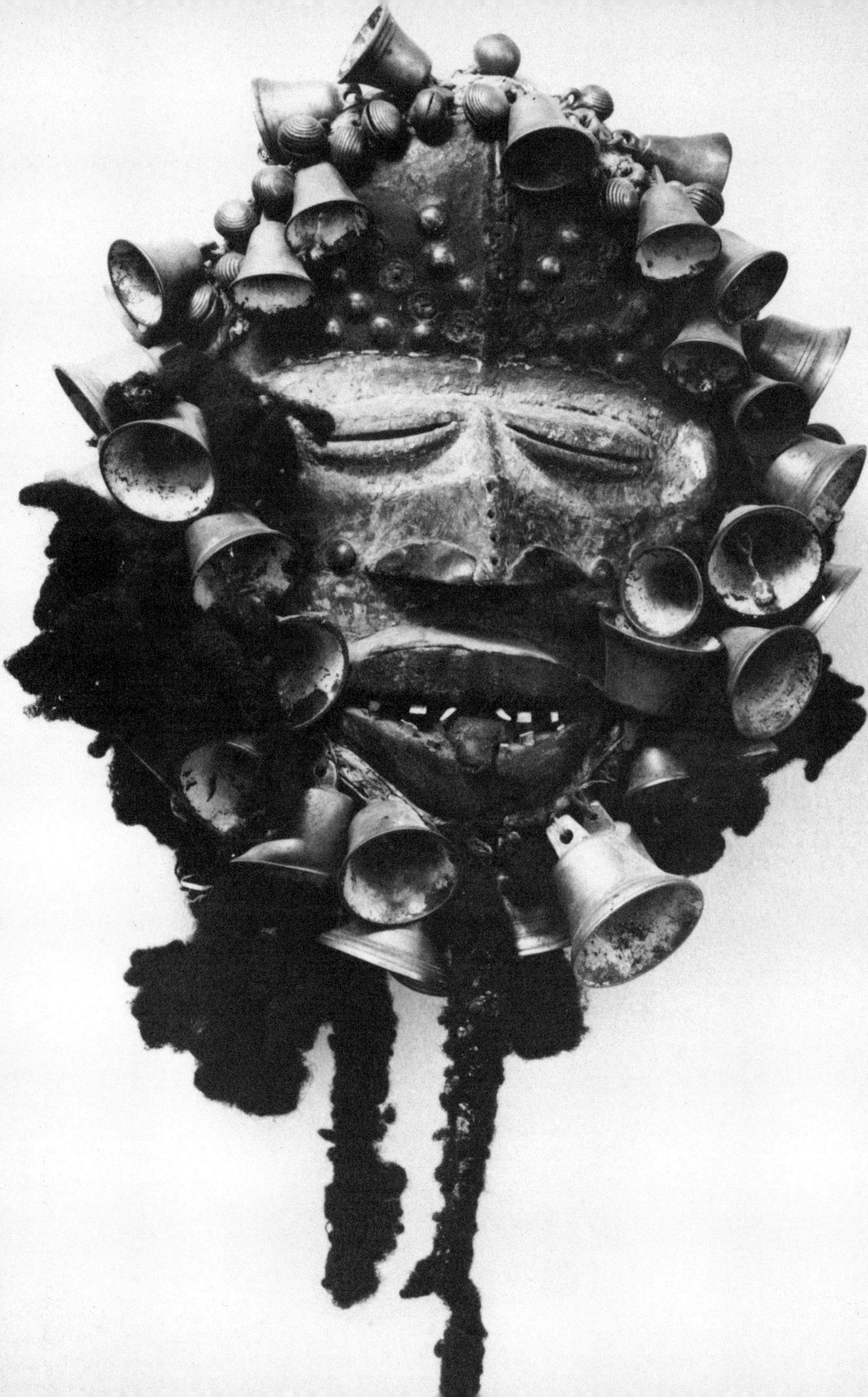

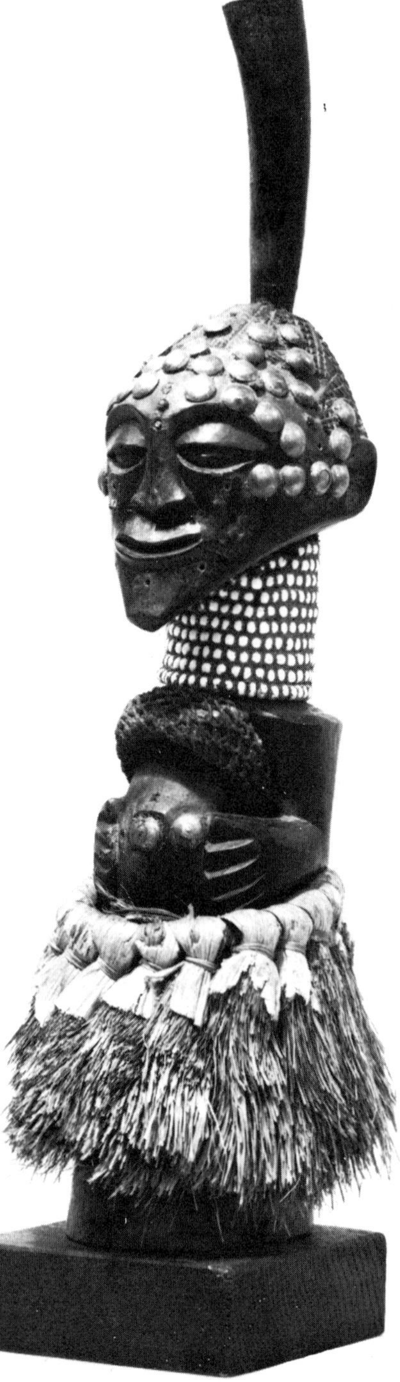

A Way of Thinking
Theodore Sturgeon

I'll have to start with an anecdote or two that you may have heard from me before, but they'll bear repeating, since it's Kelley we're talking about.

I shipped out with Kelley when I was a kid. Tankships, mostly coastwise: load somewhere in the oil country—New Orleans, Aransas Pass, Port Arthur, or some such—and unload at ports north of Hatteras. Eight days out, eighteen hours in, give or take a day or six hours. Kelley was ordinary seaman on my watch, which was a laugh; he knew more about the sea than anyone aft of the galley. But he never ribbed me, stumbling around the place with my blue A.B. ticket. He had a sense of humor in his peculiar quiet way, but he never gratified it by proofs of the obvious—that he was twice the seaman I could ever be.

There were a lot of unusual things about Kelley, the way he looked, the way he moved; but most unusual was the way he thought. He was like one of those extra-terrestrials you read about, who can think as well as a human being but not *like* a human being.

Just for example, there was that night in Port Arthur. I was sitting in a honkytonk up over a bar with a red-headed girl called Red, trying to mind my own business while watching a chick known as Boots, who sat alone over by the jukebox. This girl Boots was watching the door and grinding her teeth, and I knew why, and I was worried. See, Kelley had been seeing her pretty regularly, but this trip he'd made the break and word was around that he was romancing a girl in Pete's place—a very unpopular kind of rumor for Boots to be chewing on. I also knew that Kelley would be along any minute because he'd promised to meet me here.

And in he came, running up that long straight flight of steps easy as a cat, and when he got in the door everybody just hushed, except the jukebox, and it sounded scared.

Now, just above Boots' shoulder on a little shelf was an electric fan. It had sixteen-inch blades and no guard. The very second Kelley's face showed in the doorway Boots rose up like a snake out of a basket, reached behind her, snatched that fan off the shelf and threw it.

It might as well have been done with a slow-motion camera as far as Kelley was concerned. He didn't move his feet at all. He bent sideways, just a little, from the waist, and turned his wide shoulders. Very clearly I heard three of those whining blade-tips touch a button on his shirt *bip-bip-bip!* and then the fan hit the doorpost.

Even the jukebox shut up then. It was *so* quiet. Kelley didn't say anything and neither did anyone else.

Now, if you believe in do-as-you-get-done-to, and someone heaves an infernal machine at you, you'll pick it right up and heave it back. But Kelley doesn't think like you. He didn't look at the fan. He just watched Boots, and she was white and crazed-looking, waiting for whatever he might have in mind.

He went across the room to her, fast but not really hurrying, and he picked her out from behind that table, and he threw her.

He threw her at the fan.

She hit the floor and slid, sweeping up the fan where it lay, hitting the doorjamb with her head, spinning out into the stairway. Kelley walked after her, stepped over her, went on downstairs and back to the ship.

And there was the time we shipped a new main spur gear for the starboard winch. The deck engineer used up the whole morning watch trying to get the old gearwheel off its shaft. He heated the hub. He pounded it. He put in wedges. He hooked on with an handybilly—that's a four-sheave block-and-tackle to you—and all he did with that was break a U-bolt.

Then Kelley came on deck, rubbing sleep out of his eyes, and took one brief look. He walked over to the winch, snatched up a crescent wrench, and relieved the four bolts that held the housing tight around the shaft. He then picked up a twelve-pound maul, hefted it, and swung it just once. The maul hit the end of the shaft and the shaft shot out of the other side of the machine like a torpedo out of its tube. The gearwheel fell down on the deck. Kelley went forward to take the helm and thought no more about it, while the deck crew stared after him, wall-eyed. You see what I mean? Problem: Get a wheel off a shaft. But in Kelley's book it's: Get the shaft out of the wheel.

I kibitzed him at poker one time and saw him discard two pair and draw a winning straight flush. Why that discard? Because he'd just realized the deck was stacked. Why the flush? God knows. All Kelley did was pick up the pot—a big one—grin at the sharper, and leave.

I have plenty more yarns like that, but you get the idea. The guy had a special way of thinking, that's all, and it never failed him.

I lost track of Kelley. I came to regret that now and then; he made a huge impression on me, and sometimes I used to think about him when I had a tough problem to solve. What would Kelley do? And sometimes it helped, and sometimes it didn't; and when it didn't, I guess it was because I'm not Kelley.

I came ashore and got married and did all sorts of other things, and the years went by, and a war came and went, and one warm spring evening I went into a place I know on West 48th St. because I felt like drinking *tequila* and I can always get it there. And who should be sitting in a booth finishing up a big Mexican dinner but—no, not Kelley.

It was Milton. He looks like a college sophomore with money. His suits are always cut just so, but quiet; and when he's relaxed he looks as if he's just been tagged for a fraternity and it matters to him, and when he's worried you want to ask him has he been cutting classes again. It happens he's a damn good doctor.

He was worried, but he gave me a good hello and waved me into the booth while he finished up. We had small talk and I tried to buy him a drink. He looked real wistful and then shook his head. "Patient in ten minutes," he said, looking at his watch.

"Then it's nearby. Come back afterward."

"Better yet," he said, getting up, "come with me. This might interest you, come to think of it."

He got his hat and paid Rudy, and I said, *"Luego,"* and Rudy grinned and slapped the *tequila* bottle. Nice place, Rudy's.

"What about the patient?" I asked as we turned up the avenue. I thought for a while he hadn't heard me, but at last he said, "Four busted ribs and a compound femoral. Minor internal hemorrhage which might or might not be a ruptured spleen. Necrosis of the oral frenum—or was while there was any frenum left."

"What's a frenum?"

"That little strip of tissue under your tongue."

"Ongk," I said, trying to reach it with the top of my tongue. "What a healthy fellow."

"Pulmonary adhesions," Milton ruminated. "Not serious, certainly not tubercular. But they hurt and they bleed and I don't like 'em. And acne rosacea."

"That's the nose like a stop light, isn't it?"

"It isn't as funny as that to the guy that has it."

I was quelled. "What was it—a goon-squad?"

He shook his head.

"A truck?"

"No."

"He fell off something."

Milton stopped and turned and looked me straight in the eye. "No," he said. "Nothing like anything. Nothing," he said, walking again, "at all."

I said nothing to that because there was nothing to say.

"He just went to bed," said Milton thoughtfully, "because he felt off his oats. And one by one these things happened to him."

"In *bed*?"

"Well," said Milton, in a to-be-absolutely-accurate tone, "when the ribs broke he was on his way back from the bathroom."

"You're kidding."

"No I'm not."

"He's lying."

Milton said, "I believe him."

I know Milton. There's no doubt that he believed the man. I said, "I keep reading things about psychosomatic disorders. But a broken—what did you say it was?"

"Femur. Thigh, that is. Compound. Oh, it's rare, all right. But it can happen, has happened. These muscles are pretty powerful, you know. They deliver two-fifty, three hundred pound thrusts every time you walk up stairs. In certain spastic hysteriae, they'll break bones easily enough."

"What about all those other things?"

"Functional disorders, every one of 'em. No germ disease."

"Now this boy," I said, "*really* has something on his mind."

"Yes, he has."

But I didn't ask what. I could hear the discussion closing as if it had a spring latch on it.

We went into a door tucked between store fronts and climbed three flights. Milton put out his hand to a bell-push and then dropped it without ringing. There was a paper tacked to the door.

DOC I WENT FOR SHOTS COME ON IN.

It was unsigned. Milton turned the knob and we went in.

The first thing that hit me was the smell. Not too strong, but not the kind of thing you ever forget if you ever had to dig a slit trench through last week's burial pit. "That's the necrosis," muttered Milton. "Damn it." He gestured. "Hang your hat over there. Sit down. I'll be out soon." He went into an inner room, saying, "Hi, Hal," at the doorway. From inside came an answering rumble, and something twisted in my throat to hear it, for no voice which is that tired should sound that cheerful.

I sat watching the wallpaper and laboriously un-listening those clinical grunts and the gay-weary responses in the other room. The wallpaper was awful. I remember a nightclub act where Reginald Gardiner used to give sound-effect renditions of wallpaper designs. This one, I decided, would run "Body to *weep* . . yawp, yawp; body to *weep* . . yawp, yawp," very faintly, with the final syllable a straining retch. I had just reached a particularly clumsy join where the paper utterly demolished its own rhythm and went "Yawp yawp body to *weep*" when the outer door opened and I leaped to my feet with the rush of utter guilt one feels when caught in an unlikely place with no curt and lucid explanation.

He was two long strides into the room, tall and soft-footed, his face and long green eyes quite at rest, when he saw me. He stopped as if on leaf springs and shock absorbers, not suddenly, completely controlled, and asked, "Who are you?"

"I'll be damned," I answered. "Kelley!"

He peered at me with precisely the expression I had seen so many times when he watched the little square windows on the one-arm bandits we used to play together. I could almost hear the tumblers, see the drums stop; not lemon . . . cherry . . . cherry . . . and *click!* this time but tankship . . . Texas . . . him! . . . and *click!* "I be go*dd*am," he drawled, to indicate that he was even more surprised than I was. He transferred the small package he carried from his right hand to his left and shook hands. His hand went once and a half times around mine with enough left over to tie a half-hitch. "Where in time you been keepin' yourse'f? How'd you smoke me out?"

"I never," I said. (Saying it, I was aware that I always fell into the idiom of people who impressed me, to the exact degree of that impression. So I always found myself talking more like Kelley than Kelley's shaving mirror.) I was grinning so wide my face hurt. "I'm glad to see you." I shook hands with him again, foolishly. "I came with the doctor."

"You a doctor now?" he said, his tone prepared for wonders.

"I'm a writer," I said deprecatingly.

"Yeah, I heard," he reminded himself. His eyes narrowed; as of old, it had the effect of sharp-focusing a searchlight beam. "I heard!" he repeated, with deeper interest. "Stories. Gremlins and flyin' saucers an' all like that." I nodded. He said, without insult, "Hell of a way to make a living."

"What about you?"

"Ships. Some drydock. Tank cleaning. Compass 'djustin'. For a while had a job holdin' a insurance inspector's head. You know."

I glanced at the big hands that could weld or steer or compute certainly with the excellence I used to know, and marvelled that he found himself so unremarkable. I pulled myself back to here and now and nodded toward the inner room. "I'm holding you up."

"No you ain't. Milton, he knows what he's doin'. He wants me, he'll holler."

"Who's sick?"

His face darkened like the sea in scud weather, abruptly and deep down. "My brother." He looked at me searchingly. "He's . . ." Then he seemed to check himself. "He's sick," he said unnecessarily, and added quickly, "He's going to be all right, though."

"Sure," I said quickly.

I had the feeling that we were both lying and that neither of us knew why.

Milton came out, laughing a laugh that cut off as soon as he was out of range of the sick man. Kelley turned to him slowly, as if slowness were the only alternative to leaping on the doctor, pounding the news out of him. "Hello, Kelley. Heard you come in."

"How is he, Doc?"

Milton looked up quickly, his bright round eyes clashing with Kelley's slitted fierce ones. "You got to take it easy, Kelley. What'll happen to him if you crack up?"

"Nobody's cracking up. What do you want me to do?"

Milton saw the package on the table. He picked it up and opened it. There was a leather case and two phials. "Ever use one of these before?"

"He was a pre-med before he went to sea," I said suddenly.

Milton stared at me. "You two know each other?"

I looked at Kelley. "Sometimes I think I invented him."

Kelley snorted and thumped my shoulder. Happily I had one hand on a built-in china shelf. His big hand continued the motion and took the hypodermic case from the doctor. "Sterilize the shaft and needle," he said sleepily, as if reading. "Assemble without touching needle with fingers. To fill, puncture diaphragm and withdraw plunger. Squirt upward to remove air an' prevent embolism. Locate major vein in—"

Milton laughed. "Okay, okay. But forget the vein. Any place will do—it's subcutaneous, that's all. I've written the exact amounts to be used for exactly the symptoms you can expect. Don't jump the gun, Kelley. And remember how you salt your stew. Just because a little is good, it doesn't figure that a lot has to be better."

Kelley was wearing that sleepy inattention which, I remembered, meant only that he was taking in every single word like a tape recorder. He tossed the leather case gently, caught it. "Now?" he said.

"Not now," the doctor said positively. "Only when you have to."

Kelley seemed frustrated. I suddenly understood that he wanted to do something, build something, fight something. Anything but sit and wait for therapy to bring results. I said, "Kelley, any brother of yours is a—well, you know. I'd like to say hello, if it's all—"

Immediately and together Kelley and the doctor said loudly, "Sure, when he's on his feet," and "Better not just now, I've just given him a sedat—" And together they stopped awkwardly.

"Let's go get that drink," I said before they could flounder any more.

"Now you're talking. You too, Kelley. It'll do you good."

"Not me," said Kelley. "Hal—"

"I knocked him out," said the doctor bluntly. "You'll cluck around scratching for worms and looking for hawks till you wake him up, and he needs his sleep. Come on."

Painfully I had to add to my many mental images of Kelley the very first one in which he was indecisive. I hated it.

"Well," said Kelley, "let me go see."

He disappeared. I looked at Milton's face, and turned quickly away. I was sure he wouldn't want me to see that expression of sick pity and bafflement.

Kelley came out, moving silently as always. "Yeah, asleep," he said. "For how long?"

"I'd say four hours at least."

"Well all right." From the old-fashioned clothes tree he took a battered black engineer's cap with a shiny, crazed patent leather visor. I laughed. Both men turned to me, with annoyance, I thought.

On the landing outside I explained. "The hat," I said. "Remember? Tampico?"

"Oh," he grunted. He thwacked it against his forearm.

"He left it on the bar of this ginmill," I told Milton. "We got back to the gangplank and he missed it. Nothing would do but he has to go back for it, so I went with him."

"You was wearin' a *tequila* label on your face," Kelley said. "Kept tryin' to tell the taxi man you was a bottle."

"He didn't speak English."

Kelley flashed something like his old grin. "He got the idea."

"Anyway," I told Milton, "the place was closed when we got there. We tried the front door and the side doors and they were locked like

Alcatraz. We made so much racket I guess if anyone was inside they were afraid to open up. We could see Kelley's hat in there on the bar. Nobody's *about* to steal that hat."

"It's a good hat," he said in an injured tone.

"Kelley goes into action," I said. "Kelley don't think like other people, you know, Milt. He squints through the window at the other wall, goes around the building, sets one foot against the corner stud, gets his fingers under the edge of that corrugated iron siding they use. 'I'll pry this out a bit,' he says. 'You slide in and get my hat.' "

"Corrugated was only nailed on one-by-twos," said Kelley.

"He gives one almighty pull," I chuckled, "and the whole damn side falls out of the building, I mean the second floor too. You never heard such a clap-o'-thunder in your life."

"I got my hat," said Kelley. He uttered two syllables of a laugh. "Whole second floor was a cathouse, an' the one single stairway come out with the wall."

"Taxi driver just took off. But he left his taxi. Kelley drove back. I couldn't. I was laughing."

"You was drunk."

"Well, *some*," I said.

We walked together quietly, happily. Out of Kelley's sight, Milton thumped me gently on the ribs. It was eloquent and it pleased me. It said that it was a long time since Kelley had laughed. It was a long time since he had thought about anything but Hal.

I guess we felt it equally when, with no trace of humor . . . more as if he had let my episode just blow itself out until he could be heard . . . Kelley said, "Doc, what's with the hand?"

"It'll be all right," Milton said.

"You put splints."

Milton sighed. "All right, all right. Three fractures. Two on the middle finger and one on the ring."

Kelley said, "I saw they were swollen."

I looked at Kelley's face and I looked at Milton's, and I didn't like either, and I wished to God I were somewhere else, in a uranium mine maybe, or making out my income tax. I said, "Here we are. Ever been to Rudy's, Kelley?"

He looked up at the little yellow-and-red marquee. "No."

"Come on," I said. *"Tequila."*

We went in and got a booth. Kelley ordered beer. I got mad then and started to call him some things I'd picked up on waterfronts from here to Tierra del Fuego. Milton stared wall-eyed at me and Kelley stared at his hands. After a while Milton began to jot some of it down on a prescription pad he took from his pocket. I was pretty proud.

Kelley gradually got the idea. If I wanted to pick up the tab and he wouldn't let me, his habits were those of *uno puñeto sin cojones* (which a Spanish dictionary will reliably misinform you means "a weakling without eggs"), and his affections for his forebears were powerful but irreverent. I won, and soon he was lapping up a huge combination plate of beef *tostadas,* chicken *enchiladas,* and pork *tacos.* He endeared himself to Rudy by demanding salt and lemon with his *tequila* and despatching same with flawless ritual: hold the lemon between left thumb and forefinger, lick the back of the left hand, sprinkle salt on the wet spot, lift the *tequila* with the right, lick the salt, drink the *tequila,* bite the lemon. Soon he was imitating the German second mate we shipped out of Puerto Barrios one night, who ate fourteen green bananas and lost them and all his teeth over the side, in gummed gutturals which had us roaring.

But after that question about fractured fingers back there in the street, Milton and I weren't fooled any more, and though everyone tried hard and it was a fine try, none of the laughter went deep enough or stayed long enough, and I wanted to cry.

We all had a huge hunk of the nesselrode pie made by Rudy's beautiful blond wife—pie you can blow off your plate by flapping a napkin . . . sweet smoke with calories. And then Kelley demanded to know what time it was and cussed and stood up.

"It's only been two hours," Milton said.

"I just as soon head home all the same," said Kelley. "Thanks."

"Wait," I said. I got a scrap of paper out of my wallet and wrote on it. "Here's my phone. I want to see you some more. I'm working for myself these days; my time's my own. I don't sleep much, so call me anytime you feel like it."

He took the paper. "You're no good," he said. "You never were no good." The way he said it, I felt fine.

"On the corner is a newsstand," I told him. "There's a magazine called *Amazing* with one of my lousy stories in it."

"They print it on a roll?" he demanded. He waved at us, nodded to Rudy, and went out.

I swept up some spilled sugar on the table top and pushed it around until it was a perfect square. After a while I shoved in the sides until it was a lozenge. Milton didn't say anything either. Rudy, as is his way, had sense enough to stay away from us.

"Well, that did him some good," Milton said after a while.

"You know better than that," I said bitterly.

Milton said patiently, "Kelley thinks *we* think it did him some good. And thinking that does him good."

I had to smile at that contortion, and after that it was easier to talk. "The kid's going to live."

Milton waited, as if some other answer might spring from somewhere, but it didn't. He said, "No."

"Fine doctor."

"Don't kid like that!" he snapped. He looked up at me. "Look, if this was one of those—well, say pleurisy cases on the critical list, without the will to live, why I'd know what to do. Usually those depressed cases have such a violent desire to be reassured, down deep, that you can snap 'em right out of it if only you can think of the right things to say. And you usually can. But Hal's not one of those. He wants to live. If he didn't want so much to live he'd've been dead three weeks ago. What's killing him is sheer somatic trauma—one broken bone after another, one failing or inflamed internal organ after another."

"Who's doing it?"

"Damn it, *nobody's* doing it!" He caught me biting my lip. "If either one of us should say Kelley's doing it, the other one will punch him in the mouth. Right?"

"Right."

"Just so that doesn't have to happen," said Milton carefully, "I'll tell you what you're bound to ask me in a minute: why isn't he in a hospital?"

"Okay, why?"

"He was. For weeks. And all the time he was there these things kept on happening to him, only worse. More, and more often. I got him home as soon as it was safe to get him out of traction for that broken thigh. He's much better off with Kelley. Kelley keeps him cheered up, cooks for him, medicates him—the works. It's all Kelley does these days."

"I figured. It must be getting tough."

"It is. I wish I had your ability with invective. You can't lend that man anything, give him anything . . . proud? God!"

"Don't take this personally, but have you had consultations?"

He shrugged. "Six ways from the middle. And nine-tenths of it behind

Kelley's back, which isn't easy. The lies I've told him! Hal's just *got* to have a special kind of Persian melon that someone is receiving in a little store in Yonkers. Out Kelley goes, and in the meantime I have to corral two or three doctors and whip 'em in to see Hal and out again before Kelley gets back. Or Hal has to have a special prescription, and I fix up with the druggist to take a good two hours compounding it. Hal saw Grundage, the osteo man, that way, but poor old Ancelowics the pharmacist got punched in the chops for the delay."

"Milton, you're all right."

He snarled at me, and then went on quietly, "None of it's done any good. I've learned a whole encyclopedia full of wise words and some therapeutic tricks I didn't know existed. But . . . ." He shook his head. "Do you know why Kelley and I wouldn't let you meet Hal?" He wet his lips and cast about for an example. "Remember the pictures of Mussolini's corpse after the mob got through with it?"

I shuddered. "I saw 'em."

"Well, that's what he looks like, only he's alive, which doesn't make it any prettier. Hal doesn't know how bad it is, and neither Kelley nor I would run the risk of having him see it reflected in someone else's face. I wouldn't send a wooden Indian into that room."

I began to pound the table, barely touching it, hitting it harder and harder until Milton caught my wrist. I froze then, unhappily conscious of the eyes of everyone in the place looking at me. Gradually the normal sound of the restaurant resumed. "Sorry."

"It's all right."

"There's got to be some sort of reason!"

His lips twitched in a small acid smile. "That's what you get down to at last, isn't it? There's always a reason for everything, and if we don't know it, we can find it out. But just one single example of real unreason is enough to shake our belief in everything. And then the fear gets bigger than the case at hand and extends to a whole universe of concepts labelled 'unproven.' Shows you how little we believe in anything, basically."

"That's a miserable piece of philosophy!"

"Sure. If you have another arrival point for a case like this, I'll buy it with a bonus. Meantime I'll just go on worrying at this one and feeling more scared than I ought to."

"Let's get drunk."

"A wonderful idea."

Neither of us ordered. We just sat there looking at the lozenge of sugar I'd made on the table top. After a while I said, "Hasn't Kelley any idea of what's wrong?"

"You know Kelley. If he had an idea he'd be working on it. All he's doing is sitting by watching his brother's body stew and swell like yeast in a vat."

"What about Hal?"

He isn't lucid much any more. Not if I can help it."

"But maybe he—"

"Look," said Milton, "I don't want to sound cranky or anything, but I can't hold still for a lot of questions like . . ." He stopped, took out his display handkerchief, looked at it, put it away. "I'm sorry. You don't seem to understand that I didn't take this case yesterday afternoon. I've been sweating it out for nearly three months now. I've already thought of everything you're going to think of. Yes, I questioned Hal, back and forth and sideways. Nothing. N-n-nothing."

That last word trailed off in such a peculiar way that I looked up abruptly. "Tell me," I demanded.

"Tell you what?" Suddenly he looked at his watch. I covered it with my hand. "Come on, Milt."

"I don't know what you're—damn it, leave me alone, will you? If it was anything important, I'd've chased it down long ago."

"Tell me the unimportant something."

"No."

"Tell me why you won't tell me."

"Damn you, I'll do that. It's because you're a crackpot. You're a nice guy and I like you, but you're a crackpot." He laughed suddenly, and it hit me like the flare of a flashbulb. "I didn't know you could look so astonished!" he said. "Now take it easy and listen to me. A guy comes out of a steak house and steps on a rusty nail, and ups and dies of tetanus. But your crackpot vegetarian will swear up and down that the man would still be alive if he hadn't poisoned his system with meat, and uses the death to prove his point. The perennial Dry will call the same casualty a victim of John Barleycorn if he knows the man had a beer with his steak. This one death can be ardently and whole-heartedly blamed on the man's divorce, his religion, his political affiliations or on a hereditary taint from his great-great-grandfather who worked for Oliver Cromwell. You're a nice guy and I like you," he said again, "and I am not going to sit across from you and watch you do the crackpot act."

"I do not know," I said slowly and distinctly, "what the hell you are talking about. And now you *have* to tell me."

"I suppose so," he said sadly. He drew a deep breath. "You believe what you write. No," he said quickly, "I'm not asking you, I'm telling you. You grind out all this fantasy and horror stuff and you believe every word of it. More basically, you'd rather believe in the *outré* and the so-called 'unknowable' than in what I'd call *real* things. You think I'm talking through my hat."

"I do," I said, "but go ahead."

"If I called you up tomorrow and told you with great joy that they'd isolated a virus for Hal's condition and a serum was on the way, you'd be just as happy about it as I would be, but way down deep you'd wonder if that was what was really wrong with him, or if the serum is what really cured him. If on the other hand I admitted to you that I'd found two small punctures on Hal's throat and a wisp of fog slipping out of the room—by God! see what I mean? You have a gleam in your eye already!"

I covered my eyes. "Don't let me stop you now," I said coldly. "Since you are not going to admit Dracula's punctures, what are you going to admit?"

"A year ago Kelley gave his brother a present. An ugly little brute of a Haitian doll. Hal kept it around to make faces at for a while and then gave it to a girl. He had bad trouble with the girl. She hates him—really hates him. As far as anyone knows she still has the doll. Are you happy now?"

"Happy," I said disgustedly. "But Milt—you're not just ignoring this doll thing. Why, that could easily be the whole basis of . . . hey, sit down! Where are you going?"

"I told you I wouldn't sit across from a damn hobbyist. Enter hobbies, exit reason." He recoiled. "Wait—*you* sit down now."

I gathered up a handful of his well-cut lapels. "We'll both sit down," I said gently, "or I'll prove to your heart's desire that I've reached the end of reason."

"Yessir," he said good-naturedly, and sat down. I felt like a damn fool. The twinkle left his eyes and he leaned forward. "Perhaps now you'll listen instead of riding off like that. I suppose you know that in many cases the voodoo doll does work, and you know why?"

"Well, yes. I didn't think you'd admit it." I got no response from his stony gaze, and at last realized that a fantasist's pose of authority on such matters is bound to sit ill with a serious and progressive physician. A lot less positively, I said, "It comes down to a matter of subjective reality, or what some people call faith. If you believe firmly that the mutilation of a doll with which you identify yourself will result in your own mutilation, well, that's what will happen."

"That, and a lot of things even a horror story writer could find out if he researched anywhere else except in his projective imagination. For example, there are Arabs in North Africa today whom you dare not insult in any way really important to them. If they feel injured, they'll threaten to die, and if you call the bluff they'll sit down, cover their heads, and damn well *die*. There are psychosomatic phenomena like the stigmata, or wounds of the cross, which appear from time to time on the hands, feet and breasts of exceptionally devout people. I know you know a lot of this," he added abruptly, apparently reading something in my expression, "but I'm not going to get my knee out of your chest until you'll admit I'm at least capable of taking a thing like this into consideration and tracking it down."

"I never saw you before in my life," I said, and in an important way I meant it.

"Good," he said, with considerable relief. "Now I'll tell you what I did. I jumped at this doll episode almost as wildly as you did. It came late in the questioning because apparently it *really didn't matter* to Hal."

"Oh, well, but the subconscious—"

"Shaddup!" He stuck a surprisingly sharp forefinger into my collarbone. "I'm telling you; you're not telling me. I won't disallow that a deep belief in voodoo might be hidden in Hal's subconscious, but if it is, it's where sodium amytal and word association and light and profound hypnosis and a half-dozen other therapies give not a smidgin of evidence. I'll take that as proof that he carries no such conviction. I guess from the looks of you I'll have to remind you again that I've dug into this in more ways for longer and with more tools than you have—and I doubt that it means any less to me than it does to you."

"You know, I'm just going to shut up," I said plaintively.

"High time," he said, and grinned. "Now, in every case of voodoo damage or death, there has to be that element of devout belief in the powers of the witch or wizard, and through it a complete sense of identification with the doll. In addition, it helps if the victim knows what sort of damage the doll is sustaining—crushing, or pins sticking into it, or what. And you can take my word for it that no such news has reached Hal."

"What about the doll? Just to be absolutely sure, shouldn't we get it back?"

"I thought of that. But there's no way I know of getting it back without making it look valuable to the woman. And if she thinks it's valuable to Hal, we'll *never* see it."

"Hm. Who is she, and what's her royal gripe?"

"She's as nasty a piece of fluff as they come. She got involved with Hal for a little while—nothing serious, certainly not on his part. He was . . . he's a big good-natured kid who thinks the only evil people around are the ones who get killed at the end of the movie. Kelley was at sea at the time and he blew in to find this little vampire taking Hal for everything she could, first by sympathy, then by threats. The old badger game. Hal was just bewildered. Kelley got his word that nothing had occurred between them, and then forced Hal to lower the boom. She called his bluff and it went to court. They forced a physical examination on her and she got laughed out of court. She wasn't the mother of anyone's unborn child. She never will be. She swore to get even with him. She's without brains or education or resources, but that doesn't stop her from being pathological. She sure can hate."

"Oh. You've seen her."

Milton shuddered. "I've seen her. I tried to get all Hal's gifts back from her. I had to say all because I didn't dare itemize. All I wanted, it might surprise you to know, was that damned doll. Just in case, you know . . . although I'm morally convinced that the thing has nothing to do with it. Now do you see what I mean about a single example of unreason?"

" 'Fraid I do." I felt upset and quelled and sat upon and I wasn't fond of the feeling. I've read too many stories where the scientist just hasn't the imagination to solve a haunt. It had been great, feeling superior to a bright guy like Milton.

We walked out of there and for the first time I felt the mood of a night without feeling that an author was ramming it down my throat for story purposes. I looked at the clean-swept, star-reaching cubism of the Radio City area and its living snakes of neon, and I suddenly thought of an Evelyn Smith story the general idea of which was "After they found out the atom bomb was magic, the rest of the magicians who enchanted refrigerators and washing machines and the telephone system came out into the open." I felt a breath of wind and wondered what it was that had breathed. I heard the snoring of the city and for an awesome second felt it would roll over, open its eyes, and . . . *speak*.

On the corner I said to Milton, "Thanks. You've given me a thumping around. I guess I needed it." I looked at him. "By the Lord I'd like to find some place where you've been stupid in this thing."

"I'd be happy if you could," he said seriously.

I whacked him on the shoulder. "See? You take all the fun out of it."

He got a cab and I started to walk. I walked a whole lot that night, just anywhere. I thought about a lot of things. When I got home the phone was ringing. It was Kelley.

I'm not going to give you a blow-by-blow of that talk with Kelley. It was in that small front room of his place—an apartment he'd rented after Hal got sick, and not the one Hal used to have—and we talked the night away. All I'm withholding is Kelley's expression of things you already know: that he was deeply attached to his brother, that he had no hope left for him, that he would find who or what was responsible and deal with it his way. It is a strong man's right to break down if he must, with whom and where he chooses, and such an occasion is only an expression. But when it happens in a quiet sick place, where he must keep the command of hope strongly in the air; when a chest heaves and a throat must be held wide open to sob silently so that the dying one shall not know; these things are not pleasant to describe in detail. Whatever my ultimate feeling for Kelley, his emotions and the expressions of them are for him to keep.

He did, however, know the name of the girl and where she was. He did not hold her responsible. I thought he might have a suspicion, but it turned out to be only a certainty that this was no disease, no subjective internal disorder. If a great hate and a great determination could solve the problem, Kelley would solve it. If research and logic could solve it, Milton would do it. If I could do it, I would.

She was checking hats in a sleazy club out where Brooklyn and Queens, in a remote meeting, agree to be known as Long Island. The contact was easy to make. I gave her my spring coat with the label outward. It's a good label. When she turned away with it I called her back and drunkenly asked her for the bill in the right-hand pocket. She found it and handed it to me. It was a hundred. "Damn taxis never got change," I mumbled and took it before her astonishment turned to sleight-of-hand. I got out my wallet, crowded the crumpled note into it clumsily enough to display the two other C-notes there, shoved it into the front of my jacket so that it missed the pocket and fell to the floor, and walked off. I walked back before she could lift the hinged counter and skin out after it. I picked it up and smiled foolishly at her. "Lose more business cards that way," I said. Then I brought her into focus. "Hey, you know, you're cute."

I suppose "cute" is one of the four-letter words that described her. "What's your name?"

"Charity," she said. "But don't get ideas." She was wearing so much pancake makeup that I couldn't tell what her complexion was. She leaned so far over the counter that I could see lipstick stains on her brassiere.

"I don't have a favorite charity yet," I said. "You work here alla time?"

"I go home once in a while," she said.

"What time?"

"One o'clock."

"Tell you what," I confided, "le's both be in front of this place at a quarter after and see who stands who up, okay?" Without waiting for an answer I stuck the wallet into my back pocket so that my jacket hung on it. All the way into the dining room I could feel her eyes on it like two hot, glistening, broiled mushrooms. I came within an ace of losing it to the head waiter when he collided with me, too.

She was there all right, with a yellowish fur around her neck and heels you could have driven into a pine plank. She was up to the elbows in jangly brass and chrome, and when we got into a cab she threw herself on me with her mouth open. I don't know where I got the reflexes, but I threw my head down and cracked her in the cheekbone with my forehead, and when she squeaked indignantly I said I'd dropped the wallet again and she went about helping me find it quietly as you please. We went to a place and another place and an after-hours place, all her choice. They served her sherry in her whiskey-ponies and doubled all my orders, and tilted the checks something outrageous. Once I tipped a waiter eight dollars and she palmed the five. Once she wormed my leather notebook out of my breast pocket thinking it was the wallet, which by this time was safely tucked away in my knit shorts. She did get one enamel cufflink with a rhinestone in it, and my fountain pen. All in all it was quite a duel. I was loaded to the eyeballs with thiamin hydrochloride and caffeine citrate, but a most respectable amount of alcohol soaked through them, and it was all I could do to play it through. I made it, though, and blocked her at every turn until she had no further choice but to take me home. She was furious and made only the barest attempts to hide it.

We got each other up the dim dawnlit stairs, shushing each other drunkenly, both much soberer than we acted, each promising what we expected not to deliver. She negotiated her lock successfully and waved me inside.

I hadn't expected it to be so neat. Or so cold. "I didn't leave that window open," she said complainingly. She crossed the room and closed it. She pulled her fur around her throat. "This is awful."

It was a long low room with three windows. At one end, covered by a venetian blind, was a kitchenette. A door at one side of it was probably a bathroom.

She went to the venetian blind and raised it. "Have it warmed up in a jiffy," she said.

I looked at the kitchenette. "Hey," I said as she lit the little oven, "coffee. How's about coffee?"

"Oh, all right," she said glumly. "But talk quiet, huh?"

"Sh-h-h-h." I pushed my lips around with a forefinger. I circled the room. Cheap phonograph and records. Small screen TV. A big double studio couch. A bookcase with no books in it, just china dogs. It occurred to me that her unsubtle approach was probably not successful as often as she might wish.

But where was the thing I was looking for?

"Hey, I wanna powder my nose," I announced.

"In there," she said. "Can't you talk quiet?"

I went into the bathroom. It was tiny. There was a foreshortened tub with a circular frame over it from which hung a horrible cheerful shower curtain, with big red roses. I closed the door behind me and carefully opened the medicine chest. Just the usual. I closed it carefully so it wouldn't click. A built-in shelf held towels.

Must be a closet in the main room, I thought. Hatbox, trunk, suitcase, maybe. Where would I put a devil-doll if I were hexing someone?

I wouldn't hide it away, I answered myself. I don't know why, but I'd sort of have it out in the open somewhere . . .

I opened the shower curtain and let it close. Round curtain, square tub. "Yup!"

I pushed the whole round curtain back, and there in the corner, just at eye level, was a trianguler shelf. Grouped on it were four figurines, made apparently from kneaded wax. Three had wisps of hair fastened by candle-droppings. The fourth was hairless, but had slivers of a horny substance pressed into the ends of the arms. Fingernail parings.

I stood for a moment thinking. Then I picked up the hairless doll, turned to the door. I checked myself, flushed the toilet, took a towel, shook it out, dropped it over the edge of the tub. Then I reeled out. "Hey honey, look what I got, ain't it *cute?*"

"Shh!" she said. "Oh for crying out loud. Put that back, will you?"

"Well, what is it?"

"It's none of your business, that's what it is. Come on, put it back."

I wagged my finger at her. "You're not being nice to me," I complained.

She pulled some shreds of patience together with an obvious effort. "It's just some sort of toys I have around. Here."

I snatched it away. "All right, you don't wanna be nice!" I whipped my coat together and began to button it clumsily, still holding the figurine.

She sighed, rolled her eyes, and came to me. "Come on, Dadsy. Have a nice cup of coffee and let's not fight." She reached for the doll and I snatched it away again.

"You got to tell me," I pointed.

"It's pers'nal."

"I wanna be personal," I pointed out.

"Oh all right," she said. "I had a roommate one time, she used to make these things. She said you make one, and s'pose I decide I don't like you, I got something of yours, hair or toenails or something. Say your name is George. What is your name?"

"George," I said.

"All right, I call the doll George. Then I stick pins in it. That's all. Give it to me."

"Who's this one?"

"That's Al."

"Hal?"

"Al. I got one called Hal. He's in there. I hate him the most."

"Yeah, huh. Well, what happens to Al and George and all when you stick pins in 'em?"

"They're s'posed to get sick. Even die."

"Do they?"

"Nah," she said with immediate and complete candor. "I told you, it's just a game, sort of. If it worked believe me old Al would bleed to death. He runs the delicatessen." I handed her the doll, and looked at it pensively. "I wish it did work, sometimes. Sometimes I almost believe in it. I stick 'em and they just *yell.*"

"Introduce me," I demanded.

"What?"

"Introduce me," I said. I pulled her toward the bathroom. She made a small irritated "oh-h," and came along.

"This is Fritz and this is Bruno and—where's the other one?"

"What other one?"

"Maybe he fell behind the—down back of—" She knelt on the edge of the tub and leaned over the wall, to peer behind it. She regained her feet, her face red from effort and anger. "What are you trying to pull? You kidding around or something?"

I spread my arms. "What you mean?"

"Come on," she said between her teeth. She felt my coat, my jacket. "You hid it some place."

"No I didn't. There was only four." I pointed. "Al and Fritz and Bruno and Hal. Which one's Hal?"

"That's Freddie. He gave me twenny bucks and took twenny-three out of my purse, the dirty—. But Hal's gone. He was the best one of all. You *sure* you didn't hide him?" Then she thumped her forehead.

"The window!" she said, and ran into the other room. I was on my four bones peering under the tub when I understood what she meant. I took a last good look around and then followed her. She was standing by the window, shading her eyes and peering out. "What do you know. Imagine somebody would swipe a thing like that!"

A sick sense of loss borne in my solar plexus.

"Aw, forget it. I'll make another one for that Hal. But I'll never make another one that ugly," she said wistfully. "Come on, the coffee's—what's the matter? You sick?

"Yeah," I said, "I'm sick."

"Of all the things to steal," she said from the kitchenette. "Who do you suppose would do such a thing?"

Suddenly I knew who would. I cracked my fist into my palm and laughed.

"What's the matter, you crazy?"

"Yes," I said. "You got a phone?"

"No. Where you going?"

"Out. Goodbye, Charity."

"Hey, now wait, honey. Just when I got coffee for you."

I snatched the door open. She caught my sleeve.

"You can't go away like this! How's about a little something for Charity?"

"You'll get yours when you make the rounds tomorrow, if you don't have a hangover from those sherry highballs," I said cheerfully. "And don't forget the five you swiped from the tip plate. Better watch out for the waiter, by the way. I think he saw you do it."

"You're not drunk!" she gasped.

"You're not a witch," I grinned. I blew her a kiss and ran out.

I shall always remember her like that, round-eyed, a little more astonished than she was resentful, the beloved dollar signs fading from her hot brown eyes, the pathetic, useless little twitch of her hips she summoned up as a last plea.

Ever try to find a phone booth at five A.M.? I half-trotted nine blocks before I found a cab, and I was on the Queens side of the Triboro Bridge before I found a gas station open.

I dialed. The phone said, "Hello?"

"Kelley!" I roared happily. "Why didn't you tell me? You'd 'a saved me sixty bucks worth of the most dismal fun I ever—"

"This is Milton," said the telephone. "Hal just died."

My mouth was still open and I guess it just stayed that way. Anyway it was cold inside when I closed it. "I'll be right over."

"Better not," said Milton. His voice was shaking with incomplete control. "Unless you really want to . . . there's nothing you can do, and I'm going to be . . . busy."

"Where's Kelley?" I whispered.

"I don't know."

"Well," I said. "Call me."

I got back into my taxi and went home. I don't remember the trip.

Sometimes I think I dreamed I saw Kelley that morning.

A lot of alcohol and enough emotion to kill it, mixed with no sleep for thirty hours, makes for blackout. I came up out of it reluctantly, feeling that this was no kind of world to be aware of. Not today.

I lay looking at the bookcase. It was very quiet. I closed my eyes, turned over, burrowed into the pillow, opened my eyes again and saw Kelley sitting in the easy chair, poured out in his relaxed feline fashion, legs too long, arms too long, eyes too long and only partly open.

I didn't ask him how he got in because he was already in, and welcome. I didn't say anything because I didn't want to be the one to tell him about Hal. And besides I wasn't awake yet. I just lay there.

"Milton told me," he said. "It's all right."

I nodded.

Kelley said, "I read your story. I found some more and read them too. You got a lot of imagination."

He hung a cigarette on his lower lip and lit it. "Milton, he's got a lot of knowledge. Now, both of you think real good up to a point. Then too much knowledge presses him off to the no'theast. And too much imagination squeezes you off to the no'thwest."

He smoked a while.

"Me, I think straight through but it takes me a while."

I palmed my eyeballs. "I don't know what you're talking about."

"That's okay," he said quietly. "Look, I'm goin' after what killed Hal."

I closed my eyes and saw a vicious, pretty, empty little face. I said, "I was most of the night with Charity."

"Were you now."

"Kelley," I said, "if it's her you're after, forget it. She's a sleazy little tramp but she's also a little kid who never had a chance. She didn't kill Hal."

"I know she didn't. I don't feel about her one way or the other. I know what killed Hal, though, and I'm goin' after it the only way I know for sure."

"All right then," I said. I let my head dig back into the pillow. "What did kill him?"

"Milton told you about that doll Hal give her."

"He told me. There's nothing in that, Kelley. For a man to be a voodoo victim, he's got to believe that—"

"Yeah, yeah, yeah. Milton told me. For hours he told me."

"Well all right."

"You got imagination," Kelley said sleepily. "Now just imagine along with me a while. Milt tell you how some folks, if you point a gun at 'em and go bang, they drop dead, even if there was only blanks in the gun?"

"He didn't, but I read it somewhere. Same general idea."

"Now imagine all the shootings you ever heard of was like that, with blanks."

"Go ahead."

"You got a lot of evidence, a lot of experts, to prove about this believing business, ever' time anyone gets shot."

"Got it."

"Now imagine somebody shows up with live ammunition in his gun. Do you think those bullets going to give a damn who believes what?"

I didn't say anything.

"For a long time people been makin' dolls and stickin' pins in 'em. Whenever somebody believes it can happen, they get it. Now suppose somebody shows up with the doll all those dolls was copied from. The real one."

I lay still.

"You don't have to know nothin' about it," said Kelley lazily. "You don't have to be anybody special. You don't have to understand how it works. Nobody has to believe nothing. All you do, you just point to where you want it to work."

"Point it how?" I whispered.

He shrugged. "Call the doll by a name. Hate it, maybe."

"For God's sake, Kelley, you're crazy! Why, there can't be anything like that!"

"You eat a steak," Kelley said. "How's your gut know what to take and what to pass? Do *you* know?"

"Some people know."

"You don't. But your gut does. So there's lots of natural laws that are goin' to work whether anyone understands 'em or not. Lots of sailors take a trick at the wheel without knowin' how a steering engine works. Well, that's me. I know where I'm goin' and I know I'll get there. What do I care how does it work, or who believes what?"

"Fine, so what are you going to do?"

"Get what got Hal." His tone was just as lazy but his voice was very deep, and I knew when not to ask any more questions. Instead I said, with a certain amount of annoyance, "Why tell me?"

"Want you to do something for me."

"What?"

"Don't tell no one what I just said for a while. And keep something for me."

"What? And for how long?"

"You'll know."

I'd have risen up and roared at him if he had not chosen just that second to get up and drift out of the bedroom.

"What gets me," he said quietly from the other room, "is I could have figured this out six months ago."

I fell asleep straining to hear him go out. He moves quieter than any big man I ever saw.

It was afternoon when I awoke. The doll was sitting on the mantelpiece glaring at me. Ugliest thing ever happened.

I saw Kelley at Hal's funeral. He and Milt and I had a somber drink afterward. We didn't talk about dolls. Far as I know Kelley shipped out right afterward. You assume that seamen do, when they drop out of sight. Milton was as busy as a doctor, which is very. I left the doll where it was for a week or two, wondering when Kelley was going to get around to his project. He'd probably call for it when he was ready. Meanwhile I respected his request and told no one about it. One day when some people were coming over I shoved it in the top shelf of the closet, and somehow it just got left there.

About a month afterward I began to notice the smell. I couldn't identify it right away; it was too faint; but whatever it was, I didn't like it. I traced it to the closet, and then to the doll. I took it down and sniffed it. My breath exploded out. It was that same smell a lot of people wish they could forget—what Milton called necrotic flesh. I came within an inch of pitching the filthy thing down the incinerator, but a promise is a promise. I put it down on the table, where it slumped repulsively. One of the legs was broken above the knee. I mean, it seemed to have two knee joints. And it was somehow puffy, sick-looking.

I had an old bell-jar somewhere, that once had a clock in it. I found it and a piece of inlaid linoleum, and put the doll under the jar at least so I could live with it.

I worked and saw people—dinner with Milton, once—and the days went by the way they do, and then one night it occurred to me to look at the doll again.

It was in pretty sorry shape. I'd tried to keep it fairly cool, but it seemed to be melting and running all over. For a moment I worried about what Kelley might say, and then I heartily damned Kelley and put the whole mess down in the cellar.

And I guess it was altogether two months after Hal's death that I wondered why I'd assumed Kelley would have to call for the little horror before he did what he had to do. He said he was going to get what got Hal, and he intimated that the doll was that something.

Well, that doll was being got, but good. I brought it up and put in under the light. It was still a figurine, but it was one unholy mess. "Attaboy, Kelley," I gloated. "Go get 'em, kid."

Milton called me up and asked me to meet him at Rudy's. He sounded pretty bad. We had the shortest drink yet.

He was sitting in the back booth chewing on the inside of his cheeks. His lips were gray and he slopped his drink when he lifted it.

"What in time happened to you?" I gasped.

He gave me a ghastly smile. "I'm famous," he said. I heard his glass chatter against his teeth. He said, "I called in so many consultants on Hal Kelley that I'm supposed to be an expert on that—on that . . . condition." He forced his glass back to the table with both hands and held it down. He tried to smile and I wished he wouldn't. He stopped trying and almost whimpered, "I can't nurse one of 'em like that again. I can't."

"You going to tell me what happened?" I asked harshly. That works sometimes.

"Oh, oh yes. Well they brought in a . . . another one. At General. They called me in. Just like Hal. I mean *exactly* like Hal. Only I won't have to nurse this one, no I won't, I won't have to. She died six hours after she arrived."

"*She?*"

"You know what you'd have to do to someone to make them look like that?" he said shrilly. "You'd have to tie off parts so they mortified. You'd have to use a wood rasp, maybe; a club; filth to rub into the wounds. You'd have to break bones in a vise."

"All right, all right, but nobody—"

"And you'd have to do that for about two months, every day, every night." He rubbed his eyes. He drove his knuckles in so hard that I caught at his wrist. "I *know* nobody did it; did I say anyone did it?" he barked. "Nobody did anything to Hal, did they?"

"Drink up."

He didn't. He whispered, "She just said the same thing over and over every time anyone talked to her. They'd say, 'What happened?' or 'Who did this to you?' or 'What's your name?' and she'd say, 'He called me Dolly.' That's all she'd say, just 'He called me Dolly.' "

I got up. " 'Bye, Milt."

He looked stricken. "Don't go, will you, you just got—"

"I got to go," I said. I didn't look back. I had to get out and ask myself some questions. Think.

Who's guilty of murder, I asked myself, the one who pulls the trigger, or the gun?

I thought of a poor damn pretty, empty little face with greedy hot brown eyes, and what Kelley said, "I don't care about her one way or the other."

I thought, when she was twisting and breaking and sticking, how did it look to the doll? Bet she never even wondered about that.

I thought, action: A girl throws a fan at a man. Reaction: The man throws the girl at the fan. Action: A wheel sticks on a shaft. Reaction: Knock the shaft out of the wheel. Situation: We can't get inside. Resolution: Take the outside off it.

It's a way of thinking.

How do you kill a person? Use a doll.

How do you kill a doll?

Who's guilty, the one who pulls the trigger, or the gun?
"*He called me Dolly.*"
"*He called me Dolly.*"
"*He called me Dolly.*"
When I got home the phone was ringing.
"Hi," said Kelley.
I said "It's all gone. The doll's all gone. Kelley," I said, "stay away from me."
"All right," said Kelley.

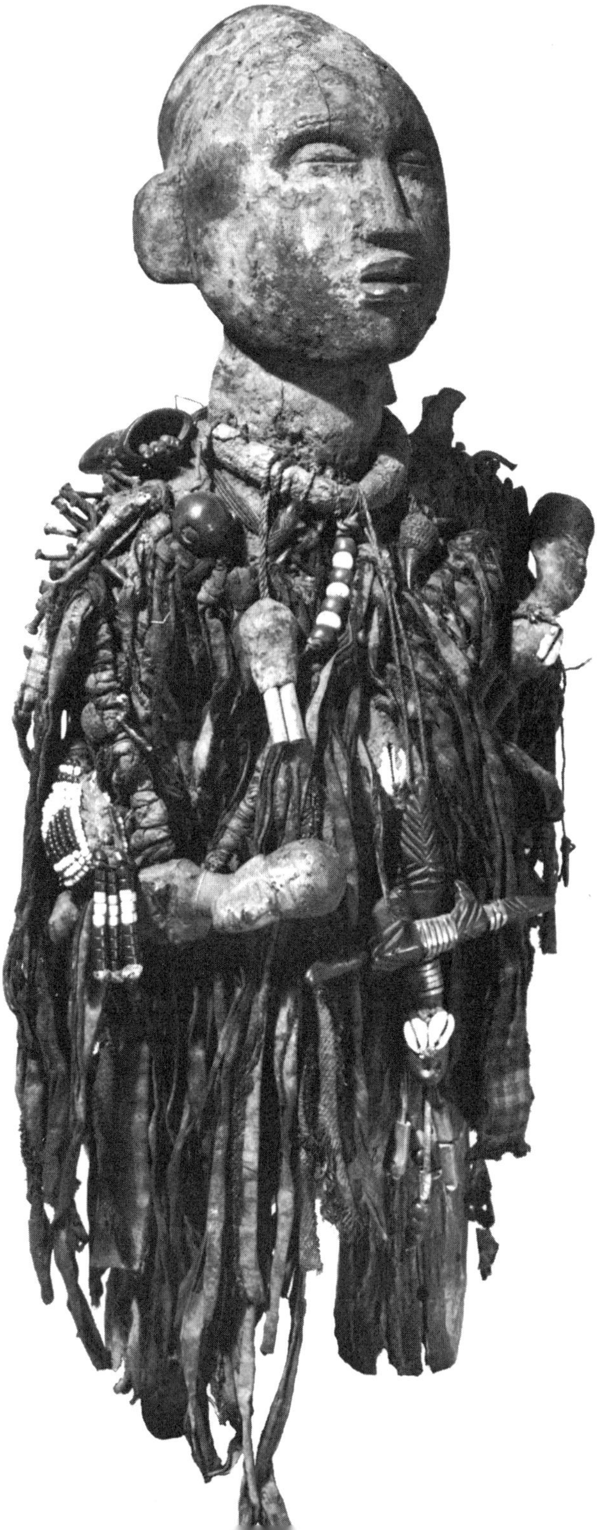

Acknowledgments

The Associated Press: For "The Real Dracula" by James F. Donohue from the San Francisco Chronicle, January 9, 1972. Doubleday & Company, Inc.: For "The Furnished Room" from *The Four Million* by O. Henry. Houghton Mifflin Company: For "Charts of 'The Universe,' 'Purgatory' and 'Hell'" as Conceived in Dante's Europe from *The Divine Comedy*, translated by Charles Eliot Norton. Indiana University Press: For "Readings, Forecasts, Personal Guidance" from *New and Selected Poems* by Kenneth Fearing. Harold Matson Company, Inc.: For "The Man Upstairs" by Ray Bradbury; copyright 1949 by Ray Bradbury. Scott Meredith Literary Agency, Inc. and the author's Estate: For "In the Vault" by H. P. Lovecraft. Random House, Inc.: For "The Demon Lover" from *Ivy Gripped the Steps* by Elizabeth Bowen; copyright 1941, 1946, renewed 1969 by Elizabeth Bowen. The University of Michigan: For "Footsteps Invisible" by Robert Arthur; copyright 1940 by Popular Publications, Inc., copyright renewed 1967 by Robert Arthur. A. Watkins, Inc.: For "... Dead Men Working in the Cane Fields" from *Magic Island* by William Seabrook; copyright 1929 by Harcourt, Brace & World, Inc., renewed 1957 by Constance Seabrook. A. P. Watt & Son: For "The Tradition" from *Tales of the Uncanny and Supernatural* by Algernon Blackwood; by permission of The Public Trustee and the Hamlyn Group. The authors and editors have made every effort to trace the ownership of all copyrighted selections found in this book and to make full acknowledgment for their use.

Illustration

The British Museum, cover; The Art Institute of Chicago, 8; Kunsthistorische Museum, 20; Museum of Modern Art, 24, 115; Kunsthalle Bremen, 34; Schloss Charlottenburg, 43; Whitney Museum of American Art, 53, 54; Private Collection, 80; Boston Museum of Fine Arts, 94, 144, 192; The National Gallery of Art, 103; Metropolitan Museum of Art, 128; Library of Congress, 130; Photographie Giraudon, 134, 143; Museum of Primitive Art, 146, 162, 189; Courtesy of the Tishman Collection, 161.

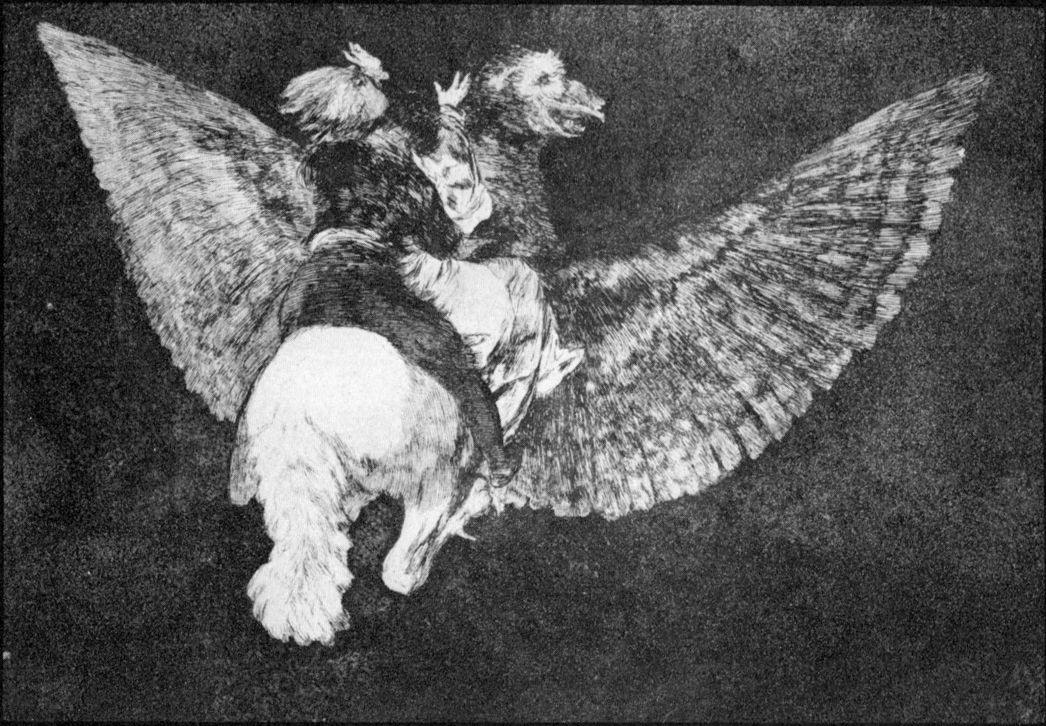